THE SHIFTING HEART

Bryn Colvin

First Magic Carpet Books, Inc. edition August 2005

Published in 2005

Manufactured in the United States of America
Published by Magic Carpet Books, Inc.

Magic Carpet Books, Inc.
PO Box 473
New Milford, CT 06776

Library of Congress Cataloging in Publication Date

The Shifting Heart by Bryn Colvin
$11.95

ISBN# 0-9766510-6-8
Book Design: P. Ruggieri

For Jonathan Colvin, Kate Brookes and Dave James,
with thanks for the support and inspiration.

Chapter One

"We aren't going to make it," Ivy said.

The wind caught her words of warning, tearing them from her frozen lips as the snow began to pelt down on the two young women. With heads lowered and backs bowed, they struggled on. The storm – which had blown in from Siberia or some other frozen place – punished the flat landscape. A few hours previously the vast expanse of sky had been clear, but a sudden wind had brought a fierce ice storm to put the travelers in real peril.

Megan put her hand on her servant's arm, afraid of separation in the blinding onslaught. "We must make it," she said, trying to mask her mounting concern.

They were a fair way from home and the blizzard was relentless. Fields and hedges vanished, bleached to pure whiteness in an instant. There had been snows earlier in the week, but while the fields remained covered the roads had been cleared by people, carts and animals, creating trails of frozen mud and filthy slush the brave or foolhardy could navigate, but all that had gone now, depriving them of landmarks.

Normally, neither young woman would have been out on such a wintry day, but there had been something of an emergency. Mrs. West knew that the Galls out by the Ely road were expecting another baby. The family was desperately poor and hardly had the means to look after themselves. They needed food and tea. Mrs. West would have gone herself had she not been inflicted with a dreadful, rattling cough. Megan had willingly offered to go in her mother's place. As daughter to the local minister, she took her charitable duties seriously. Assisted by her father's servant, the young lady had carried food and blankets to the couple, and their fast expanding brood of undernourished children. The house was small and squalid, filled with hungry, filthy infants and the weeping of a newborn. Megan and Ivy bestowed their gifts, and then departed with all haste.

As they hurried on, the falling snow blanketed them. It covered coats and bonnets alike, seeping moisture into heavy garments and giving both young women a spectral look. Ivy thought they must resemble a pair of ghost girls, and shivered at the thought. This storm could easily be the death of them, and they would not be the first young women to die in the open country. There were terrible myths in this region about girls who had met grim fates and whose shades still haunted desolate places. All they could do was keep walking and pray for good fortune.

On they trudged with frozen feet, their lungs aching from the frigid air, eyes stinging and bodies shaking with cold. Even their thick winter clothes could not keep out an ice storm. Then without warning the wind abated, drawing breath for another cruel blast. Straightening her back, Megan gazed at the white and featureless world. The snow was still falling and, though she turned, there were no discernable landmarks in any direction. The Gall's tiny cottage had long since vanished from sight.

"I cannot see the spire," she said.

"Nor can I, Miss," Ivy replied through chattering teeth.

On a clear day you could see the spire of every church in the district; little markers against the sky that told of villages and havens in the bleak landscape. With the falling ice shards hiding even these from view, and the path buried, they were well and truly lost. Familiar scenery vanished into the storm, transforming the land into a dangerous, unknown place.

"Ivy!" Megan cried plaintively, the fear in her voice undisguised.

"We've got to get shelter, Miss, even if we can't get home. Standing here's no use to us."

"But I cannot see the way!"

"Nor can I, but we must do the best we can and pray no harm comes to us. Here, take my hand."

They continued walking for a while. Having paused for breath, the storm exhaled with a vengeance, pelting the two numbed women with a fresh barrage of snow. Clinging to each other, they struggled on as best they could despite having no idea where they were going. It seemed as though they fought their way onwards for an eternity, chilled to the bone and all the time unable to see more than a few feet in front of them. What little light there was beneath the weight of cloud was fading fast. Night was falling. To be out in the dark in such a storm would mean death. The walk home should have taken no more than an hour, returning them to safety well before sunset. They had already been abroad longer than that, yet no familiar trees or houses came into view. Ivy knew they were lost, and guessed they had strayed out across the expanse of the fen. She hoped Megan did not perceive the extent of their danger. The young mistress was flighty enough at the best of times and easily frightened.

"I can see someone!" Megan cried. "This way... I see someone... there must be a cottage nearby. We are saved!"

Ivy peered blindly into the snow, squinting, unable to discern much. Her eyes detected no signs of human life and she hesitated to follow her mistress' sudden change of direction as she she broke away from her.

"Hello?" Megan called out, her voice sounding pitifully small against the howling wind.

There was no sign of a dwelling place or of any rescuer approaching. Megan was ahead of Ivy now, and the cloud of snow made them less obvious to each other. Ivy quickened her pace, trying to close the gap between them.

Megan's feet seemed to slide out from beneath her. Ivy grasped for her, managing to cover the remaining distance and catch one flailing hand. She fought to keep them both upright, but the glove slipped from Megan's fingers as she fell, the mitten staying in Ivy's grip while the precious hand escaped her. The ground beneath Megan's feet melted away and Ivy stood powerless as she realized with horror what had happened. They were standing on the edge of some road or field and Megan had fallen into a dyke hidden by the snow. Instinctively, Ivy took a step back, not knowing where the ground would be treacherous. Megan had vanished into a dark hole. Her scream was terrible to hear.

"Megan!" Ivy cried out.

"Help me!" Came the desperate reply.

Dropping to her knees, Ivy tried to see into the hole. There was no reaching Megan. "Can you climb out?" she called.

"I cannot. Ivy, I'm cold... it's wet... it's so cold..." Her voice was trembling. Shock, ice-water, both could kill.

Ivy fought back the panic and tried to think. She pulled off her coat and, gritting her teeth, tried to lower her garment down the hole. "Reach for my coat!" She felt the tension in the garment as Megan obeyed her.

"I have it..."

Standing, Ivy pulled with all her might. Slipping, she struggled to inch herself backwards. Her frozen hands could barely grip the fabric and her arms ached from effort, but there was no other way of rescuing Megan. "Give me strength," she prayed under her breath. "Help me, God, help me. Don't let her die." The wind lashed her as though determined to knock her to the ground. The coat slid in her hands, but she dug in, trying to stay firm. Refusing to admit defeat, she started tugging on the cloth again conscious that with every moment Megan would be less able to help herself.

"Hey!"

The cry came from nowhere, cutting through the muffling snow and igniting a beautifully warm hope in Ivy's heart. It was a strong, male voice.

She stood her ground, hardly daring to look, and then suddenly there were two men at her side. One of them took the coat from her hand and, without asking, began pulling on it. The other man skidded down into the dyke, creating a second hole. Between them, they pulled Megan from the icy water. She was almost blue with cold, her eyes wide with terror and her limbs shaking uncontrollably.

"You'd best come home with us," one of the young men offered. "We live close by, and her needs a fire and a dry or it'll be the death of she."

Ivy nodded. There were no choices. It might not be entirely proper, but with Megan soaked to the skin and ready to faint away, she had to accept.

One of the men hoisted Megan up in his arms, carrying her easily over the snow. Ivy and the other rescuer followed behind.

The cottage was so small that they could have passed yards from it and never known it was there. A fire burned in the hearth of the single room. There were two simple wooden chairs, a table, a few cooking implements hanging above the hearth, and several boxes, little to give comfort or cheer.

The man who had been carrying Megan placed her gently on a chair and backed off slightly. "I'll get water for a brew," he said, and vanished back out into the storm. His trousers were sodden from plunging into the dyke, but he seemed oblivious to the cold.

"I'm freezing," Megan whispered.

"I've got to get you out of those wet things," Ivy told her. She glanced at the other man, realizing for the first time that he was hardly older than she.

"There's a bed in the attic. It's not much, but you two shall have it. I'll see to that. You do what you must. I'll throw down a blanket."

Ivy was badly chilled herself, and weary almost beyond thinking. She feared for Megan, and banished thoughts of her own discomfort to attend to her mistress. The fire was warm and comforting, the house a blessedly welcome shelter from the cruel night.

By the time the other young man returned, Megan had been wrapped in a blanket to preserve her modesty and to help warm her up. Her sodden clothing hung from the mantelpiece, dripping occasionally onto the rough stone floor.

"Better?" Ivy asked.

"Warmer now…"

"Get some tea in her," the one who had just returned said, "make sure her's not going to die of fright, then get she to bed."

The men kept their distance, busying themselves about the room, fetching in more wood and tending the fire. Each opening of the door brought another hideously cold blast of air, reminding Ivy of the fate they had so narrowly escaped. Once Megan was warm and past the worst danger, the one who had carried her in hoisted her up the ladder to the attic bedroom. Ivy followed to see that all was well, and then returned to warm herself before the fire.

"Thanks to the both of you," she said. "We could have died out there."

"You must be mad, out walking on a day like this," one of them said.

Ivy made no attempt to explain or excuse their foolishness. She had quietly advised against it, but Megan was determined; the Galls were in severe distress and needed aid. With the Reverend West needed on the far side of the village, and Mrs. West laid up with yet another illness, there had been no one to go with Megan but Ivy – their loyal and long suffering servant. She appreciated that the Galls desperately needed the food and tea, but another day might not have made much difference.

"I know you," said one of the young men. "Ain't you Ivy Jenks? Albert's sister."

"I am."

"I knowed him from school. Him was always a right smart one."

"Still is," Ivy said proudly. Albert was working on the railways now, which was much better paid than the land work both his parents depended on. "You'd be Ben then," she said, having finally remembered him. He had changed a bit since she saw him last. "You're Old Moocher's little old boy."

"And him's me brother." Ben grinned and gestured to the long-limbed youth squatting on the other side of the fire.

"I thought you was an only one."

"He's a quiet one, aren't you, Seth?"

Seth nodded. "I'm off," he said gruffly as he rose to his feet. "I'll see you in the morning. You'll need help getting home."

"You can't…" Ivy began, but did not finish her assertion.

Seth vanished into the night, closing the door gently behind him.

"Don't you worry about him," Ben remarked.

"He'll catch his death out there," she protested.

"Not him."

There was something in Ben's tone that discouraged further questions. She was perplexed. Seth seemed to be of an age with them, but she couldn't recall having seen him, or even heard mention of him before. Old Moocher had been notorious – poacher, wart charmer, odd job man and teller of tall tales. He had lived with a gypsy woman for a few years – Ben's mother – then brought up his illegitimate child alone. They must have been the most talked about family in Burnham and all the other villages around as well. It seemed impossible to Ivy that there could be a brother she hadn't heard of.

"Is he really your brother?" she asked, thinking perhaps Seth was a cousin.

There had been quite a few Tucks in the previous generation, although she thought all of them had either died or left the area.

"Half-brother, different mothers. Him don't like people much."

Ivy nodded.

"You two was lucky," Ben said. "You might've died. Aunt of mine died that way, fell in a dyke in a snowstorm and when they found she, her were frozen to death."

Ivy shivered, not wanting to think how close to disaster they had been. "We're in your debt," she said.

"Don't think on it. It were lucky we saw you."

"Is your aunt the one they says walks as a ghost?"

"That's she."

There were a lot of stories about local ghosts, but the girl who died in the snowstorm was notorious. Ivy had not realized she was connected to the Tucks, or that her demise was so recent.

"So they says, but I've not seen her. There's supposed to be a few ghosts in these parts, ghost girls who wander at twilight. Bad luck to see one," Ben remarked.

"We didn't see her," Ivy said. "Couldn't see anything much in all that snow."

She tried not to think about Megan's words before she fell. Had she truly seen someone or had she just imagined it? Had she been lured off the path to her fate? Without the timely arrival of the Tuck brothers, she would undoubtedly have died from the cold. Ivy wondered what strange fate had preserved them and drawn them to this, of all houses. Ben was almost as disreputable as his father had been before him, and yet looking at him where he sat on the other side of the fire, she thought he seemed kind and gentle enough. There was a mischievous smile on his face and his blue eyes shone.

"You'd best get you to bed," he suggested. "I can sleep by the fire."

* * *

The bed was lumpy and uncomfortable. Megan tossed and turned restlessly for a long time. After the traumas of the day, she wanted somewhere safe and familiar, not this chilly attic and a bed that smelled of a man she barely knew. Whenever she closed her eyes her thoughts were filled by the face of her rescuer as the moments of her greatest terror replayed themselves... *The cold water sapped her strength and she believed she would die where she had fallen. His hand reached through the snow to her, warm and certain. His blue eyes burned dark fire...* Silent, strong, and mysterious, he had rescued her from certain death and carried her to this unlikely refuge. No men aside from her father and the doctor had ever laid hands upon her before. The strength in his body, the power in him as he bore her away, had intoxicated her even through the shock and cold. The intensity in his face haunted her now. How had he come out of the snow to save her life? Feverish and in turmoil, she fell eventually into a troubled sleep

When she dreamed it was not of rescue but of a slow death in the ice. While most dreams tended to be hazy, this one was painfully distinct. She could see the stitching on her gloves, the rough edge of a coat sleeve that was too small in the arms. Names fell from her lips like prayers, names of men she thought might rescue her – father, brothers, her lover... in the dream it all made sense, but on waking it seemed a detailed nonsense, and she put it out of her head at once.

Chapter Two

By morning the storm had blown itself out, leaving the countryside still and peaceful. The little spire of Burnham Church was visible only a few miles away. In daylight the landscape became familiar once more, the spires of Bury and Norsey easily discernable while more distant churches remained lost in the haze.

"Go down to that old hawthorn there, and beyond it you'll come to the road. The dyke's not too deep there and you'll cross safe enough. I can walk you down if you want," Ben offered.

"I'd be glad of that," Ivy replied, not inclined to take her chances with another snow-covered dyke.

Megan kept to herself as they walked. She scanned the vast horizon, wondering where the other young man had gone. Feeling a prickling sensation on the back of her neck, she turned. A figure stood outside the cottage. He did not move and for a while she was frozen, too. A shiver of eerie presentiment trickled down her spine. Reluctantly, she turned and followed their guide. Her parents would be anxious and she was obliged to return home with all speed.

"I do not believe I know either of them," Megan remarked once the two women were alone together on the road.

"Them's not church folk," Ivy replied.

Megan knew very few people outside her father's congregation. The vicar's daughter had not been schooled in the village and seldom heard any of the local gossip.

"Who are they? Do you know them, Ivy?"

"Them's Ben and Seth Tuck. Ben's mother were a gypsy woman who ran off when he were only a little one. Seth's mother I don't know about. I've not heard of her. Their dad, he was a right rum old boy."

"Does he live in Burnham?"

"Him's dead. Finished queer as anything. They found him down on the river bank one May Day a few years back and he was…" Ivy trailed off, realizing the end of the story could not be expressed to one of a genteel background.

"Yes?"

"I can't really say, Miss. It weren't proper, that's all."

"Oh, do tell me!"

Ivy glanced at her employer's daughter, startled by this sudden change of character. Megan was usually a quiet, demure girl. Maybe the storm had touched her mind a little, but she seemed less herself this morning. Lowering her voice, even though there was no one for miles around who could hear them, she said, "Him didn't have a scrap of clothes on him. Not a scrap."

Megan's hand flew to her mouth and her eyes grew wide. "Truly? What happened to him?"

"Well, that were always a mystery. There weren't a mark on him, not so much as a scratch. Our Albert said him were stiff as a board, just lying there on the river bank. When they come to bury him, this little eel came wriggling down out of his nose."

Megan squeaked with horror.

"I hadn't seen Ben in years," Ivy continued. "Him were at school with my brother."

"Was he the one who guided us this morning?" Megan asked.

Ivy nodded her reply.

"So the brother who pulled me from the dyke would be Seth?"

Ivy nodded again. "Them Tucks are a queer lot, everyone says it. My old grandmother, she used to say there'd been Tucks on this land before it were even land. And you do hear some tales about them."

"What sort of tales?"

It occurred to Ivy she had probably gone too far. "Odd things happen to them, or so folks say. Them's never had much luck. There was one old boy lost a foot a few years back, and no one ever knew how it happened. Him died not long after, mind."

Megan looked back over her shoulder. She was losing interest in the conversation. The landscape behind her remained white and still, unbroken by movement. She half expected to discover they were being watched, but there was no observer apparent.

* * *

It took Megan nearly an hour to assure her father no serious ill had befallen her. He fussed and worried like a mother hen, questioning the dryness of her clothes, the state of her joints and a dozen other details. She was patient with him, answering his queries and trying to assuage his concerns.

"I went out with a lantern, but the storm was terrible and I could barely see my hand before my face," he confessed, clearly distressed by his inability to rescue his only child.

"We were caught out, father, but took shelter in one of the cottages."

"I had hoped as much. With whom did you stay?"

"Some people Ivy was at school with," Megan replied tactfully.

She had no desire to tell her father exactly what had happened. Learning they had been alone with two young men would only provoke further doubts and questions.

"I did not tell your mother, Megan, she believes you came back and went to bed with a headache."

She nodded. Her mother was delicate at the best of times and they both took great care not to alarm her. "How is she?"

"Better today. The doctor is coming to visit her later. Can I suggest you change your clothes and sit with her for a while, if you are not too fatigued, of course?"

"I am quite well. I will go to her at once."

This was the life Megan knew, safe in the coziness of her family home and sheltered by loving parents. Her role as dutiful daughter was clearly defined. She helped her mother with charitable acts, assisted at her father's school in the village by teaching the girls how to sew, and generally made herself useful. She attended his services, poured tea at village events, and kept herself a model of modest good behavior. Soon or later one of the suitable young men to whom she was occasionally presented would propose to her. Then she would marry, have children of her own and undertake to be as good and dutiful a wife as she had been a daughter. Her future had always been thus mapped, and she had accepted it with the good grace that characterized her attitude to life.

Waking in a strange bed, with her servant at her side, and two strange young men close to hand, had affected her more than she could have anticipated. A peculiar disquiet had taken hold of her soul. Standing in her bedroom, she gazed out at the vast white plain of the fens. She was on the wrong side of the village to be able to see in the direction of the cottage where she had passed the night. A small dark figure moved across the landscape, tiny and anonymous against the monotonous expanse of snow. The sky was steely grey, threatening more blizzards. She wondered who was walking out in the frozen fields, and Seth's face appeared in her mind once more, angular and uncompromising. His eyes seemed to be burning into her heart, but there was no knowing if that was him out walking.

Seated in the master bedroom with its soft furnishings and tranquil atmosphere, Megan poured tea for her mother and added a spoon of soft sugar.

"How were the Galls?" Mrs. West enquired.

"Much as might be expected. They are even more cramped now there is another one, and the house smelled very close and musty. It did not seem at all healthy. They were very grateful for the parcel you sent."

Mrs. West nodded slowly. None of this appeared to surprise her. "If only they could restrain themselves a little. These large families are impossible to support on a laborer's money," she remarked, and sighed to herself.

Restraint was a frequent motif in her conversations. Megan wondered what, in this instance, they were supposed to be refraining from. Gin was the most usual culprit, followed by beer, but that had no obvious connection with the arrival of children. She was conscious there were matters she did not understand. She had never sought to enquire, trusting her parents would tell her anything she needed to know. As children were a matter for married people, she supposed she did not need to understand exactly where they came from until she had a husband of her own. The idea made her feel uncomfortable, and slightly threatened. She preferred not to dwell on it.

"Might you read to me for a little while?" Mrs. West enquired.

Megan smiled, and reached for the book her mother indicated.

Chapter Three

Days when Frederick West took any time to indulge his enthusiasms were rare. Most commonly he found some means to have his enjoyment serve a higher purpose and bring benefit to others. After his morning service, and an excellent lunch cooked by Ivy Jenks – his all-purpose servant – West set off with his daughter to visit one of his parishioners. The winter sun had little warmth in it but shone down brightly on the drifts of snow, the glare of it almost blinding at times.

Mrs. Hare was an elderly widow who was comfortable enough in her dotage that she could afford to pay a girl to do the work around the house. Injured by a fall some years previously, she had never properly recovered and could do little more than hobble around her cozy home. When the weather was good she had a boy push her to church in a bath-chair, but the winter months made this impossible. Reverend West often called in on her, as she was a genuinely devout woman who did not merely attend church out of social convention. They read from the Bible together for an hour or prayed while Megan undertook whatever little tasks Mrs. Hare considered too challenging for her serving girl. Most usually there was a little fine sewing for the vicar's daughter to do.

With this duty performed, West indulged himself in a leisurely walk home, enjoying the fresh air before his presence was required for the evening service. This was one of the few periods of relaxation he allowed himself. His work in the parish – both for the spiritual and the practical wellbeing of his flock – was demanding. There were not hours enough in the day or days enough in the week to manage all that was required.

Megan walked quietly at her father's side. The road was free from snow,

but the mud had frozen unevenly, churned up by feet and the hooves of hors-
es. It was difficult to walk upon, especially with the further encumbrance of
a skirt that swept almost to the ground. The sun was sinking low in the sky,
making the shadows long. Megan watched the ground before her, not daring
to pay too much attention to the snowbound landscape.

"Sometimes I feel that all we do here is race with all our might, merely
to slide gently backwards," he confessed as they walked.

"You achieve a great deal, father," Megan replied.

"But I fear it is never enough. Half the children leave my school able to
do little more than write their names. If they attended more often we might
have some chance, but some of the older boys are barely there a dozen days
of the year."

"I think they benefit from what learning they have."

"And the poverty…" He sighed helplessly. Poverty was endemic, and
they both knew it.

"I think you do much good, father. They would be far worse off were it
not for your efforts," she answered earnestly.

They fell into thoughtful silence and were almost back in the village
when the touch of her father's hand upon her arm startled her out of her
introspection. He made a low hushing noise, and pointed out across the
nearby fields.

Following the direction of her father's finger, Megan peered into the
sunlight, trying to see what had drawn his attention. Something small and
dark rolled in a lolloping gait across the snow.

"Lutra Lutra," West breathed reverentially.

Megan recognized the words were Latin, but her knowledge of the proper names for creatures was non-existent. Still, as the large mammal
approached, she did not need a translation. "Otter," she answered under her
breath.

Neither of them moved for fear of disturbing the creature. The animals tended to be shy and startled readily, although this one seemed bold and brazen enough. Otters were a frequent sight at dusk and dawn, foraging in the dykes and wandering in the fields, nevertheless, the appearance of one so close by enchanted father and daughter alike. Side-by-side, they watched its progress intently.

When a young man, West had been a keen naturalist. His priestly duties left him little time for such pursuits, but he would not deny himself the delight of watching a creature when it came so close to him. He had raised his daughter to share his love for God's creatures, and whenever they walked together he pointed out the flora and fauna around them. "A male, given the size of it, and the shape of its head," he whispered.

Megan nodded, although she would not have ventured an opinion herself.

A second otter appeared from beneath a low hedge. Apparently oblivious to the other, it also approached the road. It gave every impression that it was watching the human duo just as keenly as they were watching it.

"Another male," West observed.

As though hearing him, the second otter turned to look in the direction of the first. The two creatures stared at each other and chattered angrily. Their cries rose up from the field, muted but unmistakable. As though by some pre-arranged signal, both otters charged at once, crashing into each other with claws flailing and teeth bared. They rolled in the snow, flattening a swathe of it into hard ice. For a few moments it looked as though some vicious, territorial feud was under way. Megan could hardly bear to watch. She hated seeing anything hurt or killed.

West chuckled to himself. "I do believe they might be play-fighting," he observed. "Perhaps they are siblings from last spring."

"Perhaps…"

He was right, the initial frenzy had not led to any actual damage to either creature and there seemed to be little real aggression in what they did, even though it had at first looked violent and bloodthirsty. The fight descended into gentle squabbling, until at last the two staggered to their feet and loped off across the field together. Each looked back – one after the other – turning and pausing for a few moments to consider the watchers on the road before departing.

West smiled indulgently after them. "We had best hurry home," he said. "I should dearly like a nice cup of tea before I am obliged to go out and preach my second sermon."

Chapter Four

Attendance at the school was very poor the week the snow finally melted. Most of the fields were flooded and, although the roads were passable, many of the children were ill with influenza. Megan considered the absent ones with a heavy heart. It was very likely some of them would never return to her sewing classes; the winters often claimed a child or two. Living in such large families, with ten or twelve of people cramped into tiny cottages and no money to pay for proper food or medicine, they were terribly vulnerable. Her father did what he could, but the battle against abject poverty seemed to be one they could never win.

There were so few girls present that she dismissed them early, knowing their return would be helpful to overstretched mothers. Finding she had a little time on her hands, Megan slipped into the church. It was an ancient building, built when the wool trade was at its height and money flowed through the district. Those days of prosperity were more than a century gone, but the church remained, beautiful and tranquil in spite of everything.

Sitting in one of the pews she gazed up at the ceiling, considering the bosses, with their ornate foliage, before turning her eyes to the altar and the stained glass window behind it. Hands clasped as though in prayer, she whispered into the otherwise silent and empty space. "Help me to do more, and to be strong. Please bless me with the courage to do what I can, and the forbearance to accept when I can do nothing. I do not understand why there has to be so much suffering in this world." It was a thought that had been increasingly on her mind of late as she paid her visits to the poorest among the congregation and tried to find the means to help them.

Her reverie was broken abruptly, although Megan could not have said what disturbed her. Straining her ears, she could discern no change within the small church. Still, her skin crawled and her shoulders prickled as though fingers were teasing against her back. The slight creak of the pew behind her proved finally that she was not alone, but it would be unthinkable to turn around.

Bare fingers brushed against the back of her neck, finding the tiny area of exposed flesh between the collar of her coat and her hair. She shivered and closed her eyes. *No one should touch her in that way. It was too intimate.* She hardly dared breathe feeling the rough fingertips glide back and forth over her skin, slipping around her slender throat and then up over her chin to brush lightly against her lips. Megan was trembling, her being fluttering like a leaf in a Fen blow, powerless and in danger of being torn from its rightful place. Moving under a compulsion that she barely understood, she caught those wandering fingers with her own hand. The fingers she had captured were long and slender, the palm narrow, the back dotted with soft, dark hairs – a delicate hand but a male one, with dirt under the nails. The shirt cuff was worn and threadbare in places, the jacket too short in the arm. Each tiny detail absorbed her, a revelation in its own right as his fingers tangled with hers, arousing a sensitivity she had not known her hands possessed.

"Beauty," a voice whispered low, caressing her ear with its passionate tone.

She sighed.

"I know you!" he said, and the words sounded like recognition of her soul, not a mere acknowledgement of acquaintance.

She dared to turn her head, slowly.

Eyes of the darkest blue she had ever seen returned her gaze. She stared at him openly, meeting his intense stare with her own searching scrutiny. He had sought her out; there could be no other explanation.

"Seth," she whispered his name into the echoing church.

He nodded. "You?"

"Megan West."

"Megan…" he tried the name, almost as though he was tasting it. In his mouth it sounded musical and exotic. His long fingers stroked along her wrist, sliding easily under her sleeve to the tender skin of her forearm, his soul-divining gaze never leaving her face. "Do you know… that tumble-down place… over the way?" He spoke awkwardly, as though having to think carefully about every word.

"Do you mean the old abbey ruins not far from the road to Norsey?"

He considered this for a moment. "Looks like stone trees."

"That would be the abbey," she said, wondering how on earth he could fail to know so simple and obvious a thing.

"I'll be there in the afternoon," he said, "tomorrow… any afternoon. I'll be there."

She realized what he meant, the implied invitation in his words. He smiled, and she found herself nodding.

Once he had gone, she stared into the space of the church, searching her soul. She should have resisted his advances and protested against those uninvited, improper caresses. She should never have suggested she might meet with him in that lonely place. *It was not right or appropriate*, she thought. It was not what she, as the daughter of a vicar and an upstanding member of society, should be doing. He could hardly ask for her hand in marriage. His intentions therefore must be less than honorable, whatever that actually meant. Megan had been taught to guard her honor without having any real idea what it might need guarding from. Even though he had gone, it still felt as though he was touching her. The skin he had tantalized with questing fingertips still hummed, making her acutely aware of the way in which she had been explored. It had been a fleeting thing but, now that he was gone, she hankered after more.

Chapter Five

The garden at this time of year was a sorry sight. Those plants that would produce fresh leaves come spring still had the dead and joyless look of winter about their haggard forms. In a few weeks the first of the spring greens might be ready for picking, but until then the household must depend on roots stored for the winter. This time of year was always the same for Ivy as she hankered after something green, something fresh that she could put in her mouth and savor.

The only thing suitable for picking was the thyme, which grew in happy profusion despite the cold. Its tiny leaves were hard and unyielding, the taste of them strong. It was better than nothing. She cut a few straggly stems, meaning to flavor the dumplings with them, and then looked around to see if there was anything else. The rosemary looked tempting, even though she knew it was not at its best. Dawdling because she wanted to feel the sun on her skin for just a little longer, she inspected the other herbs and plants, wondering how they would fare in the months to come. A flicker of movement drew her eyes and she looked more closely, thinking it was most likely a blackbird or thrush in search of worms.

There was a hedge around the vicarage garden that sheltered it from the road and the fields, making a private haven. The hawthorn and blackthorn were so close entwined that, even when they had no leaves, the hedge was a dense barrier through which it was difficult to see. Down at the base of it something large was moving. At first Ivy thought it must be a cat or dog that had wandered in from one of the farms, but as she looked more closely she saw, to her considerable surprise, that it was an otter. It had been years since she had last seen one.

The Shifting Heart

They were solitary beings, she knew that. Most of the time they content-ed themselves with eels from the dykes and you never saw them at all. Her father always said that if an otter was hungry it could be as wily as a fox. They would take anything then – rabbits, ducks, hens from in the hen house, even eggs from under the very hen herself. They would eat carrion as well, he said. A starving otter would do the most unlikely things. There was a tale about an old farmer who kept a few cows and found in the winter that they gave no milk at all. He suspected poor people or gypsy folk of stealing it by night, so he sat up with his shotgun to watch and listen. Still the milk went and he detected nothing. Eventually he tried keeping vigil with a lantern so the thieves would know he was there. That night he saw a badger, an otter and a hedgehog all creep in to suckle from his cows. He shot all three of them, and after that the milk supply was plentiful once more.

Ivy supposed that with the weather being so bad there would be little for any of the wild creatures to eat. She could hear the otter snuffling about in the hedge, no doubt looking for a meal. On impulse, she slipped back into the house and fetched a few pieces of bacon rind left from the previous day. These she left on the path, not wanting to venture too close to the hedge for fear of driving off this twilight visitor. She supposed it would smell the meat. Watching from the shadow of the kitchen door, she was soon rewarded with the sight of its long form emerging from the shadows to snatch the offered bacon. It looked up fleetingly, and she had the impression it saw her and gazed critically in her direction. Then it slipped away as secretively as it had come.

She stayed still for a while, hoping it might come back. Its presence had been almost companionable, and there was precious little of that in her life. Most of her days were divided between working alone and running round after Mrs. West, whose ailments required ongoing attention. Ivy understood she was no more than a tool in the household. Her job was to serve and be useful in whatever capacity they required. It would occasionally occur to

Megan to ask if she was well or in need of anything, but that was as much notice as she ever got on her own account. Ivy felt no bitterness over this. She considered it better than field or factory work and, as employers went, the Wests were certainly better than many she had heard tell of. When the otter did not return, she slipped back into the house.

Chapter Six

Lying had proved all too easy. It was almost true for Megan to say she wanted to go walking, to look for the violets and primroses where they peeked out beneath the hedges. Her father was teaching, as he often did in the afternoons. Her mother had undertaken to visit an elderly neighbor, and agreed that a little fresh air would do the girl a great deal of good. It had been a long time since Megan had intentionally spoken falsely to her parents. It gave her the most terrible, powerful, unfettered feeling. By the time she set out along the road she was shocked by what she had done and half afraid of what might yet happen. It hardly seemed as though she was doing these things herself. Yet how else could it be? She was walking out to an assignation with a young man, having willfully misled her parents on the matter. Megan knew she was longer their docile child and that she was breaking all sorts of unspoken rules.

The road to Norsey was higher than the surrounding fields. Where sometimes cattle grazed or heavy horses pulled their ploughs, birds now skittered across recently formed lakes. In a few days the melt water would be gone and those many folk who survived by tilling the land would be back at their labors. With the fields flooded, there was no one much about. The abbey ruins loomed on the horizon, visible for a long time before she drew near them. They looked foreboding, dark shadows against the pale sun of early spring. Megan wondered what she would do when she reached that spot – if she would climb down from the road and walk amongst the remains of ancient piety or turn back for the safety of home. The thought of Seth's brooding expression and the touch of his fingers on her neck drew her onwards.

The Shifting Heart

Grass grew bright and luscious where the feet of penitents passed in years gone by. Pillars that had once supported a great arching roof now stood alone or lay where they had fallen. They were indeed like great stone trees, she realized. The place was still and empty. Above her the vast expanse of blue stretched to the ends of the world. There might be no people to see her, but there was no secrecy under so open a sky. The abbey stood a little way above the water, connected to the roadway by a broad swathe of muddy ground. Aside from the ducks bobbing on the flood there were no signs of life at all...

Movement at the periphery of her vision caught her attention. She turned. For a moment, she thought there was someone standing in the shadow of a crumbling wall watching her. She had the impression of a pale face and long, loose hair. The wind caught at the overhanging ivy, turning it, and the illusion of a woman melted away. Megan laughed at her own guilty nervousness and at the tricks her untamed imagination could play upon her.

Having assured herself she was quite alone, she walked down towards the water, being careful on the slippery ground. It crossed her mind he might have been teasing her, and the possibility saddened her somewhat. He might never have meant to meet with her; this might be some cruel jest at her expense.

A dark ripple of movement caught her eye. Bubbles trailed on the shimmering surface, rising through liquid so muddy it almost looked black. A dark spot broke through the flood-water, and the shiny head of an otter emerged. Amazed to see one of these creatures again so soon after her previous sighting, Megan watched in fascination. If nothing else, this would give her something to share with her father. Water slid from the animal's thick pelt as it confidently approached, its body undulating as it moved. It paused a few feet away from her, keen little eyes turned in her direction, whiskers twitching. She half expected it to turn and run, but it remained.

She squeezed her eyes tightly shut, opened them, and blinked again. It seemed to Megan that her eyes were playing tricks on her. The otter looked bigger somehow than it had on first emerging. As she watched in utter disbelief, the lithe creature shimmered and shook. With every breath she took, the thing she saw looked less like an otter. With her heart drumming a wild tattoo and her stomach lurching, she backed away until she felt cold stone behind her and could retreat no further. The Lord's Prayer was on her lips, chanted instinctively as the only defense she could reach for, but all it served to do was calm her terror a little as the insanity before her continued. Where there had been fur now there was naked flesh, lean and muscular in the sunlight. She could not have said which shocked her most – the impossible transformation she had witnessed, or the vision of nude masculinity that now stood before her. Paralyzed like some prey that knows it cannot escape the fox, Megan could only stare open mouthed at the man who appeared before her.

Seth's dark hair still sparkled with drops of water. His narrow face showed no traces of otter features, and his long limbs looked human enough. Megan knew she ought not to look, but her gaze was drawn down from his compelling eyes to the breadth of his shoulders and the bare skin of his chest. Then further did she dare to examine, skimming over his smooth, flat stomach to the rod that stood out from between his thighs. She had no idea what it was even as somewhere deep within her, something primal and hungry stirred. Her mind might have been kept innocent of men, but her body understood.

He strode over the grass towards her, his domination of the situation absolute. It seemed to Megan he was king of the moment, ruler of the soil beneath his feet, of the beautiful afternoon, and her own delicate body. There was no escaping his hands as he sough her breasts and hips. His mouth covered hers and she surrendered to his tongue, letting him penetrate between her lips to steal away her reason. Crushed against the wall, she was overwhelmed. All of her upbringing screamed out against such wild, improper behavior, but her body was his co-conspirator, responding to his questing hands as buttons were pulled open and cloth dispensed with. He pushed her jacket from her shoulders, opened her blouse, and pressed kisses onto her bare shoulders. Somehow his fingers found their way down the front of her stays, teasing at her small breasts until she was giddy from sensation.

"I should not..." she began, but his mouth closed over hers again, stifling the protest.

He stepped away, fixing her with his smoldering gaze. Megan realized her breasts were heaving and that she could barely breathe. She hardly knew what was happening to her. Reaching for his hand, she drew it to her lips and kissed each fingertip in turn.

"I want you," he said simply.

The words sent a thrill through her even though she could not fully grasp their significance.

"What do you want me for?" she asked innocently.

"I want to touch your body."

She flushed scarlet at this, but he had not finished.

"I want your skin against mine," he continued.

A deep yearning inside her rose up at this.

"Let me lie with you." He stepped closer, pulling up her skirts. She felt his fingers between her thighs, caressing her through her undergarments. The sensation shocked her and filled her with fear. This seemed wrong, and right, all at once. She craved more of it, but begged him to stop. Those long and lethal fingers of his were at play, skillfully mastering the mysteries of her clothing.

"No," she whispered.

He laid her down in the sodden grass, pulling her clothing away so her bare skin was upon the peaty earth. She tried to cover herself with her hands, but he pulled them away also, placing his mouth on her breasts and then her thighs, kissing the places she had been ashamed to show him. His fingers explored the dark triangle of her hair between her legs, prizing her open and exploring her virgin cleft. It was an uncomfortable, troubling feeling.

"Please…" She hardly knew if she wanted him to stop or continue. He took her words as encouragement, working his fingers deeper inside her.

"You've not had a man before," he observed.

"No!" she breathed.

Their eyes met, and her fear melted in the face of his desire. He pushed a little harder. His lips closed over each of her delicate nipples in turn, tasting them to the full. She reached for him then, finding the courage to touch his chest and arms. In response he smiled at her, a sweet reward for her daring. She continued, exploring the small protrusions of his nipples and wondering if she dared to touch that curious manifestation between his legs.

Some strange alchemy had been worked upon her body. The discomfort melted away, leaving a sweet sensation in its stead. She lay still, gazing up into his face, compelled by the hunger in his eyes to surrender as he worked some of his magic upon her.

"Don't fight it," he commanded.

She trembled, gasped, and wriggled beneath his hands.

"That's it," he said.

He moved onto her, resting his weight on his elbows and looking down into her face. The shock of his cock piercing her was startling indeed. She gasped, not knowing if what she felt was pain or pleasure. He rocked slowly upon her, filling her body with shivering, tremulous feelings and painful delight as he possessed her.

When it was done, he slipped hurriedly from her. There were no soft words or explanations. He sauntered down over the muddy grass and plunged into the water, vanishing beneath the surface with barely a sound.

Shocked and ashamed by what she had done, Megan dressed rapidly. There was blood on her thighs, the traces of her deflowering showing crimson on her skin. Grabbing a handful of grass, she tried to wipe it away, but it was drying already. She pulled on her dress, covering the mud on her back and the stains on her body. The water was still, the afternoon tranquil once more. *Surely, it could not have happened?* She must have dreamed it all, so impossible did the afternoon seem. When she rose and walked, there was a profound ache in her loins. He could not have come to her wearing the skin of an otter and seduced her body so utterly. She could hardly believe she had lost her honor so quickly. She understood now what the words from the wedding service meant – man and woman joined as one flesh. *It is not so simple as that, surely? She must have dreamed it.*

Megan knew she was no longer pure or good, that she had transgressed and tasted the forbidden fruits of pleasure. She could hardly think, but tidied herself as best she could and stumbled home. There was no doubt at all in her mind that she would go back to the ruins as soon as she could to see if it had been but a moment's madness.

Chapter Seven

On Tuesday afternoons, Ivy had a few hours that were hers to dispose of as she saw fit. Her habit was to return to her mother's house for a while, often with a pocket full of good things from the West's kitchen. Her employer had always been generous.

"How's things?" May asked. She was evidently tired and worn and obviously pregnant again.

"You've another one coming, then. Can't you get father to leave off you a while?"

May ignored her daughter's comment. She never talked of such things, treating every new baby as a surprise that no one could have anticipated.

"I brought you some cake and a pat of butter."

May managed the suggestion of a smile. "Them's good to you," she said.

"I knows it."

"That vicar before them, you'd not remember him. Him were all fire and brimstone and precious little charity. Oh, but the squire in them days, he were a right hard one. If him heard you'd missed church, and you wasn't dying or laid up with a babe, you'd get no work from him."

Ivy nodded. She had heard tales of the unpopular Reverend Patterson for most of her life. Reverend West, on the other hand, was much respected and loved by the local people, and had won a place in their hearts despite being an outsider.

"Did you ever hear about how old Patterson got himself one of them horseless carriages?"

There were innumerable local tales of the man's antics, but Ivy was not sure she knew this one.

The Shifting Heart

"Come all the way from London, I heard, although some said all the way from America, but I think that were nonsense. Must have cost more than a decent man would earn in a year. Yellow it were, the most undignified, immodest yellow you've ever seen in all your blessed life. How him loved that machine. Him'd spend hours just polishing it, like some house-proud old spinster him were. He went right silly over it."

May brightened considerably as she talked.

"Anyway, this one day he were driving along the Bury road when this great big pig ran out in front of him. Now this little old pig, him were so big he stopped that beast of a machine dead in its tracks. Now that old boar he were right angry, and he pushed that vicar and his shiny yellow machine right off the road and down into a dyke. I were only a little one at the time, but I saw it all and I laughed. I laughed till I wet my drawers. He weren't none to happy about it neither, so he crawled out all covered in mud, and with frogs in his pockets, and Lord alone knows what else. He were back next day to try and move it, but it wouldn't budge, it were stuck fast." May paused, laughing at her own memories. "Him'd come and look at it every day, his face so long it were down to his knees. And just to make it worse, what do you think should happen but a duck went and made a nest right on his nice old seat. I went by one day and there were a fox sleeping on it, plain as you like. Him never did get another."

Ivy chuckled and made her excuses. Even though she and her sister Gladys were living out, and the older boys, Albert and Fred, lodged with an uncle, there was still little room in the cramped cottage. Going home always made Ivy melancholy. The squalid conditions, the horde of siblings that she barely knew, and the desperation in her mother's face, it was all depressing. Her mother's stories were usually good, when she was in a bright mood, but some visits could be dire indeed.

At twenty one, Ivy was an old maid by village standards; most girls married long before then. Marriage was a fate she had been glad to escape, pre-serving her virginity and her independence, knowing the latter depended chiefly on the former. She did not want her mother's life.

With her duties performed, she took a leisurely stroll back to the vicarage. Instead of walking along the lanes, she chose a more circuitous route, winding through the fields. The men were out ploughing, leading the enormous hors-es back and forth across the land, preparing the soil for planting. In the hedgerows, small birds sang joyfully and the first leaves were emerging. Ivy tugged off handfuls of opening hawthorn buds, crushing them between her teeth and enjoying the taste much as she had done as a child. Now she ate them just for pleasure, not to satisfy the cravings of a never-full stomach. The long damp grass soaked the hem of her plain print dress, but she did not care. It was Spring and she had a few moments of freedom to relish.

In one of the fields, two men were digging out the ditches, removing the leaves and debris of several years neglect. Keeping the dykes clear was a never-ending job, essential now that the flat land was below sea level and vulnerable to flooding. The older man, with a rust- colored jacket that had seen better days, whistled cheerily as he worked. As she drew closer, Ivy recognized the younger man as Ben Tuck. Although she had not laid eyes upon him since the snowstorm, she raised a hand and called out a cheery hello. Both men stopped in their work, taking the chance to ease aching backs.

"Afternoon, my wench," the older man said.

Ivy vaguely knew him – he was one of the Normans, a huge sprawling family who seemed to be related to every other person in the village.

"Afternoon," she said.

She was conscious of Ben's eyes upon her, twinkling in amusement even as he looked her up and down. She raised her eyebrows at him, meaning to challenge his audacity, but found herself smiling playfully instead. He was a handsome young man with his auburn hair and wicked smile. His lips parted slightly and she looked away, unable to face the suggestive leer in his expression. As she carried on her way, he broke off from his work and followed her.

"And where do you think you be going?" she asked pointedly.

"Walk you home. Don't want you getting in trouble again."

She turned, giving him a hard look.

"Don't you try any nonsense with me, Ben Tuck."

"Would I?" he teased.

"Wouldn't you just? I hear you're as bad as ever your old Dad were."

"I'll not put a hand on you unless you ask it of me. There's a promise."

Ivy kept walking. "I'll not waste your time," she told him. "I like how I am. I've not got a young man, and I don't want one."

"You're canny. You don't want to be poor with a dozen little ones to mind."

"That's right," she sighed. "I could've stayed on with school, had a scholarship and all, but I had to go into service instead. Thought I'd never get over that, but I did."

"Must be dull, though, keeping house for the likes of them."

"The Wests? Them's a good, decent family. I got no grounds to complain."

They had reached the gate onto the road. She planned to go back that way, arriving at the vicarage in time to prepare afternoon tea.

"Well?" he asked.

"Well what?"

"Are you going to ask for a kiss then?"

His teasing was beginning to unsettle her. Much as she hated to admit it, she was tempted to ask. There was no denying she was attracted to him. However, he was trouble, and she had a very different sort of life planned for herself; she had a fair idea what that sort of thing led to.

"No," she said.

"Suit yourself. You'll be asking sooner or later, I'm reckoning."

His arrogance affronted her. With a harrumph of disagreement, she opened the gate and escaped onto the road, resisting the temptation to see if he had gone or if he was watching her. Within a dozen paces her anger had fled, leaving a whisper of regret that made her cross with herself.

To her surprise, she caught up with Megan, who was also walking back to the house. The young lady seemed distracted, as she often had of late. Ivy said nothing, waiting to see if Megan would speak to her. In days past they had been sociable enough when out on small missions for Mrs. West. Ivy wondered about the silent girl who walked at her side. She was of a marriageable age as well, but had shown little interest in that life. Until recently she had been a practical creature, hard working and faultlessly polite. Now she daydreamed and spent long hours walking the lanes on her own. Ivy wondered that the West's didn't do something for her, but they were so concerned with their good works they could not seem to see a crisis brewing in their own family.

* * *

The touch of his hands on her body and the certainty of his mouth against hers... these things were real, as real as his transformation and her deflowering. Megan was a maiden no more, and her lover was a being of uncanny power who defied all the reason she had ever been taught. She had gone to him repeatedly to assure herself of these truths. He was reliably there, either waiting in the long grass for her, alluringly bare and careless, or arriving shortly after she did. Each time she saw him her confidence grew, and each parting became harder. When they were apart she did little but think of him, remembering the feel of his skin on hers. The taste of his seed in her mouth and the memories of pleasure he invoked could steal up on her at the most unlikely of times. She would wake as if from a dream to find her sewing untouched in her lap and a whole morning passed in reverie.

It seemed to Megan he could not get enough of her. Each time he seemed hungrier for her flesh than ever. Over their long afternoons she began to learn the rhythms of his body and the mysteries of pleasure. From the first stirrings of desire, he led her along a path that wove through ever greater delights. Megan knew she was becoming a slave to his beautiful cock, addicted to the push of it inside her, to the hot gush of his release, and the quivering intensity of her own responses to his driving strength. When she thought of him, her nipples ached at the recollection of his erotic assaults upon them, and she grew warm and moist between her legs.

There were too many afternoons when work or weather kept her from him. In days past, she felt blessed to have such responsibilities and discharged her charitable duties admirably. Now they seemed futile and restricting. What did it matter if her seven-year-old pupils learned embroidery? Most of them would find no use for it in later life. There were endless gifts to be bestowed as her parents continued sending out food to those in need, but it was like one man trying to dig through a mountain. When she was with Seth, she could forget the miseries of the world and be truly happy for a while. She supposed it was sinful and weak to be so drawn to fleshy pleasures and self indulgence, but it was so rare that anyone enquired as to what she might want or need for herself. Sometimes Seth asked such things, at others he simply divined them. She had never previously appreciated what it felt like to be wanted simply for herself and not with some view to the service she might provide.

Chapter Eight

They rattled over every bump in the road as the huge traction engine drew the long trailer at its full speed of five miles an hour. Bury was nearly ten miles away, and the party from Burnham set out early in the morning all dressed in their best clothes. Even the adults were bright-eyed and enthusiastic when they departed. Mothers sat with babies on their knees while older children were already warming up to the mischief ahead. The annual treat – a trip to the Bury May Fair – was one of the vicar's few acts of secret self indulgence. He adored traction engines with their stink of hot grease and their belching smoke. It was his happy privilege to stand on the small platform beside the driver and to occasionally be allowed to take the wheel on quiet stretches. His innocent obsession gave the young people a license to misbehave in the trailer behind him, and various weary parents struggled to assist Megan and Ivy with the onerous task of keeping this unruly mob in hand. Even Mrs. West was occasionally called upon to restrain a child who hung precariously over the side, or to discourage other silliness.

On arrival, they were first greeted by the aroma of hot food, then the smells of exotic animals and the sounds of excited youngsters already enjoying the swing-boats and merry-go-rounds. Like an unleashed pack of hounds, the children bolted from their seats and vanished into the throng, leaving Reverend West with his mouth open, his speech on decorum and moderation unvoiced. He shrugged and smiled to himself. Children would be children after all. The real difficulty would be in rounding them all up at the end of the day. As his more sedate passengers descended, West smiled indulgently at his daughter and Ivy. The young woman had been a servant with them for so long he almost considered her a part of the family.

"You young people should enjoy this fine day," he said.

"I would be happy to stay with you father," Megan replied, knowing her parents preferred sedate activities to the wild turbulence of a fairground.

"Nonsense," her mother gently chided, "I will not hear of any such thing." She pressed a few bright coins into her daughter's hand. "We will see you for our picnic tea, but not a moment sooner."

Megan smiled gratefully, bade her parents farewell, and tried her best not to hurry too obviously as she entered the fairground. She was surprised they had let her go. In previous years, her father had chaperoned her on a few rides, and that had been her lot.

The fair was a marvelous swirl of sights and sounds. More people had assembled than the young women saw all year. Ivy had a few pennies she had hoarded and spent them carefully. Megan wanted to see everything, most especially the exotic beasts in their cages and the hall of mirrors. Ivy won a coconut, but they could think of no way to open it, and were eventually persuaded to give it to some of the village boys.

There was some disturbance outside the fat lady's booth. Neither of them saw how it began, but the crowd rolled open as two men laid into each other. It was a fast and dirty fight. Megan drew back, alarmed by the violence, but gripped by morbid fascination, such that she could not take her eyes from the scene. It was only when one of the fighters backed away, blood dripping from his ruined mouth, that they realized who the other combatant had been. Seth turned slowly, issuing voiceless challenges to other individuals in the crowd. Most of them retreated, but one stepped forwards, a murderous look in his eye. He was a big, burly man with a crooked nose and a neck thicker than his head. Seth eyed him up and down slowly, clearly untroubled by what he saw despite the considerable advantage both of height and weight his bulky opponent enjoyed.

The first few blows Seth dodged and sidestepped with graceful ease.

Megan could hardly breathe as she watched him. Although she hated violence, the sight of the man she adored overpowering his foes so completely captivated her. Over the weeks of their erotic encounters, she had come to think of him as her personal insanity, a being not truly of this world and hardly flesh-and-blood at all. Watching him fight in this crowded, human environment established for her that he had a reality of his own; he was not simply her temptation and her nightmare alone.

Everything he did was compelling, moving with such skill and precision. She had not known he was such an accomplished fighter. She thought she should be appalled by the scene, but instead she was transfixed. Watching him transported her into a trance-like state as she was hypnotized by the beauty of his movements. He had started in earnest on the other man, landing swift, telling blows one after another. His bulky opponent collapsed to his knees, but the onslaught did not abate. Beneath a few more skillfully placed punches, the man crumpled completely, his face a bloody pulp. Seth turned then, the killing look still in his eyes, and recognized her. Looking at him, she knew he could break her as though she was no more than a china doll, and she longed for him, craving the heat of his passion in the aftermath of the fight. Even from a distance she could see the lust in his eyes and his desire for her.

Ivy saw the look that bound them both. For a moment she doubted what she was seeing, but the sheer potency of their connection was unmistakable. She hoped it was a sudden attraction and not evidence of an actual affair. Megan stared at Seth and he stared back, each transfixed by the other. Looking at the young woman beside her, Ivy wondered if this was the source of Megan's recent distraction. She hoped not. If Ben Tuck was unsuitable for her, how much less so his violent brother for the gentle daughter of a vicar?

Seth advanced on the pair, oblivious to who might see them.

Ivy scanned the people around her frantically, searching for familiar faces, and was relieved to find none. "Hello Seth," she said, frantically trying to think of some way to instill reason into the pair.

Neither of them seemed to notice her.

"Come with me," he commanded.

Megan shot Ivy a pleading glance.

"You aren't…" Ivy found she could not ask what she feared most, but the fierce blush in Megan's cheeks told her more than enough. It was hardly her place to tell the woman what she ought to do, but even so, this was madness.

"Don't tell anyone," Megan implored.

"Come on," Seth growled. He seemed careless of the extreme social jeopardy in which he had placed his conquest.

"I won't say a word," Ivy promised, knowing as she spoke that she would regret it.

Megan and Seth slipped away from the mayhem of the fair, wandering along the hedgerows, stealing hungry kisses and exchanging molten looks. Eventually the sounds of merriment grew distant and they found some privacy in the seclusion of a tiny spinney. She pulled her lover close, kissing him with a violence inspired by his recent brutality. Her tongue plundered his mouth as her hands laced through his dark hair. She did not ask what the cause of the fight had been; it was of no consequence to her. His strength, and the wild passion in him, was all that mattered.

He tugged off her bonnet, casting it to one side before pulling the pins from her hair so that her long brown tresses fell free around her shoulders. When he pushed her roughly into the grass, she yielded gladly. The anger was still in him. Rage burned in his eyes, and his hands were harsh on her tender body, pinching and gripping with uncanny force. His teeth were cruelly sharp, nipping at her breasts and neck, startling her with ever shifting patterns of fleeting pain. She accepted it all, aroused by his intensity.

There was no tenderness or finesse in what they did. He pushed up her skirts and dragged down her undergarments so that he could get at her. She was ready for him. Theirs was a hurried, urgent coupling. They rolled together, partially undressed. His explosive lust infected her, and tentatively she began to respond in kind, with nips and pinches of her own, applying her teeth to his shoulders and chest. There was always something new to be learned with Seth, some previously unimaginable sensuality to be explored.

At the moment when she thought they were both about to succumb to pleasure, he stopped and wrapped his long fingers around her small throat. She could feel the lightest of pressures against her windpipe. Fearless, she gazed up at him. There were no doubts in her mind – she knew he could easily crush the breath out of her or snap her neck if he meant to. Her life was utterly in his hands. What he would do with that power she did not know or care, and the absolute nature of her vulnerability thrilled her to the core. He could take her life in this lonely place. The expression on his face was hard to read poised as he was on the edge of death or of blinding pleasure. She waited, not thinking, barely breathing, although her heart pounded in her ears. She had never felt so completely possessed in all her life. Seth owned her existence and he could snuff it out on a moment's whim…

Gradually, the fire of rage and destruction burned low in him; she watched the subtle changes in his face that marked its leaving. The moment of insanity passed, and he lowered his head to kiss her mouth. His hips rocked slowly, taking them over the edge together.

* * *

The church bells chimed four. To Ivy, the sound was dire and ominous. She had returned to the waiting trailer, catching a glimpse of the Wests and establishing her worst fear – that Megan was absent. She searched the crowds, not daring to ask for help for fear of further compromising the young lady's reputation. There was no sign of Megan anywhere.

An unexpected hand on her arm forced her to stop. "I wonder if I be the one you're rushing to find?" Ben asked her.

"No," she said angrily, and then realized he might be the one person who could aid her and smiled apologetically.

He must have seen something of the concern she felt. "What is it?" he asked.

Stepping closer to him, she lowered her voice. "You're brother, him's made off with our Megan."

Ben laughed.

"She? What's her want with Seth?"

"What do any girl want with a handsome man?"

Ben became serious. "I know him's taken a fancy, him don't talk much, but lately it's been nothing but she."

"She's been right queer for ages and all," Ivy observed.

"He's not for her, nor she for him."

"I know. Her's supposed to be back for tea, and her ain't, and it'll be trouble."

"We'd best find them."

"I were looking."

"He'll be gone. Him don't like crowds."

They went together, searching through the fields and exploring the hedgerows in pursuit of the missing couple. The Church chimed one quarter after another. A flash of dark pink – the color of Megan's attire – drew Ivy's attention. She advanced quickly. The sight of the young man and woman together halted her in her tracks. Megan's dress had been pulled down to reveal her small breasts. Seth lay with his head on her stomach, his back bare to the warm sunshine. Both appeared to be sleeping.

"What's her done?" Ivy murmured, hardly able to believe what her eyes told her.

"What any pretty wench does with a man," Ben replied, coming closer.

"You shouldn't be looking," Ivy chastised.

"Nor should you."

They glanced at each other, realizing the difficulty of their circumstance.

"I'm half afraid her's in love with him," Ivy confessed.

Ben shook his head. "Him's not for the likes of she."

"I know."

"You don't know the half of it," Ben replied.

Ivy shot him a questioning look.

"Come on, you, time's up," Ben called out.

Seth raised his head, and gave his brother a dark look.

"Come on, lad, her's got to get back to her folks or there'll be a right to do."

Seth prodded Megan into wakefulness, rising to stretch himself.

Megan moved languorously, opening her eyes like a sleepy, contented cat. When she saw Ben, she squealed, covering her breasts with her hands and sitting up to hide herself.

Ivy hurried to her, helping her dress. "I'm sorry, Megan," she whispered. "You should've been back an hour since. I'd never have found you else."

Megan hurriedly pulled her clothes up around her.

When Ivy looked round, there was no sign of Seth, but Ben was gathering up a bundle of garments. She almost questioned his absence, but decided it was better he had gone. "We'd best get back," she said.

Megan walked on alone, resolutely silent and unapologetic. She kept her head high and her back rigidly straight.

Ivy quietly concluded there was nothing she could do or say that would help. Best not to embroil herself any further, she decided. If the young lady could not guard her interests, there was little point trying to explain matters to her.

"If they're set on each other, we'll not stop them," Ben observed.

"I weren't going to try."

"Has her been strange of late?"

"Her has, now you come to mention it. Her's been right strange all this Spring. Not her right self at all."

Ben nodded, as though this was only to be expected.

"What ain't you saying?" Ivy asked.

"You'd not believe it," Ben replied.

"You just try me."

He stopped walking and turned to face her. His gaze was searching and wary. "Him's otter born. Him's my half brother all right, but him's otter born."

"What are you getting at?" Ivy demanded, utterly perplexed. The words made no sense to her at all.

"He ain't human, not entirely, any road."

She raised her eyebrows. There were enough stories of strange goings on in the fens, but she had never heard such a claim made before. This was not something to be believed or disbelieved. She would need the evidence of her own eyes. Questions floated through her mind… How had Ben's father got a child on an otter? Did this have anything to do with the grotesque circumstances of Old Moocher's death? What did it mean for Ben? Was the young man simply trying to tease her again? Ivy thought he seemed very serious, but she did not trust him and thought this might be some joke at her expense. "We'll see," she said.

"You don't believe me."

"Him's a rum one, that brother of yours, but it sounds like a tall story to me and I think you're trying to make a fool of me, Ben Tuck."

"I swear to you, Ivy, this is the truth. Him's not what he seems, and your Megan had best watch herself."

"She ain't my Megan."

The conversation faltered. They were almost back to the carnival field.

Megan was waiting for them by the hedge. "You'll not say anything, will you? Either of you?" Her voice was gentle and pleading. She seemed very much like the Megan of old; the well-behaved, dutiful Megan. The shift was startling.

"We can say as you caught a touch of sun and had to lie down in the shade a while," Ivy said.

"Ivy, you are a darling."

"I don't want trouble. What you do must be on your own conscience, Miss. That's all I'm saying."

Megan hurried away to her waiting parents.

"Will you take a turn around the stalls?" Ben asked.

"All right then," Ivy said. She was in need of distracting from her thoughts, and at least in Ben's company there was no need to pretend that all was well.

"Him's not easy, Seth isn't," Ben confided.

"So I see. And she looks to be getting much the same. Maybe we should leave them to it."

"I doubt we'll stop them."

"I think you might be right, but I don't want to think about them two."

He took her round the hall of mirrors and they laughed at each other's distorted images in the crowded tent. When the church clock chimed for six, Ivy returned to the trailer. She was sorry to be going back to her work, and the dangerous lies Megan was embroiling her in.

"How you getting back?" she asked Ben as they were about to part.

"I'll be walking later, won't take me more than a couple of hours. I'll watch out for you, Ivy. I seen you some Tuesdays in the fields."

"That's my afternoon off."

"Thought as much. I'll watch for you and you let me know if there's any trouble.

When it comes to people, Seth don't have an awful lot of sense."

On that note, they parted. For a moment Ivy thought he might try to kiss her, but he made no move at all, and she climbed aboard safely untouched and slightly regretful. As the traction engine pulled away, she glanced back, but Ben had disappeared into the crowds.

Chapter Nine

It was her fascination for a mystery that got the better of Ivy in the end. She needed to know if Ben had been telling the truth. He had not embellished the tale, nor had he confessed to a playful lie, which made it all the more curious. Usually a tall tale was spun out over an evening at most, and the fun was in revealing your cleverness in exploiting other people's desire for a good story. Ben had made his assertion, and left it at that. Ivy had spent many hours while her hands were occupied with monotonous work considering the possibility. If there could be ghost girls in the fens, then why not a man who was part otter? The one was no more incredible than the other, she decided.

The more she thought about it, the more the desire to know grew within her. She would find herself remembering the scene of two lovers clasped together, Seth's back exposed to the sun, his muscles shifting when he moved. He was a fine looking man. Then there was his sudden disappearance, apparently without his clothes. It was difficult thinking of him entirely unclad; the notion made her hot and uncomfortable. It became clear to Ivy that the only solution must be to see for herself. She needed to know if there was indeed some uncanny transition between man and creature.

It did not take long to learn when Megan was slipping away to be with her lover. There was usually an afternoon or more in every week when Reverend West was involved at the school or with another important Parish duty, and his wife had some concern to attend to. On these afternoons, Megan would disappear for an hour or more, oblivious to a mere servant's careful attention. All Ivy had to do was anticipate the occurrence of such a day, and rise earlier than usual. Knowing the ins and outs of the household, she was as well placed as Megan to determine when a suitable afternoon might arise. With the greater part of her work completed by noon, she merely had to wait for the tell-tale click of the door, and follow wherever the young mistress of the house went.

Once they were out of the village, Ivy lagged behind, not wanting to be noticed or recognized. It was impossible to move in the open fenland without being apparent for miles around. The last thing she wanted was that Megan should notice this intrusion; it was not something she wanted to explain. After a while she realized there was but one spot her quarry could be going to. The ruin of the old abbey was the only secluded place for miles around in this direction.

Other people were out in the fields now that the weather was better. The distinctive scent of peaty soil filled the air. Some of the first flowers were ready for picking, and the smallholders and tenant farmers were cutting the blooms ready for sending to London. As a child, Ivy had helped her mother harvest chrysanthemums, taking days off school when needed to toil in the fields alongside her siblings. Pursuing Megan was easy, but Ivy took her time, uncertain of what she was doing. She watched the distant workers in the fields and the birds fluttering overhead.

She had not set out with the intention of spying on their lovemaking; it was not until she was some way along the road that Ivy started considering what might be going on amongst the ruins. Recollections of Megan's bare breasts and the exposed length of Seth's back trickled into her awareness. The possibility of seeing him thrilled and alarmed her in equal measure. Thoughts of his lean body and intense gaze took, superseding her musings about otter forms and supernatural goings on.

There was no sign of anyone when Ivy initially approached the ruins, but then there were many hidden nooks and corners in this ruined place. She had played here herself in years gone by and knew the abbey's secret places well enough. On holidays there were always children scampering over the old rubble and playing games around the pillars. The faces might change, but their sports remained much the same.

Moving cautiously in the hopes of not making her presence too obvious, she searched for the errant couple. There were tumbledown walls half shrouded by ferns, and the remnants of long forgotten buildings everywhere. Nothing was complete. It seemed a miserable, desolate sort of place to her and she could not understand why anyone would choose it as the site of an assignation. She would have preferred one of the coppices, or the willow beds near the old mill pond. Peering over the remains of a wall, she finally saw them. Neither was facing in her direction. She froze, holding her breath for a long while as she watched the two lovers.

The act of coupling was no surprise to her. Ivy knew well enough what the farm creatures did; she had seen the stallion taken to the mares enough times for that to be no mystery. Megan's head rested on her arms, her face turned away, her usually restrained hair fanned about her like a cape. She was down on her knees and elbows. The side of one small breast and the ripeness of her hips were on full display. Ivy barely gave her a second glance. What drew her eye was the sleek muscularity of Seth's naked body. The vision of him transfixed her. She could see every shifting expression on his striking face. Every thrust he made was perfectly visible to her, as was the way his hands ran over Megan's body and the tension in his flanks as he pushed himself inside her. She had thought of stallions before, and watching him possess her mistress confirmed the image in her mind. This man was something wild; he was beyond the bounds of normal society, of that there could be no doubt. What shocked her was how he commanded her attention. She could not take her eyes from his exposed body. She swallowed, and found that her mouth was very dry. Her skin seemed to ache and buzz, her heart thrumming like some steam-driven engine. There could be no condemning Megan for such a transgression. A man like Seth could not be refused.

Ivy stayed still, the cold of the wall chilling her through her dress as she pressed close against it to keep her balance. For a while she looked away, struggling with a knot of conflicting feelings. Listening to their guttural expressions of pleasure made her skin crawl and her heart ache. The sound was too much, and she submitted to watching them again, her eyes fixed on him, her gaze running up and down the length of his perfect body and returning to the expressions on his face. Each moment his features revealed some subtle variation on a theme of mounting tension. He clenched his eyes shut digging his fingers hard into Megan's pale thighs, and the rutting girl emitted a cry of unmistakable release as he made one final, powerful thrust into the depths of her body.

His eyes flicked open and he turned his head, looking directly at Ivy as though he had known all along that she was there. She flinched under the heat of his attention, fearing he would alert Megan to her presence. Her face burned with shame at this discovery, but she could neither move nor resist the force of his staring eyes. At last he looked away and she took the opportunity to duck down and flee to the safety of the road.

Her intention had been to find out if there was anything uncanny about him. What she had seen carried her thoughts in different directions entirely. The image of him in all his naked glory would not leave her thoughts. The danger in his eyes, the raw, lustful menace of the man haunted her as she fled. Tears she could not explain stung her eyes, such that she could hardly see the ground beneath her feet. It was in this state that she almost collided with Ben.

"Hey, my wench," he said, stopping her in her tracks.

She turned away from him, unable to look him in the eye.

"Ivy? What's happened?"

There was genuine concern in his voice, and it proved to be more than she could stand. Tears cascaded down her cheeks. There was no confessing to him. She had done something she should not, and now the price of it would have to be paid. She had no room in her life for need or want. She had a good position and a simple, comfortable existence. Untamed forces had been unleashed within her and threatened to tear all that apart. "Hold me," she begged.

Fate had thrown him across her path, and she accepted it. His arms encircled her shoulders, pulling her tightly to his chest. He smelled of brackish water and mud, but she did not care.

"I knew you'd be asking one of these days, but I never thought it'd be like this. What's grieving you, wench?"

"I can't... don't ask me... I don't " Tangled phrases she could not finish fell from her lips.

His fingers caressed her back, soothing the tempest within her. After everything she had witnessed, he seemed unthreatening, a refuge of relative sanity in a world that had shifted beyond all reason. In her mind's eye she still saw Seth's face and the irresistible power in his gaze. Ben's hands glided over her hips, pulling the length of her body closer to his until they were fully touching from shoulders to thighs. It was an instinctive response to tilt back her head, offering up her lips to his. With eyes closed against the world, she felt the softness of his mouth on hers moving slowly, planting tender kisses until she melted beneath him, allowing herself to be consumed. He enabled her to forget everything else. Gradually, the tormenting image of Seth began to fade, replaced by awareness of the sensual progress of Ben's tongue in her mouth.

They stood together for a long time, and she pressed her face against his shoulder, allowing a state of calm to settle on her.

"I must go," she murmured. "I've got tea to get and there'll be trouble if they miss me."

"I'll be watching for you," he said. "And you'll find me when you've a mind to."

"I will," she promised, not knowing if she meant to or not.

She hurried the rest of the way, afraid her absence would be noticed. Reverend West might be generous in most things, but he would not tolerate her absenting herself without leave to cavort with a young man on the roadside. Her mind was reeling with thoughts of Seth, while Ben's kisses left her lips swollen and tender.

Chapter Ten

There was a fortnight in early June when the winds brought wave after wave of torrential rain. Crops suffered, fields partially flooded, and the village acquired a grim, downtrodden look. During this time Mrs. West only left her abode for true emergencies as she nursed a tremulous cough. Megan and Ivy were sent out on missions of mercy. The two young women had an uneasy truce, and they seldom spoke to each other more than was necessary. Ivy could tell there was no chance whatsoever for Megan to go out to the abbey. With her mother constantly present, the rain made all excuses of taking a little exercise impossible. The daughter of the house stalked the small rooms of her home as though they were a cage and she an imprisoned wildcat. As the rain-swept days followed relentlessly on each other's heels, Megan struggled to maintain her usual standards of gentle and cooperative behavior.

Ivy was returning to clear away the tea things when her sharp ears picked up fragments of a conversation between the Wests.

"Poor child, she is half out of her mind with worry," Mrs. West remarked gently.

"There is so little she can do. I feel for her. It tests anyone's faith to see the poorest people punished in this way," Reverend West replied. "I must confess I am at my wit's end myself. If the rain does not ease soon, the grain crops will be ruined. The flower growers are already in desperate straits. There is some hope that other crops will flourish, but even so there will be worse to come. I fear what the next winter might bring us."

"It occurred to me that we might find the room to keep a cow in the garden. That way we could distribute a little milk to the poorest children," Mrs. West suggested.

"An excellent idea, my dear, perhaps a cow and some new project would lift Megan's spirits."

"I think it might."

Ivy entered the room and saw that the well-meaning couple were pleased with the solution they had found. A cow would not relieve their daughter's frustration, only her man could do that. It amazed Ivy that these two people were unable to see what was happening before their very eyes. Megan was changing. There was something wild growing within her, and each day a little more of it showed in her face. At least there was no hint of a child. Megan was currently nurturing the feral glory of her own soul, but there was every risk her body might swell with the fruit of her passions.

Ivy had seen for herself what the weather was doing. Her family was suffering dreadfully as their early flower crops were damaged beyond all rescue. The early signs of her mother's pregnancy had vanished, un-remarked upon. Ivy knew this was not the first time such a thing had occurred. As the flowers rotted in the fields, May remained dour and uncommunicative, nursing her silent grief. Ivy knew that the money from older children – chiefly herself, Albert and Gladys – was all that was keeping the rest of them from destitution. She could only hope that later flowers might survive, that the downpour would abate and give them time to recover.

It was usually the case that Ivy was the first one awake in the morning, and the last one to retire for the night. The burden of household duties largely fell to her, although both of the other women had their tasks, and there was a boy who came to work in the garden and undertake small jobs around the house. She was tidying the kitchen by the flickering light of a single candle when there was a light tap at the window. Tensing every muscle in her body, she opened the door onto the well tended back garden.

"Hello?" she called out softly, wondering if it was some soul in distress, drawn by the light. She could see nothing in the dark garden. Rain splattered against her skin.

"Will you let me in, wench?"

The voice was low and rough. She had only ever heard him speak a few times, but there was no mistaking him.

"What you doing here?" she blurted out in panic.

"You know. Let me in."

"I cannot."

His hand emerged from the darkness, gripping her wrist with alarming force. He pushed her back against the door frame. All efforts to stand her ground and resist the intrusion were futile. Ivy became weak at his touch. A wild, futile hope grew in her that he was here for her, but she knew it was not so. He barely saw her. As Seth came into the sphere of candlelight, she realized he was utterly naked. She swallowed hard, painfully conscious of this man's proximity and his overwhelming sexuality. What sort of man wandered the night unclad? The answer was stark – a man who wears an otter's skin has no use for other clothing. Her fingers ached to touch him, and she struggled to control herself.

"Where is she?" he hissed.

Ivy considered her situation. Discovery would be terrible, both for her and for Megan. She quickly determined that assisting him was perhaps the best way of keeping them all safe, but to have this love affair conducted under the vicar's own roof seemed too much, even to her mind.

"I'll show you."

Every creak of the stairs made her stomach clench with fear. Seth was light on his feet, and she could hardly hear him as he padded behind her. He was walking in perfect step, shadowing her moves so that no one could have discerned his foot-fall from hers. All of the lights were out in the bedrooms. She opened the door to Megan's room for him, knowing she would be better able to minimize the squeak of the handle. He vanished into the darkness, and Ivy hurried to her own attic bedroom, trying not to think what might be happening in the little room below hers.

* * *

Sleep had been elusive for days. The continual patter of rain against the window was a maddening reminder of her imprisonment. Megan did nothing but think of her lover, wondering where he was, what he did, and whether he would understand that she could not escape to be with him. Without him, she was only half alive. The grey of unending rain became the emblem of her misery. It was both the source and the reflection of her suffering. Somehow over the long Spring she had made the transition from innocence to passion. The doubts and fears of months past seemed like the foolishness of childhood. Seth had awoken Megan to her sensual nature and she embraced it fully.

Darkness surrounded her, thick and cloying. Walking the borderlands between dream and wakefulness, she let her wildest fantasies run freely through her mind. She had imagined him coming to her so many times that at first, when the covers on her bed were drawn back, it seemed to be another part of her dream, but his body was too solid and certain. How he came to be there did not matter. Although she could not see him, she knew the smell of him so perfectly that she did not doubt it was him. Hands closed over her breasts and his lips sought hers. She dug her fingers into his shoulders, needing to reclaim him.

Neither of them spoke, knowing full well that any sound could lead to discovery. The language of his fingers on her skin was enough. Megan could feel the need in him. They had been apart too long, neither entirely whole without the other's touch. Seth was not a man for words. He had never said anything about love or the future. There was no need. For all the apparent differences of class and culture, they were kindred souls. The passion they shared went beyond words, a communion of wild spirits like the inevitable meeting of land and sky on the horizon.

He was hard against her, pushing into the fabric of her nightdress and nudging her stomach with tiny, suggestive thrusts. The peaty smell of his skin infected her with desire. Impatient to bare her body, he tore the front of her delicate nightdress. Lips fastened over her nipples, moving hungrily from one stiff peak to the other. She had to bite her tongue to stop herself from crying out. He moved so quickly it seemed as if he was everywhere on her skin at once. With kisses, licks and nips, he covered her stomach and hips. She raked his back with her nails. If she drew blood, it would not be the first time.

His cock seemed wider than ever before; she was almost as tight as on the day of her deflowering. She clung to him, needing the length of him filling her. His breath was hot against her ear as she wrapped her legs around his back, tilting her hips towards him, locking her ankles closer together. All the frustration and anguish of waiting fell from her mind. She was acutely alive, filled by her man and awash with sensations.

Seth took his time, his strokes long and leisurely. Although at first she was ravenous for the pleasure he could give, Megan accepted this tortuously gentle pace. Whatever he wanted she usually acquiesced to. She had spent so long suppressing her own desires that she still did not fully know how to want things for herself. He could enjoy her on any terms he wanted, she would give herself freely and utterly. Being owned by him was more akin to freedom than anything she had before encountered. Her wild soul might have found its wings, but it did not know how to fly.

They came together in a shared starburst of pleasure. He rolled easily from her embrace and drew her close so that her head rested on his chest. Megan listened to the pounding of his heart. These were the moments she loved best, the often fleeting seconds afterwards when he was easy and languid and she was truly alive to herself. Normally she opened her eyes to the vast sky and let her spirit soar amongst the clouds. They had never made love under a roof before, and she felt odd not being able to see anything. Stroking him affectionately, she let sleep take her.

In the depths of the night, he roused her with hungry kisses. She surfaced into arousal and need, welcoming him into her once more. Barely conscious, dreams stalked her waking mind, flooding her disorientated senses. Seth was upon her, but as she slipped between sleep and wakefulness it seemed as though her hands tangled in coarse fur and that there were claws raking across her body, not fingers. Whiskers brushed against her cheeks, and a sinuous tail whipped across her legs. Yet it did not matter what skin he wore, nor the shape in which he manifested, she would always know him.

A little before the dawn he woke her one last time with lips pressed against her eyelids and his hands gripping hers. She did not ask when, or if, he would return. The thoughts echoed in her, unvoiced. She knew he was going, but that he would be back at the first chance he got if she could not find her way to the ruins.

"Always," she whispered as he slipped from her bedroom into the waking day.

* * *

Ivy was already in the kitchen lighting the range and making preparations for breakfast. Every movement was an effort. The night had been difficult for her and she felt leaden from lack of sleep. She hoped Seth had long since gone.

A scream shattered the morning. A dull thud followed it, then the sounds of opening doors and voices raised in anger. Ivy ran to the bottom of the stairs, colliding with Seth as he bolted from the house. She crashed into a small bureau, bruising her legs.

"Stop him!" West shouted.

It was far too late for that. Seth would be in his other skin by now, racing beneath a hedgerow or plunging into the safety of a dyke. They would not catch him.

Ivy considered the disastrous scene. Mrs. West sat awkwardly upon the floor at the top of the stairs, clutching her head in her hands, her shoulders heaving as though with sobs. Ivy supposed that the invariably fragile woman had fainted at the sight of a naked man on her landing. White-faced and shaking, Megan clutched her torn nightdress about herself, staring from her father to her mother in turn. She was paralyzed by indecision. Reverend West was purple with rage.

"Did he hurt you?" he bellowed at his daughter. He was not a man to shout, and the anger in his voice was petrifying.

Megan shook her head.

He gestured towards her brutally damaged attire.

Megan stared back mutely, unable to explain the condition of her clothing.

West looked at the three women of his household in turn.

Ivy felt an almost uncanny calm settling over her. There would be no getting out of this mess without serious consequences, and one way or another blame would inevitably fall upon her. West was clearly in no mood to be kind.

"How did that… person get into my house?" He asked, his voice sounding more dangerous still now that he had some control over it.

His gaze was fixed upon Ivy. As the last to bed and first to rise, she was the natural suspect. With a calm that startled her, she answered him.

"I let him in last night. I had not meant him to startle you."

Megan's eyes grew round with shock, but she did not move or protest in any way.

"He spent the night in my room," Ivy added.

This was the last thing she would be able to do to protect Megan. The young lady would have to act more wisely in the future.

"How could you betray my trust in you, Ivy?"

The disappointment in his voice was worse than any angry word could have been. Ivy loved and respected the family she served. The half-lie pained her, but the truth would be worse.

"Pack your belongings and leave at once. I cannot have you under this roof a moment longer."

Ivy nodded, knowing she could not protest against such a judgment. On the landing above her, Megan fled into her bedroom. Somehow, in all the drama, the peculiarity of her torn gown had been forgotten.

Chapter Eleven

t was the first clear day in weeks, an irony that was not entirely lost on Ivy. If Seth could have waited another day for his lover, then they might all have been in a much better position.

Going home to her parents, disgraced as she was, filled Ivy with shame. Although her virtue was intact, everyone would think it lost, and what people believed was always more influential than the truth. There was no one else who might take her in, but even so, Ivy stood in the lane for quite some time, considering carrying on and taking her chances rather than having to confess to her failure. The last month had been hard on her family. How could she tell them she had lost her place, and with it the money and food that had helped them so much?

May emerged with a basket of washing to be aired. She rapidly took in her daughter's presence and condition, and her face darkened. "What on earth do you be doing here?" she asked grimly.

Ivy had rehearsed what she might say, but even so, her mouth was dry and her head suddenly empty of all intelligible thought. "They don't want me at the vicarage any more," she said.

"What fool thing have you done?"

"I let a man in, and him startled Mrs. West, so I'm to go."

"You're a bloody idiot," May responded. "So I suppose we've to take you in and do without your help and all?"

"If you and father could find room for me, I'd be glad of it. Won't be for long, I'll get something else."

"You'll be lucky. Is this man of yours going to do right by you?" May asked bitterly. She had expected better from Ivy.

"I don't reckon so."

Even though she had not explicitly claimed Seth as her lover, her mother, like everyone else, would simply assume it was so.

"You'll not get a job in a house again, that's for sure."

"I know."

"We can't keep you. If you've nowhere to go, then stay you must, but you'll have to work. You'll be on the land; you've no skill to turn to. We'll be hard pressed to feed you as it is."

Ivy nodded with resignation. She had given up all prospect of a decent future with a single act of weakness. Without a reference, she could not get another position as a servant. As soon as she went on the land, it would be guessed she had left the vicarage in disgrace and her reputation would be lost forever.

"At least it's summer. There'll be hands needed haymaking, then there's whatever corn the rain left, and more flowers in a week or two if this rain holds off. There'll be work enough. Lord alone knows what's to become of you come winter."

Ivy had pondered this question herself, and supposed the only answer would be to try for a factory job in one of the distant towns. It would mean moving away, but she could see no real alternative to that.

"You might as well help," May gestured towards the washing, and Ivy set to at once.

"You were good with rug making at school," her mother commented as they pegged out clothes together.

"I were," Ivy agreed.

It was something she had entirely forgotten about. Mrs. Norman, the school master's wife, had shown them all how to make decent rugs from scraps of cloth and Hessian sacks. Ivy found she had nimble enough fingers for the work, and could make up designs that were appealing to the eye. It was a skill she had not used for years, but supposed it might be worth considering.

"Though you've got to have something to make them from, but if you aren't too proud to go begging, maybe some folks will help you get started."

"That might do, for the winter anyways."

"It's something." May stopped working and eyed her daughter critically, studying her figure.

"There won't be no baby," Ivy assured her.

"If you've been with a man there could be."

"There won't," Ivy reiterated.

"I ain't asking, and I doesn't want to hear." She turned her back on her daughter and walked into the house. Ivy gritted her teeth and followed.

"As you're the only one here of any use at all, you can chop me some more wood for the fire."

Ivy nodded. The only significant difference between being a child in her parent's house and a servant at the Wests' was that in the latter capacity she was paid for her efforts.

For a week she helped clear the ruined flowers so that another crop could be sown. Then the later blooms came out and her father had her cutting them from dawn until dusk. Her hands, unaccustomed to such rough work, were badly scratched and she was forever bleeding but she could not afford gloves, and her back ached from being bent double all the time. At night she shared a crowded space with three younger sisters. There was only one bedroom, but her parents had put up curtains, separating the boys and the girls and allowing a little privacy for each. After having a modest attic bedroom to herself at the vicarage, this was cramped indeed.

The food in her parent's home was poorer than she had become used to – usually no more than vegetable stew with a little bread. She was conscious that her presence stretched things further, and every meal she ate left her feeling acutely guilty. The harsh combination of longer working hours and a reduced diet left her continually exhausted. She was too tired to think or feel anything much, for which she could only be grateful.

For the first time in years, Ivy found herself under no obligation to attend church. She doubted that West and his family would welcome her presence in their congregation. There were Methodists in the village as well, but she had never had much to do with them and could not imagine starting now. The first few Sundays she was too tired for anything but sitting in the little garden, shelling peas for the evening meal, while the rest of her family went to church. There were a few hard words from both parents, but she weathered them. In the end they gave up, resigned to the burden of a daughter no one would wish to employ or marry.

Gradually, her body adapted to her new life, and her energy returned. Sundays offered her the opportunity of spending a little time alone wandering in the fields, foraging in the hedgerows and forgetting about the ruin of her life. She stayed away from the abbey and from the little cottage occupied by the Tuck brothers. As it was early summer, there was always something she could pick, and adding to the meager supplies of the household helped to assuage her guilt over imposing upon them.

It was quite some distance to the river, but drawn by a growing need for solitude, her worn boots ate up the miles with ease. The worry about what she might do before the winter came was very much upon her. Ivy knew she could work through the long harvest, but after that there would be no employment for her in Burnham. She had never ventured beyond the surrounding villages. Other girls had gone to work in factories, most never to be seen again. She had no one who could help her, no friends or connections who would ease the way and find her a suitable workplace and lodgings. If she left she would have to go alone, chancing she could manage such things for herself. There was no way her parents could support her through the winter; they were barely able to feed and clothe themselves and their younger children at the best of times. There would be less work for her father then, and with her own few pennies not coming in either, they would all suffer. In failing to resist Seth, she had done herself and her family considerable harm which she could now find little means to rectify.

Ivy could see a figure approaching from the direction of the river, eel pots in either hand. A man in her position might take to poaching or fishing, but she had no such skill. Beyond a little sewing, she had no trade other than as cook and servant. Who would employ her now? She envied the distant man with work of his own. The idea of making rag rugs appealed to her, but she had no fabric and no space in which to work; the house was too crowded and dirty for such an enterprise. Her gaze returned to the toes of her boots, visible beneath the mud-splattered hem of her skirt. With head hung low, she walked, lost in troubled thought. When she next looked up, the eel man was only a few hundred yards distance. It was Ben Tuck. He approached her, stopping a few feet away to look her up and down.

"Now there's a pretty sight," he said.

She smiled wanly at the compliment.

"You not working for that vicar now? I see'd you been out in the fields."

"That I have. I'd a thought you might've heard."

"Heard what?"

"Your Seth come courting Miss West one night, and I let him in. Then him frightened poor Mrs. West in the morning and there was a right to-do. I let them think him were mine, and that were the end of it for me."

"Him's not got much sense," Ben said. "I didn't know them two were still so friendly. Him's not said much about she of late."

"Them's very friendly, indeed."

"Him's been like a storm cloud these last few weeks, lurking round the cottage with nothing to say for himself. Maybe him's not seen her since."

"Might be. Her folks won't be letting her wander about so free, I reckon. Them's had a bit of a fright."

"Or maybe she's thought better of it."

"I never had much idea what Miss Megan thought. Her seemed straightforward enough, but these last months her's been a different girl."

"Love will do that to a person," Ben said, his tone serious but his eyes playful.

"I wouldn't know about that," Ivy replied, aware she was blushing.

The last few months had changed her at least as much as they had Megan. She had lost her placid confidence and tranquility. Now she suffered irritability and sudden bouts of melancholia. If that was the consequence of love, she wanted no more of it.

"I'm sorry him have got you into difficulty."

She shrugged dismissively. The fault was as much her own as his.

"What'll you do now?"

"Work the harvest. Then there's not much here for the likes of me. I'll have to go to town, see what I can find."

"'Tis a shame. You've a good heart, Ivy, it's not right you paying for what them others done."

"I let him in."

"Could you have stopped him? There ain't no stopping Seth when he's got the mood on him."

Ivy shrugged. She had not really considered this alternative.

"You've done my brother a kindness, and he's brought nothing but trouble on you."

"What's done is done."

"That's as may be." He eyed her thoughtfully as he spoke. "You could marry me. I've not much, but it'll be better than your parents or town."

She laughed aloud, not really thinking he was serious in his proposal.

"I means it. You're a comely wench and you knows I want you."

Desperation alone might have been enough to sway her. Ivy's plans for a life of chastity and comfortable servitude had long since crumpled to dust. Marrying Ben would be better by far than any other scheme she could envisage. He evidently was serious, and she suspected it would probably be the best offer she ever got.

"All right then."

He lowered the eel pots carefully and scooped her up in his arms.

Ivy felt a tremendous weight lift from her heart. She covered Ben's face with kisses, at first from gratitude, but gradually, fledgling flutters of desire moved her. This was not the raw, terrifying lust his brother had inspired, but it felt good, and she did not fight it. Ben returned her kisses with ardor, pressing his mouth into her neck and running his hands up and down her back.

"He'll think it were you in his house that night," she said.

"Maybe that's as well," Ben mused. "Should I speak to your old dad?"

"He'll be glad to see the back of me," she replied.

"I'd be glad seeing any bit of you."

Stepping away from him, she hitched up her skirt slightly, gracing Ben with a flash of her shapely ankles.

"I could tumble you right here," he said, his tone suddenly intense.

She shivered, half frightened, half aroused by his words. "You can wait 'til we're wed."

"I'd not thought you were serious church."

"I've enough troubles already without courting more. We can be wed within the month."

"I've waited most this year already for you. I can wait a bit more," he conceded.

She returned to his arms, offering up her mouth up to his stirring kisses.

Chapter Twelve

With the haymaking under way there were few children in school and Megan's sewing class was reduced to a handful of girls. It was one of the few times during which she was allowed out of her parents' sight. Since Ivy's departure, they had become watchful and wary. She did not dare to visit the abbey, and Seth had not risked a second attempt on the house. They had employed a new girl, who could scrub and clean well enough but had little idea of cooking. Mrs. West was busily educating her. Megan found she missed Ivy's quiet efficiency, and the knowledge that she had an ally of sorts in her home. She felt trapped. Without any chance to see Seth, the days became drab and wearisome. It might be bright summer beyond the window, but her heart was in winter and she cared for none of it.

There were so few boys in her father's class that he had sent them home for the afternoon and departed himself. She expected he would call for her when her lesson was due to end. Her students were so young they could manage nothing more than a little plain sewing. She was teaching them how to make patchwork, and they were working away studiously. Gazing dreamily through the window at the quiet village streets, Megan could see a knot of the unruliest boys engaged in some violent game. They always seemed to have sticks in their hands or to be throwing things at one another. Today they were kicking something. For a few minutes she watched them. At first she thought they must have a ball or some improvised toy. Their progress along the street was very slow, and as they came closer she could hear their jeers and cheers. It was a sound she recognized from previous bouts of wildness – they had some poor victim and were tormenting it. She rose to her feet, hoping they had not assaulted some stray dog or an unsuspecting cat. Cautioning her girls to remain exactly where they were, she made her way out, determined to stop their cruelty.

On seeing her, the boys dispersed like a flock of startled birds. Megan herself might not be especially threatening, but one word from her, and Mr. Norman, their usual teacher, would be brandishing his cane in no time. Their victim lay still in the street, a bloody, broken mass of fur. It was still breathing, but only just. It tried to stand, but could not. As she approached, it tried to snap at her, its sharp teeth biting on air.

Megan looked at the wounded otter, her heart torn by rage and anguish. It showed no signs of knowing her, but why else would an otter venture into the village on a warm summer's afternoon? They were normally creatures of the twilight times, and wary of contact with people. She knelt close to him, and he snapped again. There was blood dripping from his nostrils and one eye had been crushed beyond all healing. Each breath came as a rattle. He tried valiantly to stand, but although his front legs were responsive, the back ones would not move. They had broken his spine with their sticks. He was beyond help. She wanted to take him up in her arms, to carry him out of the street and to some quiet place where she could tend him. Even as she imagined doing so, she knew it would be impossible.

A workman stopped beside her. He had an old nag of a horse pulling a rickety cart in which there were farm tools that needed the blacksmith's attention.

"Can you help me move him?" she cried out.

The laborer eyed the dying otter and retrieved a bent spade from amongst his gear. Without consulting the young woman, he stepped in and swung the blade down hard, crushing the creature's skull. Blood and bone splattered the road. Megan stared in disbelief.

"Rum things, otters," the man observed. "Don't see them here much, wonder what it were doing?"

Megan knelt down, touching the bloodied fur with both hands. The creature was deathly still. She knew there was no life left in the body.

"You all right, Missy?"

She made no reply. Her tears fell onto her hands and onto the thick pelt. She could feel a scream rising in her throat, a long howl of keening anguish which, if she dared release it, might not stop until the last breath left her body.

"I know it looks hard, but it's the kindest thing I could do for he." The laborer's tone was gentle, but firm.

By the time her father returned for her, Megan was hysterical. Mr. Norman, the cantankerous school-master, and Mr. Norman the neurotic church warden, had both come to her aid but were able to do little other than lift the wailing girl up out of the dirt of the road, and half drag, half carry her into the relative privacy of the school. Neither of them had been able to calm her or determine what exactly had caused this uncharacteristic attack.

Reverend West stood indecisive in the doorway, listening to his church-warden's tremulous account and regarding his only child with concern. "Would you be so good as to fetch the doctor for me?" he asked.

The doctor was able to transport her back to the house and gave a prescription for laudanum if her condition did not improve.

* * *

"Oh, my poor child," Mrs. West crooned softly, stroking her daughter's brow.

Megan remained still and silent. She was conscious of her mother's continued presence and occasional words, but paid little heed. They were sedating her, and she knew the muzzy calm had no reality. Inside, she was still screaming. The blood might have been washed from her hands, but the memory of it was too vivid still. She felt as if she had been bundled up in soft fabric so that every sound and sensation was muted. Inside the bundle she was trapped with her thoughts and hideous memories, but unable to respond to them. Seth's face filled her mind, yet she could not find the strength to weep and grieve for him any more. Laudanum had robbed her of all will to rage against the injustice of her loss.

"How is she?" West asked, peering apprehensively around the bedroom door.

"Much as before. She will not speak to me," his wife replied sorrowfully. "What did the doctor say?"

"That physically there appears to be nothing wrong with her beyond what can be explained by her reluctance to eat. He thinks this is most probably an affliction of the mind."

"She was always very sensitive. That dreadfully cruel incident with the otter would have shocked anyone."

"Perhaps, but that was three days ago," Reverend West sighed hopelessly.

"I think the laudanum confuses her. It always confuses me when I am obliged to take it," Mrs. West observed.

"I had wondered if it might be best to send her away for a time, to your cousin in Ely perhaps or my sister in Bath."

Mrs. West blanched visibly at this suggestion. "I would rather keep her here with us."

"It might be a change of air would benefit her."

Megan listened, aware they were discussing her fate, but not caring what decisions they made. It no longer mattered whether she lived or died. She felt as though the only part of her that had ever been vital had been destroyed on that blood-spattered roadside. She supposed that if she lay still for long enough, they would eventually bury her and have done with it.

Chapter Thirteen

"That were better than what I thought it would be," Ivy commented as they walked away from the church together.

"It makes no odds to him what we does. He'd rather have us wed and proper than living in sin," Ben smiled. He had very little time for churchmen and their ways.

"Him were looking sad, though. Didn't you think?"

"Don't he always look down in the mouth? To much praying, I'm thinking."

Ivy glared at him. The circumstances of her dismissal had not reduced her respect for Reverend West. "Him's a good old boy, and I'll not have you taking against him that way."

Ben shrugged. "We got to get us some witnesses, then. Your old dad will give you away, won't him?"

"He'd rather sell me back to the vicar, but he'll do it if he must."

"I'd wanted our Seth to stand up with me, but him's been gone this last week or more."

"You'd not get him in a church."

"Like as not you're right, but him's me only brother."

"You can borrow one of mine. I've plenty brothers spare."

Ben was quiet for a while. Ivy glanced at him as they walked wondering what was on his mind.

"Do he go off a lot?" she hazarded.

"Him's always off one place or another. Often gone a few days and I'll not see hide nor hair of him. Sometimes him'll be gone longer an' all."

"But you're mithering," she observed.

"He weren't right. Can't say what, but I know he better than anyone. He weren't right in his self, and now him's gone off."

"You think this is over Megan West? I heard from my aunt her had took a bit queer."

"I hope he's not got a child on her."

"I've not heard any gossip that way. Could be she's ill. Her mother's a right sickly old girl."

"I am worried for him," Ben admitted.

"Maybe them's had a parting of the ways or her parents have forced it. Maybe that's all it is."

"I hopes you're right."

"There's nothing to be done but wait 'til he comes back, is there now?"

"Oh, you're right enough, my wench."

She took his hand, wanting to reassure him. He might have a reputation for being troublesome, but Ben was a sweet enough lad now she had come to know him a little. Ivy felt considerable affection for him, born largely of his kindness to her. Thus far he had made no attempt to take advantage of her, for which she was grateful. Once they were married, he would probably change, but she had a few weeks grace left before it needed worrying about. She could only hope he would not be too interested in that sort of thing. She did not consider herself to be an especially sexual or sensual person and that aspect of life only troubled her. Ben was someone she found it possible to be at ease with, unlike his brother, whose mere presence was enough to fill her with the most perturbing and incomprehensible feelings. She was not entirely sorry to learn that Seth had departed.

"What will him do when he comes back?" she asked.

"Seth? What he always do, come round the house when he wants, go off when he wants."

"Do he live with you?"

"He don't sleep under the roof, if that's what you mean, but it's closest to home he's got."

"Where do he sleep?"

"Him's got a holt someplace, keeps there mostly. More otter than man is Seth."

Ben's casual attitude to Seth's condition was still something she struggled with. She supposed he had been used to it for long enough. Seth would not be around the house then. She supposed that was as well. The idea of him living under the same roof had preyed upon her mind. The thought of him being there, with the devastating intensity of his dark eyes and that too captivating body, had been alarming her. It was impossible to imagine rising early in the morning to make breakfast with him loitering in the single room, watching her. She could remember how it felt to be the subject of his scrutiny, and shivered helplessly at the thought.

"You don't like him," Ben remarked.

"It ain't that. He bother's me, that's all. Him's queer, no saying otherwise. Him's half otter, you said."

"That bother you?"

"It do."

He said nothing to that.

* * *

The wedding was a simple affair. Ivy wore her Sunday best, and most of her family was there to see the knot tied. Looking up from beneath her borrowed veil, Ivy considered the face of her vicar. He looked years older than he had when the summer began. There were dark shadows beneath his eyes and all of the warm humor was gone from his face. She was shocked by his condition and wondered what on earth had happened in that household since her departure. With Seth gone, she would have thought things might have been tranquil for them, but perhaps not. The gossip about Megan might well have some truth in it, and she hoped the young woman was not too seriously afflicted. But it was not her problem now, she told herself. There was nothing she could do for her former employer, and any troubles he might have were not her concern.

After the service, there was nothing to be done but fetch her scant possessions from her parents' cottage and trek the few miles out to Ben's isolated home. The grain harvest had not long started and no one could afford the time for celebrating the new union. Most of Ivy's family considered it an ill-omened time for a wedding.

"Them that bride twixt sickle and scythe will never survive," one of her ancient great aunts muttered before she entered the church.

Ivy smiled resolutely, hiding well the trepidation she felt.

The summer sun beat down upon them both as they trudged through the dusty fields. Ben carried her small pack of clothing and personal effects. She owned very little, and rather wished she was beginning married life with a few more things of her own. What money she had from her time at the West's she had given to her parents, and they could spare her nothing to help her set up house.

It had been many months since she last ventured inside the little cottage. Her memories from that bitterly frozen night were clear enough and little had changed. It was a cold, comfortless sort of place, and as she peered through the narrow doorway, she felt a gloom descend upon her.

Ben scooped her up in his arms and lifted her carefully over the threshold. He carried her easily and sat her down on the small wooden table. Looking up at him, Ivy could see the joy and pride in his face. A pang of guilt reverberated through her: She hoped he was not expecting too much of their arrangement. For her, it had been a way out of a life of uttermost difficulty, but she was starting to suspect he might have a far more romantic view of their situation. He cupped her face in his hands.

"I've wed you, Ivy Tuck," he said, smiling as he used the name for the first time. "Now will you come to bed?"

She smiled as best she could. She was fearful and uncertain, but had some idea what was expected of her. There was a duty to be performed, a price to be paid for having a home of her own. "Yes," she said simply, and made to get down from her tabletop perch.

"Wait." He stroked her cheek, all the while making a careful study of her face. She met his gaze as best she could, but gradually her courage failed her and she looked away. "Are you afraid to do it?" he asked.

She nodded.

"I swear I'll not hurt you, Ivy." He placed the most tender of kisses on her lips as his fingertips caressed her back and shoulders. "Come on, my duck."

He led her up the steep and narrow staircase. A shaft of sunlight illuminated the small space. Ivy remembered a grim little room, but found instead a magical bower of flowers. The floor and bed alike were strewn with countless blossoms and leaves, which gave their fragrance to the air. She supposed he must have been up with the dawn to gather so much, and it had been all for her sake. The gesture touched her heart, and she turned to him with her first unfeigned smile of the day.

He stripped off his jacket and shirt, baring his torso for her cautious inspection. He was not quite so muscular as his brother, but well enough built for all that. She ran her fingers down his chest, and blushed at her audacity. His smile was encouraging.

"I'll not bite," he said, "unless you want that?"

Taking a deep breath, she began the fiddly job of removing her own attire. There were various layers of over and under garments, all with small buttons and ties that her trembling fingers could barely manage. The unfamiliarity of baring her body to another's eyes and the uncertainty of what might follow made her more anxious than she had envisaged. The thought of consummating her marriage had seemed a little repugnant to her, but the details of the act had not crossed her mind to any great extent. One thing she had not anticipated feeling was an apprehension that he might not find her attractive once she had revealed herself fully before him.

Once it was done and she was stripped of all clothing, she stood, not knowing what to do next or where she should look. When he made no move, she risked a look at him. The expression of awe upon his face made her look again, and as her eyes met his, she felt the first flicker of confidence in his presence. She glanced at his trousers. It was all the encouragement he needed to discard them. He was a strong, lean man. Without taking her eyes off him, she reached for the few pins that secured her hair, and let her dark-brown curls tumble down to her waist. His fingers were in her tresses almost at once, moving the soft locks over her back and shoulders. She shuffled a little closer to him, letting her nervous hands find his narrow waist. He gathered her close, squeezing her breasts against his firm chest and cupping her round bottom in his hands. Ivy had to admit to herself that she liked the feel of him.

"You be a maid, don't you, wench?"

"Yes."

"You ever even fumbled a bit with a man?"

"Never."

He kissed her neck, starting just behind her ear and making his way down to her shoulder. Following the contours of her collar bone, he covered her skin with persistent kisses. Stooping, he lifted a nipple to his lips. Flesh that had previously been innocent of pleasure responded to the warm dampness of his mouth. Looking down at herself, Ivy could see her other nipple was already swollen in anticipation of similar delights.

"How's that?" he asked, surfacing.

She struggled to find her voice.

"You like that?"

She managed to nod.

"Lie down with me?"

Moving like one in a trance, she approached the flower bedecked bed and lay down. She could smell the perfumes of honeysuckle, meadowsweet and rose petals crushed against her skin. Ben stretched out beside her, lying on his side with his head supported by one arm. With his free hand he stroked up and down the length of her body. She could feel her skin trembling in to life as his fingers inspired unfamiliar sensations, sweet and tremulous, in response to his caresses. It wasn't so very bad really, she decided. Closing her eyes and accepting the slow arousal of her body, she found herself wondering what it would be like being taken by Seth. There would be no gentle care from him, she supposed. Instead he would be rough and urgent and she would be powerless to resist anything he did to her. It was a fantasy that left her feeling both weak and excited at once.

"There, my wench," Ben murmured.

His voice drew her back to the reality of her wedding day. Guilt trickled through her heart for a second time that afternoon. Ben was the brother she had married, and it seemed wrong to her to be thinking about his absent sibling in such an erotic fashion.

His hand prized her legs apart. Startled, she opened her eyes. He bent to taste her lips, whispering reassurances between kisses. His fingers trailed back and forth across her sex, light as thistledown. There was unfamiliar heat in her body, and without thinking she opened her legs a little further. With practiced ease, he explored her feminine secrets and she wondered how many other girls he had bedded. She lay very still as his mouth closed over her nipple again, and his fingers nuzzled against her labia, making her shiver even though she was perspiring in a feverish heat.

"It may hurt a bit at first," he warned, "you breathe easy and don't fret."

He climbed upon her then, and she could see the bulk of his manhood poised to enter her virginal body. The first pressure made her cry out in surprise. He halted in his progress to kiss her mouth and breasts. Gradually, she relaxed, and he pushed again. It felt as though her insides were being torn apart, as though some red-hot brand had been forced between her tender thighs. When he had sunk himself in to the root, he lay very still upon her, his fingers stroking her brow and cheeks. She risked opening her eyes, looking up at the man who had claimed her maidenhood. There was warmth and affection in his face. He did not burn her with looks of lust, but his kindness won her trust, and she felt her ravished sex begin to relax around him.

He rocked slowly and gently on her, coaxing her timid body into accepting his offerings of pleasure. Discomfort gradually melted away, leaving in its stead an easy, contented feeling. When at last she felt him pump his hot fluids into her moist depths, a profound sense of happiness settled upon her. It was not a wild sexual satisfaction nor the bliss of love requited, but this she could live with. It was gentle and manageable. She would be able to do her duty in his bed without too much discomfort.

Chapter Fourteen

"Megan!"

Someone was shouting at her. It took a while before she recognized the voice. A peculiar feeling of disorientation tugged at her psyche. *Where was she?* It was cold. Opening her eyes, Megan saw to her bemusement that she was outside somewhere. Her bare feet had been cut and bruised badly by stones in the path while her thin nightdress could not keep out the persistent wind blowing in across the fens.

The man shouting at her was none other than her father. He was silent and watchful now, his face deeply lined by worry. *What was he doing here? Why was she walking barefoot in the road? Where had she been going?* Megan could not remember. In the distance she could see the abbey ruins, brooding against the skyline. The sight of them filled her with feelings both of need and foreboding. She had been going there to meet Seth, she decided. Images of their time amongst the crumbling walls flickered through her confused mind. She remembered the heat of his hands on her body and the peaty taste of his skin. Then the terrible memory of a battered body in the street exploded into her recollections. Of late, when she revisited that nightmare, she did not see the broken form of an otter but the naked body of her lover, brutalized in human form. She started to cry. Her shoulders heaved and her ribs shook pitifully. She buried her face in her hands.

Her father removed his coat and draped it around her shoulders. She reined in her sudden tears, half forgetting why she had started to sob. She wondered where she was, and then thought to put her arms through the coat sleeves, feeling the warmth from her father's body in the fabric. The garment was large on her, but it kept the wind off.

The Shifting Heart

He carried her home as though she was a child again. Megan had always been a small girl, but she had grown thin and pale over the summer, her eyes losing their light and the sheen going from her hair. He did not ask where she had been going or what she meant to do. There were no questions concerning why she was abroad a little after dawn with bare feet and closed eyes.

Mrs. West looked more drawn and anxious than ever. With disheveled hair and eyes red from tears, she opened the door when at last her husband returned with their child. West lowered his waif of a daughter onto a couch and shook his head. "She was on the Norsey road again. Sleep walking."

It was the third time in the last week that she had slipped from the house at night, wandering the roads like a pale ghost with no awareness of where she went or what she did.

"What are we to do?" Ellen West asked in despair.

"I have prayed and consulted my own conscience. I cannot perform my duties while Megan is so afflicted. I am failing this Parish."

Mrs. West shook her head. He worked tirelessly, but it was true that his mind was no longer focused on his priestly role.

"I fear something dreadful has befallen her that she will not admit to," he confessed.

"She tells me nothing," she replied, "but I share your concern. There must be some reason, surely?"

They both fell silent, watching their child as she lay glassy eyed and silent where she had been put.

"I think we must leave this place. We must go somewhere where she will be free from difficult associations, if indeed there are any such. We must also seek more advanced medical assistance."

Mrs. West hung her head, accepting the words she least wanted to hear. "I think you are right, husband. Thought it breaks my heart to go, I do not think Megan will recover her wits while we remain here."

Chapter Fifteen

For long hours, Ivy stooped her way through the fields alongside the other poor women and children. There were plenty of stray stalks to be gleaned. The grain would help keep them in bread, or could be sold for a little money, while the straw made fresh bedding. It was back-breaking work, and the tough stalks were harsh on hands and legs alike. After the storms of early summer, the weather had been warm enough for the grain to recover and ripen. They knew they had been lucky.

For the greater part, she found herself working alone. She had never been especially popular or sociable but, even so, she detected a change in how the women were treating her. They were slower to smile and quicker to turn away. Ivy was proud enough to have asked no favors, but they all knew she and Ben were dirt poor. Old Moocher had a reputation for light fingers, and she overheard odd comments about her Ben that made her realize he was no better thought of. By marrying him, she had stepped away from her old circles and become something of an outcast. During the course of the first long afternoon, it occurred to her that perhaps they, as she had done, assumed Moocher only left one child. There was, she supposed, a fair resemblance between the siblings. Seth was the taller of the two, his eyes and hair were darker than his brother's, and he moved differently, but it was possible anyone who did not care to look closely might mistake one for the other and that Ben's reputation stemmed in part from the actions of his aggressive brother. The Tuck family had always been considered disreputable and troublesome. She supposed she should have guessed where her marriage would leave her socially, but it was not something she minded a great deal once she understood it; she had always felt herself to be rather on the peripheries. This confirmed her status.

When the days of field work were done, Ivy carried armfuls of gleanings to her mother's house, and accepted a few pennies in return. It was small reward for her efforts, but the best any of them could manage. She could have done nothing with the golden ears herself – there was no place at her cottage where grain might be threshed, and alone she would not have enough to be worth milling. This way provided her with a little money and benefited her family as well. They had kept her for more than a month, and she felt it was the least she owed them.

Ivy was a sharp young woman, determined not to spend the rest of her life in abject poverty. Most of her ambitions in life had been thwarted. The desire to learn and make something of herself was denied her by the impossibility of affording it. Plans for a life of comfortable servitude were recently quashed. Now she must look to married life and housekeeping, seeking her happiness in domestic ways. Ben was used to living from hand to mouth and seemed unconcerned with comfort or the trappings of civilization; however, she found him willing to accommodate her wishes. She supposed, having been raised by his father after his mother wandered off, that Ben simply did not know very much about how best to keep a house and stretch the money. He did not even have a bread oven.

It was late by the time she reached home. Her clothes and skin were dusty, and she ached from hard labor. She could smell the mouth watering aromas of cooking before she crossed the threshold. Having lived alone more than not, Ben was accustomed to making his own meals. She thought it peculiar that he had not relinquished the task entirely to her, but on days such as this one, she was grateful for his unconventional nature. By the scents rising from the single pot, she guessed there was duck. Sometimes Ben was absent when she woke in the early morning. She never asked where he went, but guessed he must be poaching. There was usually something good for the pot – rabbit, eels, ducks, and other wild creatures. She tried not to think about the dangers – that he might be shot by a gamekeeper, or prosecuted and jailed. She knew they depended on his hunting for food.

Ivy washed in rainwater from the butt. Cool rivulets of greenish water trickled down her shoulders and between her breasts as she scrubbed her face and neck. There was no sign of Ben in the tiny thatched cottage. Looking around outside, she could see no one in the surrounding fields who resembled him. She was heading inside when hands snaked around her waist and she felt him pressed against her back. He had appeared out of nowhere with an easy laugh and hands eager to explore the roundness of her breasts. She leaned back against him, letting him do as he pleased and enjoying the comfort of his presence.

"Where've you been?" she asked

"Here and there," he answered dismissively.

She had been thinking more about where he was in those minutes before he pounced on her. She supposed that in her weariness she had missed him somehow.

"There's duck in the pot," he added, making no move to release her from his embrace.

Tired and hungry though she was, Ivy felt no hurry. She liked the feel of his arms around her, the strength of his body pressed tight against her back. He was a sweet young man, as strange as people said he was, but full of kindness. She had become very fond of him in the few months since his proposal.

The fire made the room intolerably hot, so they took their steaming bowls and sat on the doorstep like a pair of overgrown children. The light was failing, and there was no one about to see them and judge what they did. The doorway was so narrow that their hips and shoulders were pressed together.

"It's good to think there'll be another Tuck on this land one day," Ben remarked.

Ivy said nothing. There was no sign of a child yet, but she appreciated that he wanted one.

"Seth's not the staying kind," Ben continued. "He'd never keep the cottage."

"Have your family lived here long?" she asked, taking his empty bowl and stacking it with her own.

"Since the dawn of time or so my old dad used to say. He said there'd been Tuck's here before it were drained, when this little spot were just a tiny island in the marshes."

Looking around, Ivy supposed the cottage was on a slight rise in the ground. She tried to imagine what the landscape would have looked like then. "How'd him know that?" she asked, genuinely curious.

"My family always told stories, father to son, mother to daughter, stories that go all the way back. Like how we were here before they drained it, back when there were only a few folks in the marshes at all."

His voice had become quiet and distant. Ivy listened, enraptured.

"Folks got about on stilts in them days," he added.

"You're teasing me."

"Never. Folks walked on stilts, and all the animals, them had longer legs, see, twice as long as they are now, longer than that for some even, so all the rabbits and sheep and everything else could go about with their heads above the water. Stopped growing them so tall when they drained the land, but sometimes even now you get one of those great big long legged rabbits, tiny little body, but it comes up to your waist all the same."

She saw the glint of wickedness in his eye, and knew he had been teasing her. "Oh, you…" She could not find a suitable appellation, so poked him hard in the ribs instead.

"Don't you start on me, wench," he threatened playfully.

"Or?"

"There'll be trouble."

She poked him again.

He grabbed her wrists, pulling her across his lap so she could not escape. For a few seconds she wondered if she had gone too far this time, and if he was going to paddle her bottom as her father had done when she was small. Instead, he secured her small wrists with one hand, and began to tickle her mercilessly with the other. She squealed.

"They'll hear you down in the village," he warned, but did not desist from tormenting her.

She struggled to catch her breath. She could tell what was happening to him. As she wriggled and squirmed in his lap, his cock was getting hard. She could feel the press of him against her arm. Before she really knew what was happening, his hand dove under her skirts, his fingers plunging between her thighs. Her gestures at fighting him off lost even the semblance of determination. He could do things to her that left her powerless and ecstatic. Back and forth his fingers brushed, summoning dampness from her cleft and whimpers of delight from her mouth. Twisting against him, she worked her own fingers around, reaching for the mysteriously powerful rod in his lap to rouse it further with kneading and caresses.

"Now I've got you," he said.

She gripped his shaft firmly through his trousers. "You don't want to go taking advantage of me," she gasped. "I can give as good as I get."

His fingers penetrated her and she stopped talking, unable to do more than respond to his persuasive touch. She pushed back against him, burying her face against his leg as the first flutterings of pleasure began in her. When she was moist and quivering, he withdrew his hand from beneath her clothing. She made a little sound of frustration.

"I've not finished with you, don't you fret," he promised, helping her to stand, his grip strong and certain on her hands as he pulled her to her feet.

The Shifting Heart

She leaned against him, listening to the steady beating of his heart. There was trust between them, and strong companionship. The last of the light was fading from the vast sky, and bed beckoned.

Rolling and tumbling together had become familiar play. His body held no fears for her now, and she learned to appreciate the ways in which he invoked pleasure in her. He was always careful to satisfy her, using his hands or his mouth if their coupling proved to be not quite enough for her. She loved to hear his satisfied sighs, and feel the thrusting, trembling conclusion of their lovemaking as he melted into her body.

This evening she was more than ready for him. Moistened and aroused by his probing fingers, she threw off her clothing with haste, eager to be in bed with her man. When he sank down upon her, she responded with kisses and with fingers that explored the length of his sinuous back. Her questing mouth found a deep gash on his shoulder that had not been there the previous day. It had scabbed over, but she could tell it had been a nasty cut. Sometimes he came home with injuries. He tended not to say where they had come from, and although it bothered her, she stopped asking once it was obvious he did not want to tell her. He winced at the pressure from her mouth.

"Sorry," she murmured, shifting her head so she was in contact with the other shoulder instead.

"Don't worry, that's nothing."

She knew it would be all the explanation she got.

With slow certainty, he began to transport her. The rhythm of his body in hers was awaking her flesh to sensual awareness as each grind of his hips inspired fresh joys. Her body sang for him, moved with his and trembled rapturously. Thrust by thrust, he carried her away from the harsh realities of the world into a pure and utterly fulfilling ecstasy.

* * *

Living a few miles outside the heart of the village, and not attending church regularly, Ivy and Ben were often isolated from the community around them. No one ever came to visit them, save for wild birds. As the harvest finished, and she was left to work in her small home, there were many days when Ben's was the only human voice she heard. Sometimes she would stand by the door just to watch distant figures on the road and men at work in the fields so she did not feel cut off from the rest of humanity.

Autumn brought heavy mists that clung to the land, swallowing up trees and landmarks alike and disguising all hints of civilization. Ivy imagined it was how things would have been before the fens were drained, when there was marsh and water haunted by bitterns, otters and only a handful of fen-landers. It was lonely in the little cottage with Ben gone for much of the day. Sometimes she walked into the village to buy bread, but most days were spent alone.

Walking past the vicarage on a chilly afternoon, she saw the curtains were gone from the windows. She noticed the furniture was missing, and the house had a cold, empty feel to it. It looked melancholy and abandoned. Curious to know what had happened, she called in at her mother's. Two of the smaller children were playing in the dirt outside the door, but the older ones were either at work or school, leaving the cramped cottage unusually quiet.

May was busy cutting down a worn jacket for one of the younger boys. She carried on working, talking with closed lips as she held pins between her teeth. Once they had exchanged a few pleasantries, Ivy launched into the subject that she really wanted to discuss.

"I were walking past the vicarage. Looks empty to me. Has them Wests gone?"

"Them has, and if you went to church like any decent Christian person, you'd know well enough. They went last Friday, and a new chap be coming in a week or so. The Reverend Septimus Gotobed him be."

"Fen man, then."

"Aye."

"Him weren't from round here, Reverend West, him were from miles away, and her were from Ely. I thought they'd be here forever. Wonder what made they go?" Ivy pondered.

"I did hear the young lady had turned right queer. Your Aunt Laura said her was out in the road in just her night clothes, bare feet and all."

"I heard her was ill, but nothing like that." Ivy was shocked by the news.

"Well, there's other folks have seen her. Had a right turn, she have."

"She weren't like that when I were there."

"You know Sarah Norman, your cousin Lucy's daughter, Lucy that were Lucy Gall afore she married?"

"I know she. We was at Sunday school together."

"Well, her went to the Wests after you gone, see, only a slip of girl, hardly knew how to do anything, but I heard it from Lucy herself, they had the doctor a-coming and a-going all the time, and the young lady wouldn't get out of bed or eat or anything."

"Maybe she were ill," Ivy hazarded, remembering Mrs. West's long periods of confinement from illness.

"Well, Lucy's girl, Sarah, her reckoned the young Miss were sleepwalking. Said you could hear her nights talking to herself and walking round the house. Right creepy it were, by all accounts."

"It's a rum do and all," Ivy observed. "What about this new vicar then, there any word of him?"

"Them's saying he's young and not wed yet. He's making a bit of a stir and he don't even be here yet."

Ivy nodded. New people were relatively rare. Some families moved on, working a year in one place and then transferring to a new estate. They were always strangers and never much considered. A new vicar could be in the village for years to come, and if he did not bring a wife and family with him, every single girl for miles around would set her cap at him. There would be much speculation about the match he might make, and every mother would be putting her marriageable daughters forward in hope of catching his eye. There had been nothing comparable to this for years, but Ivy was not much excited by the prospect.

Chapter Sixteen

The small window gave a view over the walled gardens, the backs of houses, and nearby streets. Everything seemed closed in to Megan. She missed the open sky and the views that went on for mile after mile. Living in this room she felt as though she could hardly breathe. Mostly all she did was look out the window. On some days – this being one of them – doctors came to poke, prod and question. She was weary of them, and ignored them with practiced ease. There was nothing she wanted to say. One would give her so much laudanum that she could not help but sleep, and another would take it away, leaving her aching and sick for days. Another medical man would give her something that only served to make her feel worse, and then sooner or later it would be the familiar grogginess of laudanum again. She wondered what they were trying to achieve. There was no life in her to save, and it amazed her they could not see this.

When they left her to her own devices, she spent her time daydreaming and remembering. Living in the recollections of the love she had known, she wanted nothing more than to escape into what had been and forget the unhappy present. If she closed her eyes, she could recapture the feel of his hands on her body and his searing kisses consuming her skin. Each time he had taken her was etched upon her mind, and she could recount every erotic detail of their passion. Touching herself as she had been touched, she could make herself believe she felt his breath on her neck and his hard cock in her body. Without him inside her, she was empty.

If there was anyone else close by, she remained perfectly still, keeping her memories and fantasies to herself. They asked what ailed her, but she said nothing. Sometimes they asked how she felt, and if she experienced any pain, but that only made her laugh bitterly. They did not know what horror she had endured. If she told them what she knew – that her lover had been slaughtered in his otter skin – she would only have confirmed their suspicions that she was losing her mind. Perhaps she was. Without him, Megan felt she was walking a dark shadow-land. She had fallen through the gauzy fragility of reality and haunted some darker place beneath the surface. Sometimes she could see the ordinary world that had once been hers, with parents and safety, but there could be no returning to that innocence.

There were occasions in the depths of the night when she had the feeling that he was close by, as though his spirit had ventured into her prison room. The whole world was a prison without Seth, but the tiniest part of it would be her heaven if only he could return to her. She breathed his name in the darkness and reached out to him with fingers that never found their quarry. "Always!" she whispered.

Chapter Seventeen

There were still a few small apples on the tree in the vicarage garden. The young vicar was in the process of employing the aid of a curved stick to pull down branches when he had the disturbing feeling that he was being watched. It was dusk, and looking around his shadowy garden, he could see nothing. Laughing nervously to himself, he returned to fruit gathering. Accustomed to town living, the dapper young man found the vast expanses of land and sky eerie. It would be a while, he thought, before he felt at home in Burnham. The absolute quiet on evenings such as this perturbed him, and he supposed it was no wonder he was jumping at shadows.

"You ain't West." The voice was low and slightly menacing.

The new vicar turned slowly, scanning the gloom for signs of the man who had spoken. He could see no one. He wondered if he had imagined it.

"Where's West?" the disembodied voice continued.

Remembering that the previous incumbent had indeed been one Reverend West, Gotobed cleared his throat. "He departed a month ago. May I introduce myself? I am Septimus Gotobed. Reverend Septimus Gotobed."

"Where have him gone?"

Septimus had now established some bearings for the voice and advanced cautiously on his gooseberry patch. "I could not say with any degree of confidence. Were you particularly looking for Reverend West, or might I be able to assist you in some fashion?"

"I weren't looking for him. I were looking for Megan."

"Megan?"

"Her's his daughter."

"And you would be?" Gotobed ventured.

"I need to find her."

Septimus considered his position carefully. He was aware that the Wests had left in difficult circumstances, but was unaware as to the nature of the problem. If the previous incumbent's daughter had in any way been compromised, then he had no desire to exasperate the situation. "I am not certain I would be able to assist you. If you would like to call upon me tomorrow, in the afternoon, I am sure we could discuss the matter."

Before he fully knew what was happening to him, Septimus was shoved forcefully to the ground. A knee pressed down on his chest, and a strong hand gripped his throat. He was not choking, not yet, but the threat was all too plain. He fought back the instinctive rise of panic, knowing his escape would probably depend on wits and diplomacy. Septimus was entirely aware that he lacked the strength to force his attacker off.

"Tell me where she be!"

"I do not know!"

The fingers pressed a little tighter, narrowing his windpipe, but not blocking it completely. "Tell me!" the voice was little more than a growl.

"I cannot…" His head was starting to swim. In desperation, he made a bid to push the man from him. His hands connected with bare skin. Startled, his shove lost all momentum and his one effort at defense proved utterly futile. A jolt of frustrated anger shot through his captor's body, and then the man was off him. The traumatized young vicar managed to raise himself up on one elbow in time to see his assailant leaving the garden, not making for the road as might have been expected, but for the hawthorn hedge that backed onto the fields. One minute he was there, a barely human shadow in the darkness, the next moment he was gone.

On the following morning, Septimus might have written this experience off as a nightmare had there not been visible bruises on the white skin of his neck. In the bright light of a crisp autumn day, the mystery seemed less threatening. He explored the garden, looking for signs of a breach in his hedge and finding none. There were prints of bare human feet amongst his fruit bushes, but in the mud closer to the hedge there was nothing at all. It was curious, indeed. Where could a barefooted, and at best partially clad, man have come from at twilight, and where could he have gone? He could think of no sensible explanation for the events, and resolved to be on his guard against further peculiarities.

Septimus had to admit the house he now occupied possessed a queer, brooding atmosphere, as though some previous gloom had soaked into the walls. He was not usually a superstitious man, but it was far easier to be rational in the sensible, human environment of a large town than it was here in this isolated wilderness. The landscape seemed to breed myths and irrational conjecture. After breakfast, he asked his young employee if she knew of any ghost stories associated with the vicarage, but she shook her head and said nothing. He resisted the temptation to mention the assault; the girl seemed nervous enough without him frightening her.

Chapter Eighteen

On the first sunny day for over a week, Ivy set about her washing with grim determination. On waking, she could smell the change in the air and knew there was some chance the weather might last long enough for drying. It could well be her last chance before the Spring to launder their bedding and get it aired, and she was determined to make the best of it. As was often the case, Ben had been out since first light. He had found a few days work on one of the small farms, which would bring in much needed money. Her arms ached as she stretched to pin up the damp washing. Still, it pleased her to see it flapping in the breeze.

Out of nowhere came the warm press of a man's body behind her, and hands that wandered confidently over her stomach and breasts. She smiled, closing her eyes wondering what Ben was doing back so soon. His questing fingers found her nipples, rubbing at them through her layers of clothing. It was pure delight to be touched in this way and she felt herself melting into desire. She wriggled against him suggestively and reached her hands back to return the caresses. The feel of bare skin sent the first warning signals through her mind, but her body was enraptured and aroused, making it difficult to concentrate on anything aside from pleasure.

Wordlessly, he pushed her down onto her knees and, with his hand flat on her back, pressed her towards the ground. While they often played and flirted outside the house, Ben had never sought to take her in daylight in so public a place. Something was wrong. Ivy felt a trickle of uncertainty pass through her. Glancing back over her shoulder, she saw someone who looked a lot like her husband, so much so that for a moment she half believed it was him. She could only see his shoulder and his hair. Little of his face was visible aside from one high cheekbone and the angular jut of his jaw. His hands were on her thighs, lifting her skirts and exploring her under garments. She could not see him well enough to be sure. Her mind and heart raced each other as fear and arousal competed for domination. She wanted to be taken, her body ached for it, but her alarm was growing with very moment. Ben's touch was not as rough as this.

Ivy knew she should cry out or try to resist because the strong hands that ripped away her undergarments were not her husband's. This was not Ben's way with her; he was always gentle and careful. Her seducer's fingers found her slickness, exploring the depths of her hungry sex with practiced ease. He delved into her and she did not fight him, succumbing to the pleasure he was giving her. When his hand withdrew, she knew what was coming next.

"Don't," she said weakly, but it was a protest she barely meant, and her voice was so low he might not even have heard her.

His cock drove into her, hard and insistent. Fingers dug into her hips. Everything about him was fierce and urgent. She could feel her nipples aching in their stays. Her seducer was relentless, pummeling her softness with a ferocity that left her gasping and shaking. She did not know what to do and so she did nothing, letting him make free with her. Her breath came in shuddering gasps as she pushed her fingers into the soft grass beneath her. Anyone could see her here. Anyone could find them, including Ben, and yet the perilous nature of her situation only seemed to ignite her further. Sex with her husband was sweet, but this was wildly erotic, turning her on in ways she had not known were possible.

The strength of her reactions was as startling as his ferocious possession of her body. She came as she had never come before, the climax shaking her to the very core of her being. His grip on her grew tighter, his strokes more persistent, his hips thrusting faster and harder until at last she felt the earth shattering eruption of his sex deep within hers.

When he finally let her go, Ivy collapsed down across the grass, finding that her knees could no longer support her weight. For a while she could neither think nor move. Blissful exhaustion claimed her. As her wits made their slow return, she realized she must discover the identity of the man who had taken her so utterly. She sat up, feeling bruised from the intensity of his penetrations. Raising her head, she mustered all her courage and looked the man straight in the face.

Kneeling before her, with a smile of wicked indulgence on his handsome face, was Seth. She covered her mouth, realizing the full extent of the transgression, yet her body was trembling from the violent thrill of it and longing for more.

"What you doing here?" he asked casually.

"I married your brother," she said, unable to continue looking him in the eye.

"Humph," he snorted, clearly unimpressed by this news. "Where he be?"

"Working," she answered, "back in the evening, I'd think."

"Then I'll get something for the pot."

His casualness about the whole business was more distressing than anything else, but she was roused from her attack of self-pity by a peculiar feeling on her skin, as though the air around her was prickling with energy. When she risked looking up, the man was gone, and in his place sat a sleek, bright-eyed otter. Her breath caught in her throat and she stared fearfully at the animal before her. Ben always talked about Seth's shifting as though it was something easy and natural. Even having missed the moment of change, the shock of it still overwhelmed her. She thought the otter had the same laughing expression on its face as the man had worn only a few seconds ago.

Low to the ground, the dark-furred creature set off at a rolling gait, vanishing into the long grass. When he was out of sight, she buried her face in her hands. She couldn't cry. Guilt and elation battled within her. Seth had taken her, and it had been a glorious experience. She had betrayed Ben, the dearest, kindest person she had ever known. *It was not my fault*, she tried to tell herself. *Not my fault at all.* She had not realized her husband's brother was behind her, and once she did find out, it was too late, but in her heart she knew how much she had desired him. Ever since the day when she spied on him in the ruins and watched him take his pleasure with Megan, she had wanted him. There was no denying it, not to herself.

An hour later he was back, his pelt waterlogged and a large trout in his jaws. Ivy set to work on it at once, glad of having something to do with her still trembling hands.

"Him got any clothes spare?"

She supposed he must have changed again. Resisting the temptation to look round and feast her eyes on the splendor of his naked body, she nodded.

"There's some in the box up in the bedroom. It's worn, I was going to use it for patching."

"It'll do."

She heard him pad softly up the stairs and sank her teeth into her lower lip. It was evident Seth meant to stay, and that things were going to be complicated in the extreme.

"Smells like trout," Ben called out cheerily as he stomped the mud off his boots outside the door.

Ivy looked up as he came in, struggling to find a smile and half afraid to look him the eye for fear he would see the guilt in hers. She nodded.

"Where you get trout?" he asked.

She gestured vaguely towards the ladder. "We got a visitor."

His brow furrowed, the look on his face questioning.

"Seth," she said, voicing his name as carefully as she could.

On cue, the young man loped quietly down the stairs. The trousers were almost threadbare and a little too short in the leg for him. He had not bothered to fasten up the shirt, and his muscular chest was very much on display.

Ben laughed with delight and stepped forward to embrace his sibling. "You been gone a long time. Where you been?"

"Here and there," Seth replied dismissively.

"It's good to have you home," Ben said enthusiastically.

"And you got Ivy, and I weren't here," Seth observed. "House looks different."

Ivy had made a rag rug for the living room, and it cheered the little space considerably. She had picked and dried herbs, which now hung from the wall in large bunches. It was not the stark cottage it had been before Seth's departure.

As she washed their few dishes after the meal, she decided it would be best to say nothing about the afternoon. The two brothers were happy in each other's company, talking and laughing together. She had no desire to sow discord between them or to confess her complicity in what had happened. *It had been a moment's insanity, no more.* Now that Seth knew she was pledged to Ben, he would surely respect that and leave her alone? Now that she knew he was around, she could guard herself against being led astray. But even as she was telling herself no such thing could ever occur again, part of her mind was revisiting her seduction and reveling in the memory.

Chapter Nineteen

At first he had no sense whatsoever of why he had awoken. Wind whistled around the eaves, blowing across the chimneys and making eerie sounds. Septimus listened for a while, thinking it was unlikely these noises would have disturbed his sleep; the cries of the wind were familiar to him now. A floorboard creaked in one of the other bedrooms, and then came the soft, padding sound of feet moving lightly over bare boards. The footfall was too light for hobnailed boots. Impressions and ideas flitted through his thoughts... Perhaps it was Sarah, his servant, on some strange night time wandering. Perhaps a thief had broken in and was searching for valuables. *But then, why would a thief be in an empty bedroom when there was plenty worth taking in the rooms below, with less risk of waking the household? Why would Sarah be up this late, in an empty room?* The sound continued, impossible to ignore and more unsettling by the moment.

Moving as quietly as he could, Septimus rose from his bed, his ears straining for clues regarding his unwelcome visitor. Softly, he padded across the rug. There was no light in his bedroom, but he knew where he was going and walked without error. As his hand closed over the doorknob, he heard another door creak open, and the padding feet passed close by him on the landing. After a few second's delay, he followed.

One of the curtains had not been properly drawn and a shaft of moonlight fell across the open space at the foot of the stairs. Hiding in the darkness above, the young Reverend watched, thinking he might get a glimpse of his night wanderer. When he heard the intruder stop in the gloom, Septimus held his breath, hoping no sound betrayed his presence. He caught a glimpse of something resembling a man, silhouetted briefly in the moonlight. Before his frightened eyes, the figure seemed to crumple away into nothing, evaporating almost, as though the moonlight had somehow destroyed his specter. Something dark slithered across the floor. He could hear the scraping noise it made in passing.

Terror gripped the young vicar. Something unnatural and perhaps demonic was in his house. Until recently, Gotobed considered himself a rational man free from the superstitions of ages passed and inspired by a reasoned, humanistic understanding of Christian doctrine. He did not believe in ghosts and demons or other monstrosities. He had laughed at those who did, until coming to Burnham. Now he lived in a house that reverberated with inexplicable grief, and a man had just melted away in his hallway. Terror, base and instinctive, triumphed over all other impulses. For a long time, he remained utterly frozen.

It took all the courage he could muster to go down the darkened staircase and investigate for himself. There was no sign of anything extraordinary. Still, he lit a candle and pulled a coat on over his night attire. It was only a short walk from the vicarage to the church. He wanted holy water and a few moments in the tranquility of the sacred place. Whatever dared to plague his abode would surely not trouble him in the house of God.

The first gust of wind extinguished his candle. The moon was high and full, illuminating the uneven road and recasting everything it touched in magical, silver tones. A dark shape slithered across the open ground between the houses. Septimus felt his knees grow weak at the sight of it. Only when it passed through a brighter moonbeam did he realize what it was. The rolling, sloping gait that had looked so sinister at first was only that of an otter out foraging in the night. He was surprised to see it in the village, but understood that they wandered about all over the place and even ventured into gardens. An otter, it was said locally, would carry off anything it could take in its mouth. He had been told that enough times since his arrival.

The laughter erupted out of him. At first it was just a low chuckle of dry amusement, a relief at misplaced fear and a realization of how ludicrous his position looked. There he was, a sensible, reasonable man abroad at night in his pajamas searching for holy water to ward off nothing more sinister than an otter. He tried not to think about what had happened in his hall, or the distinctly masculine figure he had glimpsed.

Chapter Twenty

For a few days things went well enough in the little cottage, although Ivy found that Seth's unpredictable comings and goings disturbed her equilibrium. There were no more improper advances, and he showed no signs of recalling what they had done. He was as distant and casual with her as ever. Ben was happier for his brother's return, and the two often walked together in the twilight, coming back when the moon was high. She felt like the outsider, the one who did not truly belong in this curious triangle. Sometimes they did not even eat with her, but vanished off on their nighttime pursuits. She supposed they poached together, but did not venture to ask. Some things, she thought, it was probably better not to know.

She wanted with all her heart to be good and true to Ben. Seth's presence was an ongoing reminder of her failings and a continual source of temptation. She could not help but want to touch him, and he drew her eyes continually. She was careful not to be caught watching him. This was a life lived on eggshells, requiring utter care and concentration at all times. The slightest slip or mistake could mean disaster.

It was too late in the season for there to be much worth foraging for in the hedgerows. In previous weeks there had been nuts and berries, small crab apples, occasional field mushrooms and the young leaves of nettles. There were all sorts of things that could be picked freely and eaten if you were hungry enough and not too proud to do it. Ivy had grown up poor and was not afraid to find her food when she could. As a child, she had often depended on the bounty of the hedgerows to ease her aching belly. Now the foraging season was over and there would be little worth having until the Spring. Dandelion roots, perhaps, if things grew desperate, but little else.

The Shifting Heart

Now that there was little point spending afternoons hunting for food, she was obliged to look for other ways of stretching what few resources they had. Keeping the small house neat and clean took a little while each day, but afterwards her time was her own. She had managed to beg and borrow scraps of rag and leftover cloth from friends and neighbors, and was hard at work on her second rag rug. The first had been uneven and she could see the flaws. It cheered the cottage, but she would have to do better with future efforts. A good rug might fetch a few shillings, and in the meantime, she would owe favors to those women who had been kind enough to help her. Her cousin Judith had already intimated that in the Spring Ivy should consider letting two of her boys sleep in the downstairs room, as Judith herself no longer had enough space for her brood.

Ivy leaned over the rug, turning it skillfully in her hands as she worked the shreds of old garments into a cheerful design. Her attention was focused entirely upon this project. Watching the rug grow filled her with pride as the rough brown Hessian vanished under a soft pile of color. There was nothing to indicate a change in the room, but her skin prickled. She felt his gaze, knowing without hearing him that she was no longer alone. Heat rose in her body, dangerous and intoxicating as it crept through her chilled limbs. Eventually she could stand it no more and looked up at him.

Seth stood only a few feet away, and the full power of his gaze was focused upon her. She met his eyes, unable to resist and, once captured, unable to look away. She was acutely aware of every last inch of her skin, and all of it cried out to be touched by him. Raw animal lust rose up in her, hot and hungry for the spells his body could weave even as her conscience screamed against so blatant a betrayal. Locked between two powerful, conflicting desires, she could neither speak nor act.

He took a step closer and leaned nonchalantly against the wall. She wanted him to speak, to say something she could react to such that she might reclaim her sense of self and not feel so helpless in his presence.

"Be I distracting you?" he asked.

Ivy looked down at her work, wishing he could have said something different. There was no answering such a question. He was distracting her dreadfully, but she did not want to acknowledge it.

"Do you want me to go?"

She should say "Yes" but to do so would be to own how deeply the mere fact of his proximity affected her. To deny it would only be to invite him to stay. She sought frantically for a phrase that might banish him without causing offence or giving away too much. "You can please yourself," she replied.

"Can I, now?"

She realized that had probably not been the best thing to say. Seth took a step closer, then his hand was on her cheek and gliding over her neck, fingers delving beneath her collar. She closed her eyes. There was no escape now. Her need for him flared up. The gentle caress became the press of nails, keen and sharply alluring. "You shouldn't..." she began, but he silenced her with a kiss, his tongue filling her mouth and drawing hers into a sensual dance. When he broke away, she tried again. "I ain't free to do this."

"Ain't you?" His hand cupped her breast, moving suggestively over the fabric of her dress.

She wanted his fingers on her nipples and that ravenous mouth of his upon her body. She struggled to hold firm against him, to resist the hungry look in his eyes and the lure of his slightly parted lips.

He knelt before her, placing his hands lightly on her feet, and then gradually sliding them up the length of her legs, pushing her skirt back as he went. "Tell me to stop," he challenged her.

Her mouth was dry. She knew what to say, but her voice would not come. All she could do was look into his dark-blue eyes, trembling under his hands, wanting more but fearing it.

"Tell me you don't want it." His voice was low and the tone commanding. His hands glided back and forth along her legs, fuelling the heat in her.

She screwed her eyes tightly shut, trying to focus her mind on resisting, but all she did was remember how he had touched her before.

"You can't." His hands stopped their teasing. "Now, tell me the truth."

She wanted him to carry on touching her, to answer the need in her body and satisfy the lust he had awoken in her.

He lifted his hands from her skin altogether. "Say it!"

His order broke down all her reserves. She could deny him no longer. "Don't stop," she whimpered helplessly.

"What do you want?"

She looked at him, her eyes pleading wordlessly. From his face she could tell he would not let her off easily. Her pussy ached with wanting him, but she would have to beg him now or he would not finish what he had begun. "Take me," she said, her voice husky.

He lifted his hand, moving his fingers suggestively before her until she flushed hot crimson. She knew what effect that action would have on her flesh. His expression was almost insolent, daring her to go further. "Show me."

She knew what he meant. Putting her rug work to one side, she rose and wriggled out of her knickers, leaving her dress in place. When she sat, he nodded slowly. She pulled her skirt up, baring her already parted legs, and eventually bringing her moist cleft into his line of sight.

"Are you wet?" he asked.

She nodded.

He raised his eyebrows, and the look was command enough. She must demonstrate the truth of what she said.

Ivy was not in the habit of touching herself between the legs. Tentatively, she used her fingers to part her nether lips, holding them open for his scrutiny, then she showed him her juice-drenched digits.

He sniffed her hand, his expression approving, then he lowered his head into her lap. She felt his tongue caress her, and then penetrate her sex as it had her mouth. Firm and dexterous, it moved within her while his lips did their work on her clitoris. There was no resisting the uncanny skill of his tongue as it danced within her, lapping and pulsing rhythmically. She climaxed almost at once and he surfaced then, his face glistening with her moisture, a look of triumph in his eyes. With one hand on her back, he used the other to free his erection, guiding it into her. She could no longer play the ravaged innocent. She gripped his shoulders, pressing herself against him as he took her.

"You want it," Seth asserted, his breath hot against her ear.

"Yes," she breathed, "yes!"

He provided the momentum, working swiftly to relieve them both. He came hard, rocking her body with the force of his orgasm. She was only a few seconds behind him, the shuddering thrusts of his final pleasure inspiring her own blinding crescendo.

* * *

"Them Wests have gone," Seth remarked as they sat together after the evening meal.

"Them's been gone a while, I heard," Ivy replied.

"Where?"

"I ain't heard that."

"What you want with them?" Ben asked.

"Megan," his brother replied.

"What, Megan West, the one as fell in the dyke last winter?" Ben asked, feigning innocence.

"Her's the one."

"I thought you were done with her when you took off."

"I thought her was done with me. Needed to think."

"And now what'll you do?" Her's gone, all right."

"Her's mine," Seth stated.

Ben appeared startled by this statement. He shook his head. "Nay lad, a wench like her's not for the likes of us. Her might have lain with you, but you'll not keep her."

"Her's mine, Ben, her's already mine, but her be gone."

"You'd gone when her went off with her folks," Ben pointed out.

Seth shrugged, indicating he did not see any great importance in this.

"She didn't come to see me. Seemed like her'd changed her mind, so I went. But her's the one, an I knows it, so I come back."

It was the longest speech Ivy had ever heard him make. The words troubled her. He had spent the afternoon in her arms, now he was talking about Megan as though the afternoon's ecstasy meant nothing to him.

"You've not got her in trouble?" Ben asked.

Seth shrugged again. "Could have. That's why I got to find her."

Ben shook his head.

"Her's mine," Seth reiterated. "I've got to find out where her's gone and fetch her back. Her belongs here now."

"Someone must know. We can ask around a bit, can't us, Ivy?"

She nodded mutely, feeling a chill of hopelessness settle on her. It was as though she did not exist for Seth; her body was nothing more than a receptacle for his frustrated lusts. Megan was in his heart, and she knew herself to be far less than that. She had not thought she loved him herself, but to hear him speak so possessively of another grieved her. She was his lover now, and she wanted that to mean something more than simple sexual expression. She stole a look at him. He was cleaning under his fingernails with the tip of Ben's pocket knife, but as though sensing her attention, he glanced up with a playful smile on his lips. He raised his eyebrows. Ivy decided she was not quite invisible to him. The expression on his face had her aching with desire, but there was nothing to be done about it.

Chapter Twenty One

Some days seemed clearer than others to Megan, it all depended on how much laudanum they had given her. On this particular morning she woke, restless and troubled, in a room she knew was not really hers. Memories of the snug vicarage bedroom came to her, sweet and nostalgic. She had grown out of childhood there. The window in that room had showed visions of farmland and fen, not the dreary monotony of houses, and that fondly remembered bed was the last place she had lain with Seth. It was where she belonged, in that familiar place with her lover at her side, his arms encircling her.

Megan had no idea where she was now or why they were drugging her. The previous months were little more than a troubled haze in her mind. This current clarity of thought was peculiar to her after so long in chaos. For a while she tried to remember what had happened, but it would not come, and she gave up trying. Eventually several realizations came to her, each definite and perfectly clear. She was not in her home. She was being kept in a stupor, and she did not know why. She had to escape. It all seemed very simple and obvious.

From the light penetrating the curtains, it appeared to be early morning. The building she was in seemed quiet enough, but if she was to move she thought she must do it now, before she was sedated again. It took her a while to find her clothes. Many of the things she remembered owning seemed to be here, including her few items of jewelry. Realizing she had no money to speak of, she bundled her trinkets into a handkerchief and tied that to her underclothes for safekeeping.

It took Megan little time to discover that the door to her bedroom had been locked from the outside. She could see the key in the latch. The one window was too small to afford escape, and she had never been much good at climbing anyway. Time was passing all too quickly. Searching frantically, she recalled that one of the drawers in the dresser was lined with paper. She tore this out, and slid it under the door. Using one of her hairpins, she managed to dislodge the key. It landed with a dull thud, and she pulled the paper under the door, bringing the key with it. In a trice she was free of the room. Looking about, she could see other closed doors, none of which had keys on the outside. She was not sure what that meant. The place was utterly unfamiliar. Fighting the urge to run, she shut her door and locked it, leaving it as it had been. Only then did she bolt for the stairs, grabbing a large coat from the stand before hurriedly opening the last barrier to freedom.

Outside, the street was largely empty. She tried to run, but she was weak and her legs lacked the strength. The best she could do was trot rapidly. She took the first turning, wanting to be out of view as quickly as possible. Then she dared to slow down and look around her, not wanting to waste what energy she had. This did not look much like Ely, which she remembered from childhood. Wandering about aimlessly, taking one turn after another with little thought for where she was going, she wondered if she could be in Cambridge. Perhaps this could be London, Bath, or an even more remote and unfriendly place. She did not dare to ask anyone for fear of being discovered. She expected at any moment to be grabbed and hauled back to her prison, but none of the few people about paid her any attention. Bells from a nearby church chimed seven.

How long would it be before they noticed her absence and came looking for her? She could not tell, but she feared it. Each passerby seemed a potential threat, someone who could capture her or inform on her escape. Ahead of her she could hear a great deal of energetic noise. Her first instinct was to hide, but after the initial fear passed she realized the sound was stationary and therefore posed no threat. Turning a corner, she came upon a vast market with stalls being erected in preparation for the day. There were a great many people about, which meant she was less obvious here than on the empty road. Trying not to draw too much attention to herself, she wandered from stall to stall, looking, thinking, and trying to suppress the attacks of fear that rose up in her each time someone glanced her way.

There were tantalizing smells of food, of fresh cooked bread and cakes. Investigating the pockets of her oversized coat, she found a few pennies. She bought a large currant bun for her breakfast and a meat pie for later, which she hid in one of the voluminous pockets. With food in her stomach, she felt more alive and capable. She could truly fend for herself, she thought. Now that she was free, it would not be so difficult a thing to find her way home. All she needed to do was work out where she was, and find the right road.

From the hectic bustle of the market she moved onwards with no sense of where she might be going. Most of the street names were either so common as to be unhelpful, or they failed to spark any recognition at all. The large, overbearing buildings evoked no recollections. Turning a corner, a sign for Trumpington Street caught her eye. That had a familiar ring to it. She paused, looking at the board and racking her brains. Eventually, she remembered there had been a village, miles to the north of Norsey with the same name. Lost as she was, it seemed as good an omen as any. With renewed courage, she set off.

Eventually, the town dissolved into the familiar vista of flat fields bounded by hedges. The sight of it came as a great relief. She knew much of the country was not as flat as her village, and she had traveled enough to appreciate the differences. There was no doubting this was some part of the fens, and her heart leapt at the discovery. She could not be so very far from home after all. The road was well used, with plenty of people on foot or on horses making their way in and out of the town. Although surrounded by this profusion of strangers, Megan was conscious that there was not a single familiar face amongst them. She had never been truly alone in her life before. The world around her seemed vast and overpowering. She knew herself to be a mere speck on the face of an ancient landscape. There was no one to guide her now or to determine her future. All safety was gone, but utter freedom was hers. She could go wherever she wished and carve her own life.

What will you do, she asked herself. She knew little of any practical use, she had no money to speak of, and there was no one to whom she could turn. *Where will you go?* Could she go back to her home in Burnham? Would her parents be there, and the life she had left behind so long ago waiting for her to step back into it like some fairytale princess, or had she been with her parents in that strange urban house? She could not remember. She held her head in her hands as she walked, trying to pry through the maddening shroud that covered her recent memories. Where were her parents? When had she seen them last? She could remember traveling out with them to the May Fair at Bury, but that seemed a lifetime ago. Then a memory surfaced in which her mother was crying. When had that occurred? Where had they been? She could not say.

Megan tried with all her might to piece together her fragmented recollections. Her time with Seth was keenly fresh, but that sweet memory belonged to early summer and she knew very well that winter was coming on. The leaves had gone from the trees and hedges while the sky wore sleety grey colors threatening rain or snow. What had happened since the spring? Where had she been? She had no answers, only hazy feelings of pain and trauma muffled by the influence of opiates.

As the darkness came down, she found a barn to shelter in. The night was painfully cold even with a roof above her head and straw to cover her. The skin on her face ached from the chill and she hardly slept at all, shivering in the darkness and waiting for the dawn. In the depths of the night, aching pains began to grip her as her body protested against the withdrawal of laudanum. She shivered and sweated in turn half believing she would never see the sun again. Her feet were sore from unaccustomed walking and her legs ached from the same. Friendless and afraid, she wondered what madness had inspired her to leave the safety of her room, the comfort of her bed. Seth's face came to her, his voice soft in her thoughts. *Where was this man?* Therein might lie her salvation.

Chapter Twenty Two

There was a long stretch of days when sleet and rain lashed the village of Burnham. The first storms of winter rolled in off the sea, ravaging the land and warning of worse to come. Those who could stayed by the fire and waited it out, huddling in gloomy cottages and hoping the roof would bear the punishment. Those others who had no choice but to work ventured out when they had to and came back frozen to the bone, with fingers blue and lips chapped. It was a grim time of year with the nights drawing in and the long expanse of winter looming before them like some unrelenting foe. Once Christmas had passed and the nights started to lighten, it might not seem so bad.

Ivy worked like one possessed, spending every waking moment on her rag rugs until her fingers ached and her eyes were bleary. It was torment to be trapped in the tiny cottage with the two brothers. For long hours Seth and Ben either talked or stared into the fire, taking turns to go for wood or water. They hunted a little, but game was scarce and there was little food for any of them. Hunger became a constant companion, fraying her already troubled nerves. It seemed as though there was never enough space to breathe or think. She had no time to herself; no privacy, and little comfort.

Being close to Seth was enough to set her thinking about him in ways she could ill afford. She could often smell him, even through the smoke from the fire. From time to time she felt the heat of his eyes on her skin and knew he was thinking the same indecent things. At night when she lay with Ben, the guilt of her confused feelings only added to the torment. She still took pleasure in her husband's arms, welcoming him as a lover, but then she loathed herself for sating the lust his sibling had inspired.

Seth kept his hands to himself, carefully avoiding getting too close to her. In some ways she was grateful for his restraint, but she hungered after the slightest touch of his hand and ached to brush close by him. Sometimes, when Ben was making love to her, she closed her eyes and dared to dream she might have both of them together, lying in the same bed and taking their turns with her. It was her darkest, deepest desire, to have both brothers without fear or recrimination. In the harsh light of day, it was impossible to believe such a taboo scenario could ever come to pass. In the darkness, with Ben moving hot and eager between her thighs as she gasped her appreciation, she pictured herself lying between the two men, each with his lips fastened to one of her nipples. By day she was frightened by what her dreaming mind dared to conjure. It was as though she had become two people – the public version, an honest Ivy who respected her marriage vows, while behind her lurked a nameless creature as wild as the fen skies unfettered by all law and convention. Ben called to her duty, Seth to the hidden, feral part of her self. She wondered if he had divided Megan from her good sense in the same way, speaking to her secret soul and inspiring cravings for transgression. Knowing now what it meant to live a double life and keep the secret of forbidden passion, Ivy could empathize with the young woman she had once worked for. At the time, she had felt nothing but anger and resentment, now she thought she understood.

A knock at their door in the late afternoon announced Nat Roberts, one of the smallholders who farmed not far from the Tuck's cottage. At the sound of fist on wood, Seth disappeared rapidly up the stairs.

"Afternoon, Tuck," Nat said as Ben let him in. The middle-aged farmer nodded a greeting to Ivy, but paid her no further regard. "That wind last night took the roof clear off my hen house. I got little old hens running about all over the place and nothing to keep them foxes off."

Ben nodded.

"Reckon I need another pair of hands to do it. I got the wood and all, but I need that hen house fixed by nightfall or them foxes'll have the lot. I ain't got much by way of ready money, but there's a few eggs and potatoes in it if you want."

Ben grabbed his coat from behind the door, grinning.

"It's a right harsh blow today," Nat added.

"You knows I'll work in any weather."

"That's why I come to you."

"You'd better get to thinking what you can make with eggs and tatties," Ben told Ivy as he departed.

The door was barely shut before Seth padded back down from the bedroom. "So, him's off working the rest of the day then," he said.

Ivy felt the now familiar thrill of erotic possibility warm her body. "That him be. We'll not be eating stale bread tonight."

It was a feeble attempt at diverting them both. She still could not reconcile herself to this unbridled lust. She tried to concentrate on her work, but to little effect. Her hands were awkward and she could hardly think about what she was supposed to be doing.

"You ain't fooling me," he said. "You smell of sex."

She flushed at this, unable to resist looking at him. That careless look in his eyes, the one he always wore when seducing her, began doing its work. He knew no rules or boundaries. Right and wrong did not seem to come into the equation for Seth, only need, lust and satisfaction. Human law, convention and religion meant no more to him than it did to the bittern booming in the marshes or to a fox stalking rabbits along the hedgerow.

He took the rug from her and dropped it to the floor, his fingers taking the place her handiwork had occupied. Closing his hands around hers, he tugged her and she rose to her feet, unable to resist the implicit command.

"Come to bed," he ordered.

Ivy flinched, thinking there was some sacrilege, surely, in taking this affair to her marriage bed. She met his eyes and knew such protests would be meaningless to him. A bed was nothing more than a place to lie or sleep, and one, at that, which he did not normally choose to utilize. He would not understand what it symbolized. Her arguments died on her lips. *Why quibble over disrespecting the symbol, when you had already betrayed what it represented?* She followed him up the stairs.

With casual ease he discarded the worn shirt that had once belonged to Ben, and cast off the trousers that were too short in the leg and going in holes at the knees. The vision of his nudity always transfixed her, wiping all other thoughts from her mind. He moved like a predator, stalking her with hungry intent. He stopped a few feet away from the bed, arms folded across his chest, his expression impatient. If he had to demand that she strip, he would be harsh with her. If pushed, he would dominate her by force of will. Sometimes that made her feel better, as though this was a thing entirely beyond her control. On other occasions, his capacity to strip her of all reason and self-possession made her detest herself.

She hurried to abandon her own attire. The room was chilly. Her best efforts to block out the wind had not yet found every crack, and there were drafts aplenty. It was too cold to remain exposed for long. With a final flutter of ill-ease, she crept under the familiar covers, holding them back for him to follow.

His hands covered her breasts and stomach as he leaned close. She closed her eyes, letting it happen to her, and the sumptuous delights of his tongue at play between her lips was enough to smother her smarting conscience. She reached for him, feeling the sleek smoothness of his skin and the tension in his muscles. They were so alike, these brothers. She was not certain she would easily tell them apart with her eyes closed. There were subtle differences in the way they smelled – Ben's aroma was earthier, Seth's was slightly sharp, and he was taller by an inch or two, but that was only obvious when the pair stood side-by-side. However, when it came to their styles of love-making, there would be no mistaking one for the other. Seth was all eager aggression, while Ben was gentle and sensual in everything he did.

After days of frustrated longing, the feel of his hard cock slipping inside her was a blessed relief. Here was the satisfaction her body craved, the heat that would melt all the chill of winter from her. She undulated beneath him, nearly drowning in his kisses and trembling at the first sweet suggestions of the violent, searing release he always brought her.

"You fuck like a bitch in heat," he remarked, and came quickly, disappointing her, for her own appetites were not yet fully sated. He slid off her and she sat up, planning to get back to her work and gritting her teeth against her dissatisfaction. "I ain't done with you yet, wench." He caught her around the waist, rolling her over and dropping her face down onto the bed. His hands moved forcibly up and down her back, and then his fingers plunged between the cheeks of her bottom, teasing her there before probing the slick cleft dripping with his cum. She moaned, parting her legs slightly to let his fingers in. He toyed with her for a long while, raising her arousal to scorching levels, but never quite taking her over the edge. One hand on her back kept her in place while the other went about its mischief, tantalizing her into a state of utter abandon and longing. She begged and pleaded with him, but to no avail.

"I could leave you like this," he threatened, evidently amused by her condition.

"Don't... oh, please don't!" she implored.

"So you want it then?"

"Yes!"

He was fond of this game, it seemed, making her confess to him the terrible extent of her lust. There could be no pretending she was being seduced when he pressed her for such acknowledgements. It was just another part of the power he had over her.

"What you want?" he asked.

"Take me!"

"You can say it better," he replied, his fingers still thrusting into her.

She knew what he wanted. They were words she had never spoken, only heard from others, words used by coarse men and fallen women. She stuttered, stumbled, hesitated. "Fuck..." she managed.

"Yes?"

"For pity's sake, just fuck me, Seth!"

He laughed at her then, and as his fingers came sliding out of her shamelessly juicing sex he moved round behind her. "On your knees, wench."

She moved at once, eager to obey the command that might lead to her supreme fulfillment.

Seth was hard for her again, and he had aroused her so thoroughly that she started to come with his first deep, hard stroke. So intoxicated was she by his power over her body that she cried out and moaned her pleasure without restraint, urging him on to greater efforts. His fingernails raked her back and thighs, each scratch a heated, searing line of sensation that spoke to the very depths of her flesh, and his pulsing ejaculation rocked her to the core.

Ivy slumped down into the bed, savoring the afterglow of pleasure.

"You two about done?"

Ben's voice cut through her thoughts like a knife. She could hardly breathe half believing this could not really be happening. She felt Seth's weight move on the bed. There was a terrible silence in the room, and she risked looking up. Her husband's usually gentle features were twisted with fury. He did not even look at her. Ivy hung her head in shame.

"Downstairs. Now," Ben ordered.

It was only the direction of his voice that marked any difference between him and Seth; the brutal command would have sounded equally convincing in the taller brother's mouth. For a second she thought he meant her. This was something between siblings, and she had no place in it.

As soon as they had gone from the bedroom, panic gripped her. She had seen what Seth could do when raised to anger. There were no sounds of voices from the room below, but then came the terrible click of the door closing. She leapt from the bed, tugging her dress on with no thought for undergarments. Barefoot, she raced down the stairs and out onto the cold grass, looking frantically for her two lovers. Hearing their raised voices, but unable to distinguish the words, she ran after them, hoping to divert their anger from each other and on to herself. She felt she deserved their hatred, their rejection. Any price would be worth paying if it stopped them from harming each other.

They had not gone far. Seth was already bleeding from a cut above his eye while Ben's coat was ripped. They circled, oblivious to her presence, and then erupted into a flurry of blows, moving so rapidly she could hardly tell which of them was which. Hands locked on throat, on shoulders, bodies entwined, wrestling and tussling until they were rolling on the ground, faster they went, the air about them shimmering. Ivy stared on in blank amazement, terrified they would kill each other, but powerless to intervene. "Stop it!" she called out in desperation, but neither of them paid her any attention. "Don't do this over me!" she begged, the volume of her voice falling. "I'm not worth this…"

They were soon so covered with mud they resembled each other completely. One (Seth, she presumed) began to shrink and twist, escaping from the lethal grasp with an uncanny shedding of skins. He was tangled in his own clothing and fought free, emerging furred and furious. The other man was little more than a beat behind, casting off all illusions of human form to continue fighting with tooth and claw. Blood and fur showered the earth as they tore chunks from one another. If Ivy had been afraid before, she was terrified now.

Ben had never told her he could change his skin as readily as Seth. The revelation left her reeling. *What else didn't she know?* One of them had the upper hand and she could see the other was flagging, bleeding heavily and failing to fight back. In these forms she could not tell them apart. Moving closer, she meant to try and intervene, but their fight carried them away from her and she was powerless to stop them. The brother who was winning opened a great gouge in the other's side, making the dark blood flow freely. Both became still, one crouching, the other lying defeated in the grass. She had no idea which was which, but the sight chilled her to her very soul. The victor turned, bounding off into the grass and vanishing into the hedgerow before she had time even to call out. He had been limping and was injured as well, although not so grievously as the sibling who remained.

"Don't move!" she shouted, her wits returning now she realized she must act.

Ivy ran for the house, grabbing her only spare sheet and hurrying back. The dreadfully wounded otter lay where she had left it, breathing unevenly. She was afraid he might have lost too much blood already, but she bandaged him as best she could, and managed to stop the flow. She knew full well that otter teeth could crush the skull of a fish or small bird and take the fingers from your hand. It was hard to think that the ravaged creature had some human element to its psyche, but she bit back her fear and doubts to do what she could for him.

The otter was too large for her even to consider carrying it, and she could hardly leave it where it had fallen. If the cold night did not kill him, the next person who found him probably would. After some deliberation, she went back for a blanket, and managed, with much perseverance, to roll the animal on to it. Dragging him home was no easy matter, with the mud to impede her, and the considerable weight of the creature to contend with, but now that there was something she could do, Ivy focused her full will on the task in hand, hauling with determination. She would not let this one die. She tried not to think about the other brother, the one who had fled limping into the undergrowth. He too might be in grave danger, but unless he came back to her, there would be no helping him.

She made up a nest of bedding before the fire, and set about cleaning the otter's wounds. She could only hope the other one would have the good sense to come home, but the fear that she might have lost one of them forever was breaking her heart.

Chapter Twenty Three

A floorboard creaked in the hall downstairs. Septimus had not slept well in a long while. Even though there had been no night-time disturbances in his house for weeks, every sound troubled him and he woke frequently. This broken sleep was taking its toll by day, making him pale and listless. He lay still, listening. There was a poker on the floor at the side of his bed, placed there to grant him some reassurance. In face of the distinctive sound of footsteps, it seemed woefully inadequate. These footfalls were light and hurried, racing up the stairs and into the empty bedroom next to his. *That bedroom again*, he noted, wondering why it was being singled out for special attention. Part of him wanted to draw the covers up over his head and try to pretend nothing had happened. He knew, however, that unless he faced this fear that it would torment him forever.

It might be Sarah, he told himself. His servant might be playing pranks or indulging in some other youthful foolishness. He tried to hold that thought in his mind and not think of ghosts, or of the strange figure he had glimpsed in his hall, or of the man who had attacked him in the garden. His hands shook as he lifted the poker, and he was so apprehensive it was all he could do to open the door of the spare bedroom.

The space was in utter darkness unrelieved by moonlight or a candle.

"I knew you would come."

The woman's voice sent a shiver down his spine. She sounded moderately cultured, but completely unfamiliar. He took a tentative step forward.

"I've missed you so much, but I knew you would find me, I knew it. If you were not here, I was sure you would be at the ruins tomorrow, even though you did not come today."

Whoever she was, she sounded very real and human even though her words made no sense at all.

"Come and lie with me," she said, her voice husky.

Septimus shivered in his night shirt. No one had ever propositioned him like that before, and the temptation to respond to this passionate stranger was shocking. However, his good sense overcame the sudden drives of his body, and he proceeded with caution.

"There is no bed, but you can lie in my arms," she went on.

He had placed the voice now and guessed that its owner was sitting on the floor close to the window.

"Will you not greet me, my love?" she whispered anxiously.

"Forgive me, young lady, but I fear you have mistaken me for someone else," Septimus said stiffly.

He heard a sudden intake of breath, followed by a shuddering sob. This was becoming more peculiar by the moment, and he wondered if he might be dreaming. Pulling the curtain back, he let what little moonlight there was into the room. There was enough light that he could just make out the crouched form hunched where he had guessed she would be. Touched by the sound of weeping, he knelt beside this latest unlikely nocturnal visitor and touched her shoulder lightly. "Why don't we go downstairs?' he suggested. 'I could make you a nice cup of tea or something stronger, if you prefer."

"Who are you?" she asked tearfully.

"Reverend Septimus Gotobed," he replied.

She sniffed. "My parents don't live here any more?"

"Your parents?" Something began to fall into place in the young vicar's tired mind. "Would you tell me your name?" he asked gently.

"Meg," she said.

"It's Megan, isn't it?" he said, remembering. "You would be Megan West." This was a difficulty he had not anticipated – the daughter of the former incumbent, tearful and un-chaperoned in his spare room. He helped her to her feet. Her small hand was very cold in his. "How did you get here?" he asked, although the real question on his mind was 'How did you get in'? After the last escapade, he had gone to some pains to secure his abode, but evidently it was in vain.

"I walked," she said.

"Where are your parents?"

"I do not know."

It was getting worse by the moment and he feared both their reputations would be seriously compromised by her arrival.

Septimus led his visitor down to the kitchen and, rather than disturb Sarah, he set about making tea himself. He knew the theory, even if he was a little rusty on the practice, but the results were drinkable enough. Although the young woman spoke like a lady of some education and breeding, she looked like a tramp. Her long hair was filthy and tangled with leaves, her coat was far too big for her and grubby, and her dress was torn and stained. She was a pretty enough thing, he mused, but the intensity in her face bordered on derangement. Her behavior hardly boded well, and he feared he might be dealing with someone who had been exiled from their better senses.

"Would you like anything to eat?" he asked, having no idea what else to do with her.

Megan nodded eagerly, and proceeded to devour the bread and ham he put in front of her. Her skin looked sallow even in the candlelight and she was decidedly thin. As she ate, Septimus considered his position carefully. He could not throw the girl out into the streets; that was unthinkable. To have her stay under his roof would be difficult in the extreme, but there was nowhere else he could send her at this late hour. It was futile to think of concealing her presence, Sarah would know everything, and the girl had family in the village, so any attempt at disguise would only make him look worse. He resigned himself to brazening out whatever ensued, and hoped he would be able to weather what he sensed was going to be a testing time for him.

"I'm sorry about before," she said suddenly.

He looked up at her.

"I thought you were someone else."

"I did rather get that impression."

She smiled then, a look of real trust in her eyes.

"I will not pry into your circumstances, but you evidently have some favored young man."

She looked at him quizzically. "There are plenty of people who would throw me out onto the street for admitting as much," she replied.

"I am not such a person. Let him who is without sin cast the first stone."

She nodded enthusiastically. "I will try not to cause you too much trouble," she said winningly.

She seemed entirely sane and rational now, yet he could not help but think her promise came rather late, and that the trouble was already caused.

"Will you help me?" she asked, her tone painfully laden with need.

He had never been one to refuse a fair damsel in distress. "I will do whatever I can," Septimus reassured her.

She waited until he went to dress himself more appropriately, and then, after filling her pocket with cheese and apples from his larder, she let herself out through the kitchen door. The key hidden in one of the herb pots was something Septimus knew nothing about.

It was just before the dawn by the time she left her old home. As the sky was free from rain clouds, there were a few people already abroad, going about their business. Megan saw a few she knew and kept her shoulders hunched and her head hung low. They shot quizzical glances in her direction, but no one greeted her and she supposed they did not know her without her fine clothes and proud posture. It was almost as though she no longer quite existed. Megan could recall the neat and tidy girl she had been – nothing at all like the wild and grubby figure she now presented. Gone were the simple, elegant dresses, the carefully arranged hairstyles and the modest dignity. Now she resembled a gypsy; tattered and carefree.

First she went to the abbey ruins, to wander there amongst the fallen stones and crumbling pillars. Here, at least, nothing appeared to have changed. Watching the clouds roll across the sky had a timeless feel, as though she could rest in this place forever. It was not a thought she cared to dwell upon. For a while she sauntered about the place, pausing in all those sacred places where she and Seth had made love only a few months before. She could remember each spot exactly, recalling what position he had chosen, and all the details of their coupling.

Early in the afternoon she glimpsed an otter coming out of a dyke near the road. It showed no signs of having seen her. A long eel trailed from its jaws, still wriggling and lively. The dark-furred creature settled on a bank and began to crunch its prey, taking the head first to stop the eel's continued resistance, and then enjoying the rest of its meal at a more leisurely pace. When it was done, it sloped off. Megan could only wonder if it truly was an otter. These days she looked at every creature askance, not knowing if there might be more to its existence than a first look might suggest.

Late in the afternoon, she accepted that her lover would not be seeking her out today. Seth had promised once that he would come to her every afternoon at the ruins if she waited for him, but that had been a long time ago. Perhaps things had changed. There was still so much she could not remember, so many troubling holes in her past into which all manner of vital things might have fallen. She brought to mind the little cottage where her beloved man lived and wondered if he might be found there now. It was a very long time since she had last ventured that way, and it was a fair walk cross country, as she remembered it. There were few alternatives worth considering, however. She supposed she could return to the curious young vicar. He had been kind to her, and might continue to be so. Otherwise she knew her only option was to find some barn or outhouse to shelter in. It was surprising to her how easily she had taken to living rough. It was hard, but there was a simple immediacy to it that appealed to her current state of mind.

The cheese was long since finished and the second apple eaten. She was hungry again. These days she ate when she could, with little fuss or concern. No more for her the world of finely sliced bread with butter and jam, or soft cakes on a Sunday afternoon. Her mother's sedate meals on fine china were like dreams of an ancient civilization. Now there was dirt under her nails and she ate with her hands.

It was almost dark when she reached the Tucks' cottage. It had proved hard to locate, squatting as it did so close against the earth, with a screen of small trees to break up its outline. From the outside nothing much seemed to have changed, but she felt peculiar looking at the place. It was a little like homesickness, a little like fear. A light glowed at the curtained window. She gazed at it for a long time, thinking Seth might be there, that in a few moments she might be safely back in his arms once more. She could almost smell him. She was half afraid to knock, as though the sound of it might dispel her imaginings and give her some harsh reality in their place.

The fear was not misplaced. It was a while before the door opened, but when it did, Megan was presented not with the angular face of one of the Tuck brothers, but with the strained, wan features of her former servant – the last thing she had expected. From Ivy's face, the recognition was not mutual.

"Ivy? It is Megan."

Ivy's eyebrows rose, and she opened the door a little further, her eyes wide and staring.

"Will you let me in?"

There was a moment of stillness and silence between them, then Ivy nodded slowly and allowed the windswept young woman to enter.

Megan surveyed the scene thoughtfully. It was warmer and brighter than she remembered, and there was something nestled before the fire... an otter, heavily bandaged. Her heart sank. Something terrible had happened to her lover. "Seth?" She approached cautiously. The otter was badly injured and made no move to acknowledge her presence. Memories came flooding back to her... Seth lying in the road, his pelt filthy and his skull crushed, her own destructive grief, and the darkness settling on her... everything welled up afresh like the gush of blood from a wound. But this could not be the creature she had seen brutalized outside the village school... dark recollections tangled with the present, each impossible in the face of the other. "Is it Seth?" she asked, no longer certain what she should believe.

"I don't know if it be he or Ben," Ivy confessed wearily. She sat down on one of the hard chairs.

"I do not understand..."

"I'm not so sure I understand myself. Didn't know Ben were a shifter as well, but them's both part otter."

"I knew about Seth. I have seen him change his skin," Megan confessed, awash with relief that she no longer had to bear this alarming secret alone. "I didn't know Ben could do it, too. I suppose that makes sense, though."

"I knew about Seth too, but Ben's never told me."

Megan considered this carefully. "What happened?" she asked at last.

"Them two got in a fight. Them were both right mad, and took to their otter forms part way through. This one took the worst of it, the other one sloped off. Him were injured too, but not so bad. I don't know which this be." She spared Megan the rest. It would not help anyone to reveal that Seth had been Ivy's lover. It was as much as Ivy could manage to convey these few phrases. Anger, grief, self-loathing and fear twisted within her. She felt more than she could ever say.

Megan listened in silence, and passed no comment. Instead, she gazed into the fire as though divining something in the flickering tongues of flame. The two of them remained quiet for a long time.

"What you doing back here?" Ivy asked at last. She had emerged a little way from her own troubles and realized there were complications afresh to be dealt with.

Megan shrugged. "Burnham's home for me. I walked back."

Ivy resisted the temptation to press more closely. This was not the Megan she knew. The skittish young lady had gone and in her stead was a thoughtful, distant creature who looked as worn as any land woman.

"Why are you here?" Megan eventually enquired.

"Ben married me."

Megan giggled.

"What'll you do now?" Ivy ventured.

Megan shrugged. She had given no real thought to anything beyond the necessity of finding her lover. "There is another man living at the vicarage now."

"There be. Reverend Gotobed, or so I hear. Not laid eyes on he myself."

"He seemed very nice." Megan smiled to herself. After a while, she rose to inspect the wounded creature by the fire. Aside from the swathe of makeshift bandages, there were cuts and blood spots in great number all over his body. "They really did fight," she observed. "How bad are his injuries?"

"Couldn't say. Looks bad, I reckon, but what do I know about otters or skin changers? Wait and see is all we can do."

"Perhaps we could fetch the doctor?" Megan suggested.

"To an otter? He'll laugh at us."

"Not that I have any money," Megan added, realizing there were numerous flaws in her plan. She yawned widely.

"You'll not go anywhere tonight. Best stop here," Ivy told her.

"Are you sure?"

"Where else can you go? Take the bed upstairs. I'll not sleep anyway."

With a grateful, almost childlike smile, Megan accepted and climbed the ladder to the bedroom.

Ivy closed her eyes. Only a few hours previously, she and Seth had played in that bed. He could be dying now for all she knew. One of them was badly injured, the other might well be in no better state, and even if health returned to them both their dispute might never find resolution. She feared for them, and wondered what would become of her when all of this was done.

She sat up through the long hours of the night, tending the fire and watching over whichever of her wounded lovers was there with her. She thought and worried, grieved, feared and agonized over all that had happened. None of it could be changed or atoned for, and her own responsibility for what had happened loomed large in her mind. The fault for this violence appeared to be hers alone. She could not blame either one of the men she adored. It was hard to accept, when she stood so close to losing both, that each had won a place in her heart. But this was no time to be thinking of love. The future looked bleak, with little scope left for reconciliation or happiness. She doubted Ben could ever forgive what she had done or that either brother would want any more to do with her.

Chapter Twenty Four

Septimus was less than entirely surprised when he found his unconventional visitor had departed. He almost expected it. The girl troubled him considerably – her physical and psychological condition, her isolation and her unlikely story. Like it or not, she had entered his house and made him aware of her plight. He now had some responsibility, he felt, to put the matter to rights. He was confident she must be Reverend West's daughter, but he thought he should check before making too much fuss. A word in the right quarters would soon locate the Wests. Matters could then be taken forward in the manner that seemed most appropriate. If he assessed the matter rightly, the young lady's parents might well be able to fetch her within the week. *That of course was assuming she had not vanished from Burnham as mysteriously as she arrived.*

Her uncanny appearance and suggestive words had left their marks on Septimus, and he felt quite peculiar each time he remembered their first exchange. His thoughts returned to that part of their encounter all too often, slipping away to recall her husky voice and indecent request until he was almost giddy from the thought of it. Gotobed comforted himself with constant reminders that he had behaved impeccably and not transgressed in any way. The trouble was, the more he considered it all, the more acutely he realized he would very much like to have done something regrettable. It was not a mode of thought he was remotely accustomed to and it vexed him considerably.

In order to fend off his lustful thoughts, Septimus focused his attention on seeking the girl's parents and making them aware of the situation. His Bishop would no doubt be able to assist in that part of the problem, and it was to this good man that Septimus addressed his first missive. The letter took some drafting, sensitive as the circumstances were. Harder yet was the second letter to be enclosed with the first addressed to the people he suspected were this Megan's parents. In the end he chose to say very little, not wanting to add to their inevitable distress should the girl indeed be theirs.

When it was done, he pondered his next move. Discovering where young Megan had gone that morning must be his immediate concern. Locating her, and then finding suitable accommodation for her until her parents could be found, was essential. It would not be easy, that much was apparent. He was sorely tempted to consider taking her into his own home, but people might well talk, and he was not certain he could restrain himself as he should.

As was his habit when he wanted some local intelligence, Septimus sauntered down to the kitchen to consult with Sarah. The girl was young, but she was sharp witted and appeared to know everyone. While her cooking left a great deal to be desired, she was well behaved and good mannered, which was worth a considerable amount. He exchanged a few words on the subject of meals and what purchases might be required for the week ahead. Then, with practiced ease, he steered her gently in the direction he wished to learn about.

"You were employed in this house before I came to Burnham, I believe?" he ventured.

"That I were. Not for long, though."

He nodded encouragingly. Sarah was not an especially discreet soul. Given time, and a little gentle provocation, she usually shared whatever gossip she had.

"There were a bit of a to-do with the previous girl, Ivy Jenks,' she went on. 'Her let some man in one night. Heard her's married him since, though."

"All is well that ends well, as they say."

"I were here a bit after that, but then Miss Megan, she got sick and they moved away."

"Was she very unwell?"

"Her was out of her wits, I reckon. Running into the road in her night-dress, sleepwalking, not eating, talking queer. Her'd gone right peculiar."

"That is very sad to hear. Was there any cause for it?"

"Not that I ever heard. Her just took peculiar and that were it."

"But it all happened after Ivy Jenks let a man in," he mused.

"That it did. Right after that it were."

"Where is Ivy now, do you know?"

"Her's married Ben Tuck, them lives in one of them small cottages away from here. Her's me cousin, as it happens. Not that we was ever close, mind."

He did not push any further. Being a fen man himself by birth, even if he had spent most of his years in town, Septimus understood how people like Sarah thought. The passion for tall tales, mysteries and peculiarities was so common that any story worth telling was rapidly embellished to suit the local palate. If he asked more questions now, the likelihood was that he would be showered with wild imaginings. The fen-man in him was entirely capable of doing that unaided. He envisaged terrible secrets – a servant girl blamed for a daughter's indiscretion, an assault swept under the carpet as these things most usually were, and a dozen other grim tales. This was a house in which he had witnessed troubling things – the violent man in his garden, searching for Megan, the man in the house who had vanished, and then the girl herself, drawn back to this place. He thought there might be some coherent explanation for it all, but even so there was deep mystery here to be pondered and solved.

Donning his hat and coat, Reverend Gotobed set off for the bakery, intent on learning more and determining the exact location of the Tuck's

cottage before the day was out. The pretext of buying bread had served him
well in the past when he required information about his parishioners.

Chapter Twenty Five

Megan was in the borderlands between wakefulness and sleeping, still hazy with dreams and imaginings. The pillow beneath her smelled of Seth; of the sharp aroma of his body, so unforgettable and evocative. It took her some time to remember where, and when, she was, in the little cottage she had been brought to after her ordeal in the frozen dyke, only months had passed since then.

Had she dreamed or was the recollection of him real? She did not know. At first the memories seemed as fickle and fleeting as true dreams, but as she grasped for them they became clearer in her thoughts. He had been with her during the night, waking her with kisses and caresses so her body was tender and aroused before her mind had fully woken to the wonder of his presence. She had tried to ask him questions, but he hushed her with the weight of his lips, and silenced her tongue with his own. Every few moments he paused in what he was doing to rest his forehead against hers. He had not done that before, not so often or so intently, and she felt the intimacy of it, his face so close to hers, his thoughts separated from her own by a narrow thickness of skin and bone.

In the darkness they had feasted upon each other, mouths consuming skin with an aching desire born of painful separation.

"I thought I had lost you forever," she whispered repeatedly.

"Never, you belong with me. You are mine, always."

For months she had wandered in darkness, her mind half broken and her wits in tatters. Now that they were together, Megan felt herself come alive. The fear and pain melted away and instead there came the most terrible and compelling clarity. She could only be fully herself when he was between her thighs, his mouth on her skin and his hard cock filling her body. She could only be truly real and happy while he possessed her. When they were apart, she was nothing at all.

"I am dead without you," she confessed.

"I'm dead without you, my wench," he answered, following the words with kisses that seemed to draw her soul out through her mouth to mingle with his.

No drug could capture and enthrall her as this man did. The madness and addiction of loving him was sweet delight in exuberant madness. She felt her body racing towards the highest expression of passion. Seth was with her. From the size of him and the way he moved, she knew his pleasure would soon be upon him.

He made her climax so powerfully that her sense of self collapsed around her. As the first burst of excitement waned, tears of joy burned on her cheeks. Again he brought her to orgasm, sending hot fire through her psyche, burning away the past with all its toils and disappointments. A third and forth time she rose breathless to meet him, trembling in ecstasy at each thrust of his body. She came again, and it was though nothing had existed before this encounter and nothing after it could ever matter. With a final shudder, he emptied himself inside her and she joined with him in a final pinnacle of sensation that broke down all barriers between them. Heart to heart and soul to soul, they trembled on the edge of full communion, two beings locked together in numinous passion.

Lying with her eyes closed, the feeling of sumptuous repose permeated her. Megan slept for awhile, blissful and requited. When she woke, she could tell at once that he had gone. She felt his physical absence keenly, but knew it to be a temporary thing. They were bound now by something stronger than human marriage. Everything that she was she had truly offered up to him. It mattered little where they went or what they did, they would always have that perfect, transcendent connection. He would return; it was inevitable. They belonged to each other and such profound love could not be denied.

* * *

In the morning, Ivy rose to relieve herself in the little privy behind the cottage. When she emerged, blinking tired eyes against the light, she saw two dead eels upon the doorstep, fresh and glistening. Both their heads were gone, bitten off by the looks of it. She glanced around her hopefully, knowing the absent sibling must have brought this gift. He had not gone far then, and was well enough to hunt. That at least was something. It suggested all was not lost.

When she carried the slime-coated eels inside, she found Megan sitting in one of the chairs, her legs folded up under her ragged dress and her expression reminiscent of a sleepy cat. The otter had not moved.

"Sleep well enough?" Ivy asked.

"Yes, thank you."

Without fuss or comment, Ivy began preparing the meat, cleaning the slime away, and then cutting one eel into small sections for cooking. She took the raw meat of the other to the injured otter, and knelt beside him to help him eat. He took a few tentative bites and managed to swallow a little, but the effort of eating was too great and he lowered his head after only a few mouthfuls. Ivy crooned encouraging noises, stroking the thick pelt with a finger as though she was tending to a child. He was struggling to do the smallest things, and she did not think it boded well.

"I believe that must be Ben," Megan said suddenly.

"What makes you think that? Ivy asked. She had done little but wonder which of the two it was, but did not know their otter forms well enough to tell. She supposed Megan might have some insight into the matter.

"I know because Seth came to me last night."

Ivy shook her head. "I reckon you must have dreamed it, he's not been up them stairs."

"He lay with me," Megan retorted angrily.

"I been awake all through the night, and no one's stirred, not you, or this otter here, or anyone else. Them stairs creaks something dreadful, if I'd nodded off I'd have heard that, or the door, or you two."

"You are mistaken," Megan said, pouting like a willful child. She did not tell Ivy that her thighs smelled of her lover's juices, or that there was a bite mark on her shoulder that had not been there the day before. Now that she was awake, she could feel where he had been inside her, his erection making her ache deliciously hours after their coupling was over.

"I don't want to fight you," Ivy said wearily, "we've enough to contend with already, no point you and me fighting like a couple of fools."

The sudden sound of rapping on the door caused both young women to start. They exchanged nervous glances. Ivy rose, and opened the door a crack. Peering through, she could see a well dressed young man, his expression sincere. "Can I help you?" she asked warily.

"I am terribly sorry to disturb you. I hope you can forgive me. Would you be Mrs. Tuck by any chance?"

"That be I."

"Good, good. I do not believe we have been introduced. I am Reverend Gotobed, I have not been in the Parish very long."

"You're the young man as replaced Reverend West then," Ivy said, relaxing a little and opening the door more hospitably.

"Indeed I am."

She stepped out of the house. "I'd invite you in, but it's a terrible mess and all," she apologized, her thoughts racing as she tried to guess what he might want.

"I was rather hoping you might be able to assist me. I am trying to find a young lady by the name of Megan West. I was wondering if you might have seen her."

Ivy kept her face carefully neutral. She guessed Megan had run from her parents and that there might well be further complications. Megan had turned more than a little queer, with a feyness to her that unsettled Ivy. "I thought her'd gone off with her folks," she said carefully.

"I believe she had, but that she might be here alone. The young lady is…" Septimus reached for the right word, not wanting to alarm or misrepresent. "She is a little troubled, I believe. A young woman appeared at my house yesterday, and I believe it to have been Miss West. As you can imagine, I am greatly concerned for her wellbeing."

Ivy wondered if Megan could hear all of this, and supposed she probably could. The young lady had fled the vicar once and had not thus far presented herself this time. She caught the sound of the stairs creaking softly, and understood that Megan did not want to be found. "This wench you saw, pretty were she?"

Septimus nodded.

"With a grubby dress and a great big coat on her?"

"That is a fair description, yes."

"Did she tell you her name?" Ivy asked innocently.

"She called herself Meg, and I surmised that she might well be Miss West."

"Ah, well, you see, I've not seen Miss West since I left serving her folks, but I do have seen Meg Tuck, her's Ben's sister."

"Truly?"

Ivy nodded, hating to lie, but feeling in her heart it was the right thing to do.

"Her's a gypsy, like her mother. Different fathers, you understand, but

Meg do come back here now and then. I suppose her'd be about the same age as Miss West, but I can promise you, them's totally different."

Septimus nodded quietly at this. His look was appraising. "Is she here now?"

"No, her was off with Ben first light, she don't like to be cooped up inside, and them's got a lot of catching up to do."

"I see. Thank you for your time, Mrs. Tuck, and for solving a little mystery for me." He doffed his hat politely, then strode off in the direction of the road.

Ivy watched him go, uncertain as to whether he had believed her lies, and wondering what on earth to do now. "Him's gone," she called out to Megan.

The young woman appeared at the top of the stairs, an anxious look on her face.

"Him's the new vicar, thought you was at his place the other day, guessed who you was and come looking for you."

"What did you tell him?" Megan asked nervously.

"That you was Meg Tuck, Ben's sister, that you're a gypsy."

"Did he believe you?"

"I don't know, but him's gone for now. I'm thinking you don't want to be found?"

Megan shook her head vigorously by way of a reply. "They locked me up and made me take laudanum until I hardly knew who I was. I don't want to go back there."

Ivy wondered who 'they' were but decided it might be better not to ask. "Well, you can stop along here, for now at any rate."

Megan smiled gratefully at this. "You are very kind to me, Ivy."

Ivy shrugged dismissively. "It don't make any odds to me."

"I am going to go out now," Megan announced. "I shall go and see Seth."

Ivy stood by the door and watched Megan make her way over the fields.

She was unsurprised to see her visitor was heading towards the old abbey ruins. Perhaps it was true that Ben lay injured and Seth would be waiting for his true love in the place they had always met. Jealousy washed through her, strong and sickly at the same time. It seemed as though all the weight of the world was bowing her tired shoulders while Megan lived a happy dream full of phantom loves. She envied the young woman her delusions, and thought how sweet it must be to ignore all the harsh truth and inhabit a make-believe realm. Her own life was in limbo, and until the otter in her house recovered and she knew what the siblings intended, there could be no peace for her.

It was obvious to her that Megan had parted company with the more common reality. She moved in a different world now, her starry eyes seeing a fen of ghosts and shape-shifters and who knew what else? Ivy was starting to envy her that escape from the difficulties that surrounded them. She would like to let her own hair fly loose and walk out into the fens chasing dreams of passion. Her sense of duty would not permit it, not yet anyway.

* * *

The days passed slowly, each much like the last. In the morning there would be some offering on the doorstep – a few eggs or a rabbit, eels, ducks and other meat. The bringer of these gifts never stayed long enough to be seen despite Ivy's best attempts to catch him. The wounded otter in the house ate little and remained listless. There was a smell of infection from his wounds and Ivy sank slowly into despair. Nothing she did seemed to help in the slightest and she no longer believed he would live. Her gloom permeated the cottage like shadows encroaching at nightfall.

Megan rose with the dawn, accepting the food she was given as though it was her right, and not considering what it might cost Ivy to provide for her. She still had the bed, while Ivy dozed when she could, resting her head and arms on the table or curling up on the floor next to her suffering creature. Sleep was elusive and the distraught woman seldom sought its solace, but Megan barely noticed this.

Before there were too many people abroad, Megan made her way to the ruins to pass the day waiting, and dreaming... the lightest breath of wind felt like the touch of his fingers on her cheek. The cries of wild birds carried echoes of his voice, and the soft, peaty earth reminded her of the smell of his body. This once restless young woman found she could sit for hours now, hardly stirring at all as the ghostly communications came to her. Seth was ever present, and she need only close her eyes to know his touch and feel the warmth of his skin against hers. When she lay back in the long grasses they tickled her face and felt like his hair on her cheeks.

She was lost in reverie, her fingers digging into the cold soil as she knelt to better recall what they had done in this place. She could remember the strength of his hands on her hips so well that it seemed real to her. Once again she felt the hot throb of cock in her body and the rhythm of his hips grinding against her thighs. Here she had knelt for him, offering herself up like a bitch otter to her mate. Here he had raked his nails down her back until he drew blood. Lying on this very patch of grass, he had fucked her relentlessly until she wept for pleasure and mercy. In those days she had been half afraid of his wildness, overpowered by his lust and determination, now she would welcome it.

"Excuse me."

The unfamiliar male voice shattered her fragile world, driving off the wealth of exquisite illusions. She looked up, angry and resentful at the intrusion. On raising her head, she saw the vicar who now lived in her father's house. She looked away from him, reining in her irritation. She did not want anyone intruding on her sacred places. "What do you want?" she asked. Much of the restrained polish had fallen from her voice of late. She sounded less like a child of the middle classes now and more like any other poor fen girl. When she was alone, she practiced speaking as her lover had done, wanting to capture Seth in any way she could.

"I happened to be passing. I thought you might be in distress."

She sneered at this, knowing he could not begin to understand how she lived or what she saw.

It was chance alone that had drawn Septimus to this spot. History and antiquity intrigued him, and when he had time to himself, it was his delight to search out ancient places. This was not his first time visiting the ruins, but he had been absent for some weeks thanks to the weather. It had been on his mind to undertake a little archaeological digging in the summer months, to which end he had made a considerable study of the ruined abbey, trying to ascertain the most promising places.

The crouching figure had at first looked to be nothing more than fallen masonry. Only on closer approach did he realize some human had prostrated themselves in the ancient chapel. For a while he watched, perplexed and fascinated. It was quite some minutes before he realized it was none other than the peculiar girl who called herself Meg. A rush of heat coursed through his body, conjuring visions of contact and seduction in his imagination. Her position was exposed and the spot so very isolated. Horrified by the fruits of his thoughts, Septimus had spoken to her for no other reason than to break the fearful spell that bound him.

For some time they remained as they were, watching each other warily. She was a mystery, indeed, with her wild hair and luminous eyes. He found himself wishing she would offer herself up to him once again. To be asked to lie in those arms, to be blessed with her kisses and caresses, was a maddening prospect. *Resist*, he told himself, but his body urged indulgence. He wanted to step forward, push up her skirts, and delve into her secrets for himself. He imagined drowning in the pool of her mystery and his heart beat faster yet.

"Can I help you?" he asked her instead. His tongue felt thick and heavy in his mouth. He could no longer bear the silence and stillness. There must be some move towards propriety and convention soon or he might lose all control of himself.

Megan stood, shaking off the animal-like pose and becoming more obviously human to him. The light in her eyes faded a little, but he still felt witness to some act of primitive ritual magic. For a while those uncommunicative portals to her soul captivated him. Then his attention turned to the fullness of her lips, the perfection of her cheekbones, and the glory of her untamed hair. The shabby dress and coat disguised her figure from his wandering eyes. She was small boned and delicate, but he imagined there would be sensuous curves to her form that might fit snugly under a man's hand. Septimus burned with the desire to be that man.

"You've got nothing I want," she said sternly, her voice cutting through his lust.

"Are you Megan West?" he asked, still unsure of her identity.

He had a feeling the Tuck woman had been less than truthful, although he could not have said why. He supposed she had seemed furtive when he visited her.

"I'm not anyone," she answered cryptically. "I'm nothing and no one at all. I'm the wind off the fen." She turned, her hands stuffed into the pockets of her coat. She pulled the garment wide around her, spinning like a feather on the breeze. "I am a heron stalking in the reeds." She giggled to herself, dancing a little closer to the young vicar. Septimus was half afraid of her, but even so, this sudden, incomprehensible display had not dampened his ardor. "I'm a bitch otter in heat."

He gulped at this declaration. All pretence at control left him. He caught her hand, touched her face, and pressed his lips to her perfect mouth. For a few seconds she was still, her proximity intoxicating. He wanted her to reciprocate, to demonstrate the desire he had heard in her voice not so many nights before. She pulled his bottom lip into her mouth, but only to nip him sharply with her teeth before she danced away, taking a part of his soul with her. His lip throbbed with pain, and he rejoiced in it. Brutality from this woman he would willingly submit to.

"You can catch me for a moment, but you can't keep me," she sang the words like a melodious blackbird.

He reached for her again, but this time she was too quick and sidestepped him so he stumbled and nearly fell.

"I'm an addiction. I'm the purple poppy you see in all the gardens, sweet dreams and nightmares. Once you've tasted me, you'll never rest." She laughed at this, joyful in her own bright visions and relishing the incomprehension in his eyes. The rest of the world was mad and she was the only sane thing in it, the only one capable of seeing things truly. She knew this with all certainty. The delirious young man might taste her mouth, he might lie with her, but he would never understand. She could show him, but he still would not see. She felt the wind take her hair, brushing its tender kisses against her skin and whispering secrets for her ears alone. She heard Seth's laughter and knew he appreciated the absurdity of the situation. He was the one person who understood, who saw things as clearly as she now did. It was time to be on her way.

Septimus leaned heavily against one of the damp walls. He felt like one in a sick fever. Sweat dripped into his eyes, blurring his vision. The girl was gone, and it seemed as though the better part of his reason had departed with her. The exchange had been pure lunacy, but he wanted her desperately. He could still taste her mouth and the feel of her skin when he grasped her hand. Thoughts of crushing her to him, of threading his fingers through her hair and pressing his mouth to hers possessed him. He staggered home like a drunkard.

Chapter Twenty Six

Ivy thought it was probably after midnight. Aside from the glowing fire it had been dark for a long time, but would be darker yet. In the room upstairs, Megan turned in her sleep, murmuring to herself sporadically. Quiet as it was, each small sound was grotesquely exaggerated in Ivy's mind. Every so often, the otter beside her took a long, shuddering breath. In the silence between these gasps, Ivy waited, hardly daring to inhale until he exhaled. It was hard to be certain of anything in the darkness with nothing to mark the passing of time. She thought his breaths were coming less often now. He had not eaten at all during the day, and had drunk precious little. She had done her best with poultices, trying to draw the poison from the wound, but it did not seem to be working. She was not much skilled with herbs, and feared she may have made a mistake. His coat looked rough and poor now, and the light had gone from his eyes.

The hours wore on relentlessly, bringing no sign of the miracle Ivy hoped for. She was too tired to cry, but fear had a tight hold on her. Having lain awake for many nights and struggled alone through unforgiving days, she was too exhausted to give vent to her distress. She thought if her lover did slip away, she would lie down at his side and breathe her last. It would be a relief for both of them not to suffer any more.

Stroking the otter's head gently, she talked, letting her thoughts run freely. Memories of childhood and fragments of her hopes meshed together in a single, impenetrable stream of half-told tales. It hardly mattered now which one of the brothers it was who lay here, and which had gone. Sometimes she wondered if there had truly been two of them or if her memory was playing tricks. It seemed so unlikely this otter who lay so still in her arms had ever worn a human skin. Sleeplessness brought its own forms of madness. Perhaps when this vigil ended she would let down her hair, smear mud on her face, and run wild with Megan. They could race to the ends of the earth.

Although he had been still for hours, the otter shifted unexpectedly, lifting his head and resting it on Ivy's arm. She was surprised by the weight of it. By the orange firelight, she saw that his eyes were open for the first time in days. They regarded each other, divided by silence, but bound by love and suffering. Ivy wondered what she could see in those dark eyes. Was it affection or terror that glinted there? Did he look at her with trust now? She wished she could tell. There was so much she wanted to say to both brothers, but without knowing which was which, she dared give voice to none of it. *Was there any point seeking forgiveness now?*

With a little sigh, the eyelids fell once more. Ivy pressed her face into his fur, feeling his whiskers against her cheek. Her hair tumbled down around them, enclosing woman and otter behind a private veil. If will alone could keep death at bay, she would see them both safely through to morning...

When Ivy woke from a shallow and restless slumber, the light of a new day glimmered at the window and the creature in her arms lay stiff and cold. No matter how she strained her ears, she could not hear the tell-tale rise and fall of breathing. The form beside her was chilly and leaden. Closing her eyes, she listened instead to the slow rhythm of her own respiration. It was a terrible sound to her, one she wanted to break off but could not stop. No matter how hard she tried to make each breath her last, the instinct for life would push forwards, making her gulp another cursed mouthful of existence. She did not want to rise from this final embrace and face the day. Her limbs seemed as lifeless as his.

For once in her life, Ivy wanted to be free from duty and necessity and not be obliged to deal with what must come next. The body must be buried.

What would happen now to the surviving sibling she did not dare to consider. In the end, the press of a full bladder forced her to relinquish the corpse of her lover and accept the unrelenting requirements of life. Outside, the air was fresh and clean even though another mild storm had blown in. She stood on the threshold of the cottage for a few moments, watching the rain sleeting down and wondering why she had not wept yet. The pain in her was so strong as to seem unreal, and nothing would be sufficient to express it.

Amongst other things, there was a shovel in the outhouse. Ivy took it and circled the cottage, looking for a suitable site. There was no escaping this miserable task – a grave must be dug. She chose a place beside the clump of elders and set to work as the rain lashed down, drenching her. As she dug, fancies born of desperation paraded through her thoughts. *These brothers were something other than human… might they not transcend death somehow?* Might she not go back inside to find the worn otter pelt shrugged off and a beautiful, smiling man naked beside the fire? Where there was impossible magic, who was to say what rules would hold sway? Then she remembered old Moocher, dead and naked on the riverbank, and she knew her lovers were as vulnerable and mortal as any other being.

The soil was waterlogged and heavy. She worked on in grim silence until her arms and back ached and her clothes were wet through. Spade by spade the hole grew wider and deeper until it last she thought it big enough. She did not see Megan emerge.

"What are you doing?" the girl asked, pulling her coat tight around her against the rain.

Ivy gave the other woman a long, hard look. She could not speak to explain it; her voice was dead within her.

Megan considered the hole, taking into account its shape and depth. Her face went a ghastly white. Shaking her head, she backed away as though sheer force of denial might make this excavation something other than a grave. Her face crumpled, her hands covered her face, and her shoulders heaved with sobs.

Somehow, the sight of Megan weeping made the tragedy human once more, and Ivy could feel the ice melt from around her own heart. She went to her sister in sorrow and held her close, their tears mingling in the rain.

"We should do this together," Megan said, her voice thick from crying. "You should have woken me before."

Between them, they managed to carry the otter from the house to the hole Ivy had dug. They lowered him down so he was lying on his side, his body curled slightly.

"One of us ought to say something," Megan suggested.

"What is there to say?"

"I wish there were flowers we could pick or…" Her thought were lost in another flood of tears.

His pelt was sodden from the rain, his eyes closed forever. Ivy knelt down and pulled off the bandages, revealing the infected wounds that had destroyed him. It seemed wrong to put him in the ground encased in cloth; he should be in his natural state. There was nothing to indicate that this wanderer of field and fen had ever been more than he now appeared; no trace exsited of the man he had sometimes been. All that remained was a small, battered body, pathetic in its lifelessness. It would be necessary to cover him over, but she hesitated, unwilling to begin that final dedication to the clay. A flurry of movement in the corner of her eye made her look round.

The other otter was approaching slowly, sniffing the air. However much Ivy had grieved before was as nothing compared to the unbearable anguish of this moment. The surviving brother crept forward to learn the terrible truth, that he had caused the other's death.

At the graveside, the living otter gazed down upon his dead sibling and emitted a high, keening sound that chilled Ivy to the heart. She watched as the form before her folded in upon itself, melting and unraveling with eerie fluidity. For a second or two it was nothing more than insubstantial light, but gradually a new shape emerged, with slender limbs and dark hair. He looked very thin and dreadfully exposed in his nudity. She was half afraid to approach this hunched and shuddering form. She still could not tell which of them it was as rain made the hair dark, and neither had been as thin as this when she last saw them. There was no knowing if he would want her care or kindness. She was the reason this had happened, and she would not blame the surviving brother for hating her. Still, she could not bear to stand by and do nothing. It was better, she thought, to offer and be rebuffed than to remain coldly aloof.

With a trembling hand, she reached out to the crouched and shivering man. His skin was cold to the touch, but he did not flinch or resist her. She saw one slender hand reach down into the muddy hole, touching the sodden pelt of the dead otter, stroking fur that was matted with blood. He turned then so she could see his tear-streaked face and haunted eyes. In that moment, Megan saw him clearly for the first time as well. Ivy heard her cry of dismay, and saw the young woman turn and run. She was too tired to give chase. Ben closed his eyes against the sight of her fleeing form. Wordless, husband and wife knelt side-by-side in the mud.

Gradually, the storm abated, leaving a heavy, grey sky above the water-logged land. Ben rose unsteadily to his feet and Ivy watched him nervously, not knowing what he might do next. She could see the pain in his eyes, and something else as fiery and dangerous as ever Seth had been. The resemblance was uncanny. With a flash of insight she realized he too would run from this scene, and that if she did not find the means to stop him then, like Seth and Megan, he too would leave her forever. As he turned away from her, she threw herself upon him, her fingers sliding on his wet skin. "Don't leave me!" she begged.

"I've killed him!" Ben raged, his voice rising in a mournful howl.

She said nothing. There was no denying what had happened.

"They should hang me for this," he said, and she could hear the desire for punishment in his voice. Like her, a part of him wanted nothing more than to lie down in that grave and surrender to death.

"They won't," she said, finding her reason in the midst of the insanity around her. "Hardly anyone knew him. Even if you confess it, they'll not hang you for killing an otter. Them'll just think you be mad."

"Him's me brother. Him's the only family I've got."

She could hear the rage and pain in him, and it cut her deeply. "I'm sorry, Ben. I'm so sorry. I've tried to keep him alive. I'd of done anything. Anything."

He turned, his fingers gripping her shoulders and digging hard into her flesh. He shook her. "You!"

She heard the accusation even though he did not fully express it. All she could do was look into his eyes, seeing the tortured expression there. What did it matter if he destroyed her as well? "Do as you want with me," she murmured.

As though disgusted by this, he pushed her roughly away.

She slipped in the mud, falling to her knees. Her wet hair hung across her face. She could not stand, but remained like a penitent, arms clutched across her body as she wept. She expected that he too would leave now and that would be the end of it. She wanted nothing more than to just lie down in the mud and give up. Pride alone kept her upright.

When at last she had cried out her misery and was too weary to shed more tears, she looked up. Ben was shoveling with grim determination, covering the otter body of his brother with dark soil. She rose shakily to her feet and watched him complete the small mound of earth. The rage had gone from him and he stood for a while, his eyes glassy and his face blank. She approached him, and although he did not look at her, there was no overt rejection. Taking his hand, she led her husband as though he was a child. There were immediate, physical things that needed doing. She could concentrate on those necessary tasks and ignore the rest for a little while. There would be time enough later to ask what came next, and for making the choices that would determine the rest of her life. For now she wanted to care for the brother who remained, to wrap his chilled shoulders with a blanket and offer him warm food and the comfort of a fire. If she could be busy and useful, she could protect herself from thinking too much. For there were dark thoughts preying on her. She had failed Seth and lost him forever. Megan too was gone, and she had failed the girl as well. There was no going after her now, she could be anywhere. Only Ben remained, and she was determined to see he at least was cared for properly.

Chapter Twenty Seven

The letter penned by Frederick West was troubling in the extreme. Septimus read it through several times, struggling with his conscience all the while. Megan West was indeed missing and had been for some time, to the considerable distress of her parents. The young lady he had described when writing to them could in fact be her. No mention whatsoever was made of her condition and no reasons were offered to explain why she ran away. He wondered how much there was to the situation he remained ignorant about.

Septimus no longer knew quite what to believe. He considered families to be vitally important and a girl adrift from her parents was hardly to be encouraged to stray. He also had good reason to think that, for one reason or another, the young lady was quite disturbed. He ought to find her again and return her to the bosom of her family, but he hesitated to go looking for her or to reply to the letter. When he closed his eyes, he could see her dancing in the ruins, her hair blowing about her and her eyes bright. Her words had been disturbing, but there was something wonderfully magical about her distraction. He knew little of what happened to the insane except that they were usually locked away for their own safety. Meg Tuck, or West, or who ever she truly was, seemed like a wild flower, like the poppy she had likened herself to. It seemed very wrong somehow to pluck her from the fields where she belonged and send her back to some hospital or another. He wanted her to be free in all her disturbing sensuality. In the secret depths of his soul, Septimus wanted to walk in the fields and have her come to him, dancing like a leaf on the wind, finally offering to share her secrets. He longed to be her choice, and the inspiration of her passion, not mistaken for another man.

The Shifting Heart

He had the feeling that a little of her madness had found its way into his own psyche. He was forever watching through the windows, gazing out over the vast expanse of rain swept fen, looking for signs of movement that might be the girl who had enchanted him. For her sake, he thought, he would willingly throw off all the trappings of civilization. There was little he would not sacrifice for one willing kiss from those luscious lips, for one kind look from those beautiful eyes. Her words of suggestion and seduction remained with him, and each revisiting generated a frenzied heat in his body. To lie with her was his constant daydream, to be welcomed into those arms, to touch and taste, lick, finger and caress…

After an existence of comfortable chastity, this sudden blossoming of lust threatened his reason. He had not known before what it meant to burn with desire and why a man might cast off all else for the sake of an alluring woman. He had preached often enough about temptation, but not understood it. The temptations of an extra slice of cake, or an extra hour in bed when there was work to be done, were easily triumphed over with little effort and no regret. To fail in face of such minor trials had few serious consequences, practical or spiritual. The heated temptation of a woman's body was another matter entirely. He thought what he should not, his imaginings filled with dreams of her thighs and loins and visions of her breasts and buttocks. To run his fingers over her delicate skin would be paradise, but this was not the religion he had given himself to. Where was his spiritual dedication to the god who glorified self-denial? He was becoming disturbingly pagan in his adoration, making a goddess of this girl whose touch of madness had imprinted on his soul. There were real dangers here. To succumb would be to fall.

Septimus could see his spiritual jeopardy all too clearly, yet try as he might to reason with himself and resist such salacious imaginings, he could not. He had found a lusty animal beneath the thin veneer of his civilization. Base instinct refused to yield to higher thought. Now he wanted to prostrate himself before his idol, pay homage to her breasts, and enact his worship between her thighs.

Behind him the door opened and Sarah entered the parlor, bringing cups and cake for afternoon tea. He turned, aware his manhood had risen and was pressed awkwardly against his trousers. He did not care if she saw it or not. Septimus had never looked properly at his servant before, disregarding her as was usually his habit with such people. She did as she was bid, and that was enough. Until Meg had roused him from sexual slumber, he had never really considered any woman in a sensual light. Looking at his hard-working Sarah now, he saw for the first time that she too was a creature with breasts and hips, with soft skin beneath that modest dress and apron. The erection in his trousers demanded satisfaction and it no longer seemed to matter quite what he did with it. He stepped forward and she looked up at him from beneath long eyelashes.

He advanced rapidly, skirting the table so he was upon the girl in no time. She was too startled to react, and did not even seem to see the danger until he had her chin between his fingers and his face close to hers.

"Sir?"

He heard the doubt and trepidation in her voice. She was in real peril now. This lust was a monstrous thing. It could switch its focus without warning and might consume any woman in its path. Septimus was afraid of himself and of what he might do. The beast was unleashed and he no longer knew how to tame it. There was a terrible power in sexuality, one that could blight lives and cause utter havoc. He knew now why his betters preached against it so rigorously. A girl seduced might have a child. A girl pregnant out of wedlock was always a social outcast, although they were never as rare as people liked to think. He wanted her, not for her own sake, but to ease the aching pressure in his loins. He pressed a kiss on her mouth, one hand reaching for the roundness of her breast. She tried to fight him off then, pushing him away with both hands and squirming to escape. It only fuelled his desire, but she managed to break away from him, her chest heaving.

"What be you doing, sir?" she gasped.

"What do you think I'm doing, wench?"

She flushed. "I be a good girl, sir!"

"Is that so? Will you be a good girl for me, Sarah? Will you give me what I need?" He could hardly believe the words as they passed through his lips. The monster of lust was speaking in its own voice and would not be restrained. It gave him power, enabling him to utter these phrases he knew to be debauched, to say things that would normally be abhorrent to him. He did not know how to read his servant's face, and could not translate the expression he saw there. There was hard calculation in her eyes, but he did not perceive it. Gotobed might have been an attractive man had he not been shy in private and perpetually awkward. He was usually pleasant and polite. Physical need transformed him, adding brightness to his eyes and color to his cheeks. She glanced down, and when she looked up again her lips were slightly parted and her cheeks flushed. A man in his position would, at the very least, have to pay her off to avoid scandal and Sarah thought it worth chancing.

"What are you needing, sir?" she ventured, stealing a glance at the bulge in his trousers.

He took her hand and guided it to his groin. As she massaged him, he set to work on the buttons of her dress, pulling her apron off, and then exposing her undergarments. It did not take him long to fetch her breasts out, sampling each rosy nipple in turn. He had never hungered like this before in all his life. He needed the sweet taste of female flesh against his lips. Megan might be beyond his reach, but this fair maid seemed willing to give her all, and he could plunge happily into her depths if she would but allow it.

In boyhood he had dreamed sometimes of fair women who let him run his hands over their dresses, and had awoken from such nights with sticky sheets and a guilty conscience. As Sarah's hand worked upon him, he recalled those dreams, recognizing the feeling that now had him in thrall. This was the true force of lust then building like a river after snowmelt, aching to burst its banks. He felt the great current burst forth, crashing out to saturate his clothing with its salty tide. The madness that had gripped him dissipated rapidly, leaving him more himself than he had been for days.

Sarah's hand dropped from his damp trousers and he felt an immediate pang of guilt that he had used his servant in so unbecoming a fashion. With an apology on his lips, he managed to look her in the eye. To his surprise, her face was flushed and she looked remarkably pleased with herself.

"Feeling better now?" she asked him.

Septimus grinned bashfully and nodded. "I should not... I hope you can... I promise it will never..." he stuttered.

She shook her head and kissed him full on the lips, her tongue flicking at his closed mouth until he opened up and allowed her in. She moved closer, pressing her body against his so that he could feel the softness of her breasts crushed against him. It was evident she wanted no apology for what he had done. He rather believed that, despite his expectations, Sarah might be keen on further transgressions. Encouraged by the seductive teasing of her tongue within his mouth he tried taking further liberties. He fondled his servant's bottom and then pulled at her dress, tugging the fabric up over her hips so he could get his fingers between her thighs.

"I likes that," she said. "Just a bit further up... there."

Her satisfied sigh as he found the right spot made him weak in the knees.

With soft words of encouragement, she guided him in, telling the young vicar how best to explore her secrets. The moist slickness of her cleft captivated him, and he could not help but think how sweet it would be to enter there and cast his seed into her body. He did just as she instructed, rubbing and thrusting with his fingers until she began to groan and clench around him. The knowledge that he was giving her pleasure made him feel more powerful than he had ever felt before.

"You are a very good girl, Sarah," he said as she clung to his shoulders and shuddered her pleasure against him.

"I like to serve you," she whispered.

"If you continue to serve me this well, I shall have to give you a pay rise."

"I could give you better service than this even," she said, pressing tight against him and moving her hips so that he could have no doubt at all of what she meant.

Chapter Twenty Eight

For a long time neither one of them said anything. Ben allowed her to bring him clothes and to dry his hair with a scrap of cloth. There was a little fish soup left over from the previous day, which she heated up for him. He ate slowly and mechanically, his eyes staring blankly at nothing at all. Ivy knew there was nothing she could say that might permeate his grief. Perhaps when he was ready, he would speak, but until then she could only offer her patience. It was painful to see him like this, so worn down and hopeless. It was obvious to her that he had not meant the fight to go so far.

"Did him suffer much?" Ben asked suddenly, his tone harsh.

"I don't think so. Him were quiet to the end."

"I always thought him were a fighter. Thought about it a lot, Seth were stronger than I, him could've taken me apart."

"Looked to me like him were fighting you," Ivy replied.

"Him weren't. I've had time enough to think on it." He shook his head. "I was angry, didn't think. Didn't bloody think. I went mad. It were the blood that stopped me, made me realize what I'd done. Too bloody late." He buried his head in his hands.

She touched his shoulder, wanting to do more but not knowing how much he would accept.

He hunched, lifting his head a little as he ventured a question. "You and him… how long?"

She looked away, deeply embarrassed by the direction their conversation had taken. She did not want to discuss what had happened, but it dawned on her that if she maintained her private silence, there would be no healing for either of them. Ben needed to know what she had done, and there were things she would need in return. "That first day him come back. I didn't know it were he, I thought it were you until it were too late."

"And then?"

"A few times. I never sought it, but him were hard to say no to."

Ben pursed his lips. "I know you didn't wed with me for love."

She opened her mouth to protest, but he gestured for silence and continued.

"You wedded I for practical reasons, I knowed that then and I knows it now. I thought you might get fond of me, with time. Did you love he?"

Ivy considered her answer carefully. "I'm not sure I knows. I think so, a little."

Ben nodded grimly. "Him's never been short of wenches," he commented.

"That don't surprise me. I were never special to he."

"Then him were as big a fool as I."

The compliment at the heart of his bitter remark startled her, and she had no idea how to react to it.

"What'll we do now?" he asked.

His use of the word 'we' gave her a flicker of hope. "I don't rightly know. If you want rid of me, I'd not blame you."

"I killed my own brother over you. You really think I want rid of you?"

"I don't know what I thinks."

There was a defeated look in his eyes, but she was not sure quite what it meant. "I still can't believe him's gone," he said.

"I know. I keep looking for he by the fire like he were these last few days, or thinking him might come in the door."

"Seems like him's come and gone all my life. Can't think I'll not see him again."

Ivy felt a lump rising in her throat. It all seemed like some impossible nightmare to her.

"If you've had enough of this life with me, I'll not stop you from going,"

Ben said gently.

It was peculiar to think she might have some real choice, but the illusion did not hold for long. If she left Ben then she might go back to her restricted parental home. Otherwise she must find some way to earn her keep in a community where there already were more laborers than employment. If she was to live at all and not risk destitution, then there were no real choice, she had to stay. It would not be easy, but she supposed if she was to stay, she had better make the best of it and try to be happy with the man she had married."I'd rather stay, if you're happy to have me," she said simply. "We weren't doing so bad before. I know this weren't ever going to be a grand romance, but we did well enough, didn't we?"

"I thought so. Was you happy with me?" he asked, still not looking at her, but sounding fragile and vulnerable.

"I were," she said, "and I could be again."

"Even now him's dead?"

"Even so. Folks die, and life goes on, and that be all there is to it. You can't keep anything forever."

"I don't know as I could ever laugh or smile again."

"I were like that when my sister Rose died. I were only little and she a year older. But life goes on."

"I didn't know."

"You'll not find many folks round here as haven't lost brother or sister sometime. It's just the way of it."She rubbed her hand back and forth across his shoulders, feeling how dreadfully thin he had become. Ben had never been an especially heavy lad, but the last days had taken a tremendous toll and the change in him was startling. "I'd best get to and finish that rug I were doing. We could use the money."

He nodded. "I wish I had your outlook, Ivy, all I can do is grieve and regret."

She said nothing to this. If he wanted to believe she had shaken the whole thing off she could not face telling him otherwise. Her role in what had befallen, and her aching sense of loss, had not dulled. Living was merely a matter of going through the routine; her heart was no longer in it. She was surviving only on the hope that time would ease her unhappiness. She sat down next to him, close enough that from time to time her arm rubbed against his.

"I know you didn't mean to do it," she said after a while.

It was a long time before he replied. "I don't know what I meant to do."

Ivy thought she knew something of how that felt, but decided it might be better not to say.

Chapter Twenty Nine

The long grass around her was damp and the ground beneath her chill. These were the first things Megan knew with any certainty. In her memory she could find only a vast black void that had consumed everything else. She knew better than to peer into it, or to ask what it might disguise. In time she might remember, but for now it was enough to simply be. She had the feeling that this loss of knowledge had happened to her before, but she could not remember when or why, not that it mattered especially. Without the past to anchor her, she was a free thing to be blown by the wind or carried by the river.

Only a few feet away from her, the thick grasses gave way to dark mud and thence to water almost black from the peat it carried. Every so often there would be a plop, splash and a brief ring on the surface to mark where some fish had risen and plunged. Despite the cold, it was a tranquil scene. She noted that she was rather chilly and that her stomach rumbled from hunger. She considered these facts with the same easy detachment she did the burbling of the river and the antics of the fish. None of it seemed especially important. Glancing around her, she determined there was nothing available to eat and no source of heat. If she stayed, then the cold and hunger would remain, and probably grow worse.

Rising to her feet, she made a slow circle, considering the almost featureless panorama around her. Here a tree crouched against the land; there a distant church spire suggested the presence of a village. None of these signs meant very much to her and she had no real sense of where she might be. With no inkling of past or future to direct her thoughts, she had only the present to contend with. She walked, keeping the river as her companion and following it as it coursed downstream. She was weary and her head was light, which made progress slow. On the opposite bank, a long-legged heron stalked slowly in the opposite direction, head lowered as it watched for fish or frogs in the murky water.

The first hints of recollection began surfacing in her thoughts, coming up through the murk of her fugue state like bubbles rising in the river. Gradually she came to appreciate that she was searching for someone, and it was of the uttermost importance she should find him. The need for this man was pressing, even though she could not root it in anything. She waited for further insight, not worrying for the present that she could not recall more than this. The details would manifest in time; she had the distinct feeling they always did.

A face began to appear... jet-black eyebrows above eyes of the deepest blue... angular bones giving a sharpness to his cheeks, nose and chin, but a mouth so soft and sensual it balanced the semblance of harshness... she saw the dark shadow of stubble on skin somewhat roughened by the seasons, and short, smooth hair a color that echoed the peaty soil... Piece by piece, the recollection of his body returned... the hard muscles of his chest, the riot of dark curls where his manhood slumbered, the strength of his long legs, the dangerous grace of his slender fingers... Hardly aware of the world around her, she revisited every curve and contour, every scar, mole and blemish. She knew them all, like landmarks beneath a familiar sky. The map of this beloved body had returned to her conscious mind, and with it came feelings both of peace and of purpose. This mole would be a shallow pool, that winding scar a road between two villages... all sorts of wonderful things might be read in the skin and understood.

Megan recalled the taste of his mouth and the feel of his skin against hers. The more thoroughly she traced out his body in her mind, the more intensely aware she became of herself, as though this was also her *form some-*

how, her skin with the myriad scars and markers. She felt then that if she only reached hard enough, she must connect with him. Certainly she was bound to find him in time, her feet must carry her to wherever he was; it was inevitable. Each breath she inhaled and each step she took was bringing her closer to this man.

When at last she found him, they would kiss as they had done before, with tongues deep in each other's mouths and hands roaming free over naked skin. They would inspire such heat in each other, such melting desire, that all else would seem but a grey haze of dullness in comparison. They would lie together in the long grasses, legs interwoven, lips locked tight together, she engulfing him with her flesh and welcoming him into the secret hollows and caves of her body. Then, and only then, would she truly know herself. In his arms, it would all make sense once more. As he rubbed against her, penetrating ever deeper into her being, she would understand everything and need nothing. It was a vision that accelerated her pulse and gave her courage. She would walk forever to find such a man.

Chapter Thirty

To assuage the grumblings of his conscience, Septimus devoted some considerable effort to locating the missing girl. He walked up to the Tuck cottage on several occasions, but found it empty. The weather had cleared a little and the first field work was underway. Tactful inquiries amongst parishioners established that no one could recall having seen the young woman aside from himself. None of his most reliable sources were aware that Tuck had any siblings, but several did mention his gypsy mother, which sat well enough with the original story. He raised the topic of a missing girl with a few of his more gossipy regulars, but to little effect.

A few days after he had given up the search, Mrs. Norman, the church warden's wife, took him aside outside the bakers. "Good afternoon to you, vicar. I've heard you been asking about a missing girl. That be so?"

"It is, indeed."

"Funny that. I couldn't help but think…"

"How so, Mrs. Norman?"

The churchwarden's wife was a little mouse of a woman, all twitches and scurrying. She never seemed to be entirely still. "There were a girl went missing before I were married. Pretty thing she were with long, dark hair and eyes like velvet. Her were one of them Tucks. Used to be a great sprawling family up in that little cottage, a dozen children if not more. They've always been a queer lot and all."

"May I ask what happened?" Septimus was confident the tale would have no bearing on his own concerns, but was inclined to humor the old woman.

"Well, her were Megan Tuck, and she were a lovely little thing. Her was a few years younger than me. Her had all this lovely dark hair, and all the boys loved her. My younger brother, Wilf, him were right sweet on she."

The name startled him, but Septimus maintained his composure.

"There was them as said the young squire had eyes for she, and there was them who said a lot worse. But you know how them all talks about big families in small houses."

Septimus nodded. He knew. There were always rumors of incest, and the more remotely a family lived, the more likely such gossip would be.

"Her vanished one night in a dreadful storm. A right proper fen blow it were, with snow coming in so hard you'd not see your hand before your face. Old Mr. Norman, him were the schoolmaster then, but not related close to the Mr. Norman we've got now, or to my Mr. Norman come to that. Where were I going?"

"You mentioned there was a terrible storm," Septimus said encouragingly.

"Ah, that were it... him were right angry, Old Mr. Norman. Him said her folks had killed her and I don't know what else. I don't know why him said that, mind, there was no proof of anything either way. Right to do, it were. Never saw her again, not to be sure it were her."

"What do you mean?" The young vicar knew this was probably just another tall tale, but could not resist asking.

"Well, every now and then someone would see a figure like she out on the road walking in the fields, out by them old abbey ruins or some other lonely spot. They'd see her, this pretty girl with her long hair and sorrowful eyes, just for a moment, and then they'd not find her. Her'd be gone. Haunting us, that's what she's been doing, haunting us, and it's dreadful bad luck to see her, it means something strange will happen to you."

"Do you think I saw the ghost of Megan Tuck?"

"I think that might just be it vicar, I reckon you might. We hadn't seen her these last ten years or more, and the younger folk, they don't remember the old tales like I do. Them knows about the ghost girls, but not who half of them was. But I've got to tell you, I saw her myself back in the autumn, I was just out at twilight and I saw her with me own eyes, her hair all hanging down loose, and just how she were as a child. Scared me half silly."

Septimus compared the description to Megan and wondered what exactly he had seen. "Did she have any connection with the vicarage at all?" he asked, wondering if his own abode was caught up in this ghostly story somehow.

"That were out by your house, now I comes to think of it. But that's not the queerest part. Her eldest brother, him were gone the next spring, never said a word, and them were old Moocher's brother and sister. You won't know about him, that's before your time. He were a strange old boy, were Moocher. They found him a few years back, him drowned in the river, and when they went to bury him, they found him was full of eels. Have you ever heard the like of it?"

Septimus agreed that he had not.

"The thing is, vicar, him were Ben Tuck's father!"

She presented this as though it should clarify the whole situation. Septimus continued nodding, although he had no idea what he was getting at.

"Them's a queer bunch, them Tucks, you mark my words, them's an odd lot."

"That was very interesting, thank you, Mrs. Norman."

"Glad I could help you Reverend Gotobed."

As Septimus walked the short distance home, he thought about the mysterious girl he had seen. *Could she have been a ghost?* She had seemed very real. Then there were other peculiarities to consider. Most especially, if Meg Tuck was a long missing girl from a generation ago, why did Ivy Tuck claim her as sibling to Ben? It seemed to the vicar that something very strange and complex was going on. Either they were trying to make a fool of him, or he had stumbled upon something genuinely uncanny. The girl he had kissed seemed warm and real enough at the time. She had eaten like a very hungry living person when she sat in his kitchen. But, then, Septimus knew, he was no expert on the nature of spirits The Bible held precious little guidance for dealing with the wild fantasies of fen tales save to discourage that sort of thing. Stronger than his inclination to rationality and his religious sensibilities was his desire to have a conclusion on a good story.

"You look worried," Sarah remarked as he removed his coat in the hallway.

"Do you believe in ghosts?" he asked her.

"Don't rightly know. I ain't ever seen one."

He could tell the topic did not especially interest her. "I heard a story about a ghost girl who is supposed to haunt lonesome spots around here. Have you heard of her?"

"She? There's lots of stories of she. Some say she drowned in the river or got buried under the snow one winter. I've heard it said that some old ancestor of the squire murdered her and all."

"Go on."

Having realized Septimus was keen on the topic, she continued eagerly. "I've had a few little old boys ask if I'd mind to go looking for her, but I reckon they meant something else, don't you think?" She raised her eyebrows suggestively.

The expression was distracting. He could not help but imagine Sarah walking out to some remote spot with a young man. "Did you ever go?"

"I never saw no ghost," she replied.

There was a suggestive look in her eyes, and Septimus found he was thinking less of mysteriously missing girls and more of the very real one in front of him.

"You busy any more, today?" she asked him.

Since their erotic escapade a few days previously, she had dropped all formality with him when no one else was in earshot. He was rather enjoying her forwardness and was eager for another bout. "I think I have discharged my duties for today," he replied.

"You got anything else needs discharging?"

"Now there's a tempting offer."

"I'll be taking that as a yes, then."

Septimus felt his manhood rise in response to her words. Sarah was not as innocent as she had first pretended. She knew all manner of delicious tricks that could be performed with hand and mouth, and on several occasions had led him astray in the most delightful ways. He was hoping her teasing meant another such indulgence might be forthcoming. "Ah, my temptress, my temptation," he murmured.

She smiled.

They retreated to the privacy of his bedroom and he lay back upon the bed, closing his eyes and surrendering to her. Her quick hands had him out in no time, caressing his length with distinct enthusiasm. Which would be the worse sin, he wondered, to take this girl out of wedlock or to encourage her to spill his seed? He was uncertain. There were some scenarios he knew no specific theological debates about. His suspicion was that the act Sarah was performing was irredeemably sinful, but he thought it best not to consult his Bishop over the matter. The warm moisture of her mouth surrounded him as her tongue swirled back and forth over the tip of his swiftly hardening penis. Her lips were firm, locked around him, working up and down with confidence. She already knew what he liked and was generous with her favors.

Strictly speaking they would not spill any seed upon the ground. Septimus laughed inwardly at his excuses. This was sheer lewd wantonness and no denying it. She dutifully swallowed when he climaxed, thus avoiding any spillages, but to take pleasure in this way was hardly a virtue. Technically it might be an entirely different matter to the act specifically proscribed against, but he had a feeling that if his sins were being notched up in some sacred place, then this abandon would stand against him. The temptation of her silken lips was one he could not resist, however. Carnal joy had him enthralled, his manhood slick with her spit and stimulated by the grip of her lips. For a while he opened his eyes, enjoying the view of her bobbing head and her obvious contentment. That she liked getting him between her teeth was only too apparent. The delectable tension in him mounted, surging and seething towards fulfillment.

"Oh, God," he groaned, but whether as apology or thanks was not apparent, even to him.

Sarah straddled him and edged up the bed, lifting her skirts so he could see her moist and glistening pussy. "I want you to do the same for me," she commanded. "I want your mouth on me. I want to you put your tongue in me."

Her demand sent a thrill of erotic delight through him. He loved the authority in her voice and this reversal of the usual balance of power. To be commanded by his serving wench was irresistible. She moved onto his face, and he set to work on her with great enthusiasm, relishing the taste of her and hurrying to obey her further commands, "More of this, less of that." She wanted his tongue first in one place, then another, and he complied without hesitation, glad to be ruled, receiving his orders with the pleasure of a willing supplicant.

Chapter Thirty One

vy was sat at the table cutting gloves from rabbit skins when they came. The knock at the door surprised her, as no one had called since the young vicar appeared over a month previously. She had grown partial to the silence and isolation. Opening the door, she stared in rude, amazement at her guests, and it was some moments before her wits returned and she managed to invite them across the threshold.

Reverend West looked knowingly around the small room, and accepted the seat he was offered. He looked much as Ivy remembered him – drawn and haggard, with dark hollows beneath his eyes. His wife was little more than a wraith. She had shrunk in every way, seeming tiny and wizened, as though she were centuries old. Ivy took all this in at a rapid glance, and concluded that Mrs. West probably did not have many months left to live. Whatever was wrong with her had proved to be serious after all.

"How may I help you?" she asked carefully, trying to mask how greatly their presence disturbed her.

"How are you, Ivy? Does married life agree with you?" West asked with forced lightness.

"I be well enough, thank you."

"Forgive me if I leave off some of the pleasantries, but there are things I must ask you," he said earnestly.

"By all means. Shall you take a cup of tea?"

Mrs. West nodded gratefully at this, and Ivy set to work, glad of having something to do other than simply standing to face their joint scrutiny. It was not difficult to guess what their visit must pertain to. Ivy thought frantically, trying to decide what best to say.

"I do not know if you are aware of this, but our daughter vanished from our residence in Cambridge over a month ago. We have been trying to find her since then," West explained.

"I didn't know that," she replied, glad that she could be safely honest in that regard.

"We are desperate to find her," Mrs. West added, her voice querulous. "Have you seen her at all?"

"Only briefly since I left your employment."

"So you *have* seen her? Reverend Gotobed seemed entirely unclear on the matter."

"I didn't know what him were about, and it were delicate," Ivy said awkwardly.

Ben chose that very moment to make his return, for which she was deeply grateful. There was a brief distraction while introductions were made. The ailing lady gave Ben a long, searching look and Ivy guessed she was thinking of Seth's intrusion into the house. Ben looked less like his sibling than ever, and Mrs. West might well wonder whom she had encountered that night.

"Ivy, I hope you hold no grudge against us for what happened. We are two people in a state of despair, and I implore you, if you have any intelligence of our daughter, please share it with us," West pleaded.

"Tell her," Mrs. West added softly.

West frowned and closed his eyes for a few seconds.

"Ellen does not have long to live and cannot bear to leave this world not knowing what has become of her only child."

Ben and Ivy exchanged glances.

"Her ran away for love Mrs. West,' she said. 'Him were a lad she'd never have got to marry, you'd not have given your blessing and her knew it."

"What manner of man was he?"

"Him were a tinker. Him were around the village all that summer, mending this and that. I don't know where her'd met him, but she begged me to help."

"That night in the house, it was him, was it not?" Mrs. West concluded.

"It were," Ivy acknowledged.

It was close enough to the truth, and she understood they needed some story they could be happy with. The truth, as she guessed it, would break their hearts. She thought Megan had most likely thrown herself into the river when she realized Seth was dead. "I did wrong by you both, just not the wrong you thought it were. I let a man into your house, but it weren't on my own account," she added, glad to be free of that deception.

"I understand you were trying to protect her," Ellen West said.

"I were part to blame. I thought that were the end of it, that I'd see no more of she, but a few weeks back, her was here, meeting up with him, and they was off."

"Do you have any idea where she might be now?" West enquired.

"Her's been gone weeks now. They was heading down Suffolk way as I heard it, but they could be anywhere by now," Ben put in.

"What was he like, this man?" Mrs. West asked.

"I worked with him," Ben said. "He was the best sort, hard working and gentle, he'd be good to her, and anyone could see they was very much in love."

"They were going to find some place them could marry proper," Ivy added, hoping this final embellishment would not prove too much.

There was a look of relief on Mrs. West's face, and Ivy knew she had done all she could. It would be better for both of them to imagine their beloved little girl living out some romantic adventure.

When the Wests departed a little time later, Ivy sank down onto a chair and buried her face in her hands. She felt Ben's fingers stroke her shoulders affectionately.

"That were the kindest you could have done by them," he told her.

"I knows it, but I never liked to lie."

"You made me proud," he said simply. "You made it sound like it should have been, her and Seth going out into the world. I'd like to think of them that way myself."

Ivy sniffed. His fingers continued to caress her, and she nuzzled against him, needing a little comfort and affection in the face of so much sorrow.

"There, my wench," he said, stroking her hair.

She was glad of his closeness and companionship. Ben was the only true friend she had ever known, and the only person to share her most troubling secrets. They carried each other's truths now, and those bonds held them firm in spite of everything else. She wrapped her arms around his waist and leaned her face into his stomach, breathing the odors of muddy water from his body. He had been fishing in his other skin during the morning, and the river was still on him.

Much to her surprise, Ivy realized he was responding to her, the hard ridge of his desire pressing into her breasts. They had not lain together in a long time, and she had not expected him to want her again. The unmistakable evidence to the contrary twitched against her bosom, and she smiled in spite of herself. It felt good to be wanted, even though she did not feel much inclined towards such play. They had not even slept together since the day of the fight. Ben now slept before the fire and she rested alone, making sure she was exhausted enough at the end of each day not to think about her ghost-filled bed. Memories of Seth, Ben and Megan could keep her from sleep all too easily.

She moved her arm, hoping it would look accidental as she touched him lightly. Ben started, and she looked up at him.

"Didn't mean to bother you with that," he said.

"It's all right. Nice to know I still catch you that way."

The faintest hint of a smile touched his lips and creased the corners of his eyes. It was the first glimmer of genuine pleasure she had seen on his face in a long time.

"Ben," she said, "I'm not promising anything, but... but you don't have to sleep down here if you don't want to." She had not dared to broach the subject before, but his erection made her bold.

"Are you sure?"

"I miss you. I like your company nights. I don't know if we... if I... but I'd rather you were with me, if you'd like that."

"Truly?"

"Truly."

He squeezed her close and bent to press a kiss into her hair. "Then I'll not sleep by the fire anymore."

They held each other tightly. Finally it seemed the long winter was over and there might be hope of Spring and new life.

Chapter Thirty Two

The skeletal form of the abandoned windmill stood stark and dismal against the fading light. Only the structural joists remained; their housing long since snatched away by jealous winds. The shattered sails still held their place although they, too, were damaged, and did not spin freely in the breeze. Whether it had been built to grind corn or pump water from the nearby fields, Megan could not tell. The old windmill looked as though it might fall at any moment, and when the wind caused the sails to tremble impotently, the beams creaked and grunted in their effort to resist collapse.

She had made her home here for some time, sheltering in the musty room beneath the revolving body. Each day merged with the last so that it was hard to tell one from another. Megan no longer knew how she lived or what she did. Great swathes of time were lost in wandering and dreaming, following the nearby riverbanks and gazing for hours into muddy pools. There were days when she remembered what she was looking for and days when she did not, but either way she was contented. Her body was free from hunger. Sometimes a memory would flicker into her consciousness... the taste of a ripe plum eaten directly after picking, the sweet juices smearing hands and chin... or the moist indulgence of cake in the afternoons, with jam and cream between the sponge layers. There were days when she could smell the yeasty aroma of fresh bread, or meat roasting in a hot oven. She might wake with the taste of honey in her mouth, and not know why.

At dawn the birdsong came to wake her, from the first tentative twitterings to the full throated melodies of blackbirds and thrushes. Sometimes she did not sleep at all, wandering by starlight feeling the soft caress of darkness on her skin. One night the moon would be a full and glowing orb, but the next would find it no more than a tiny crescent, and she did not know where the days and weeks that should have lain between the two might have gone.

There were few people in this place. Sometimes she saw men in the fields, but they kept their distance and she was afraid to speak to them. There was a black dog who skulked along the hedgerows at night, and a wan girl who usually crouched by the river, watching the water without moving or speaking. Neither of them seemed to see her. The other girl had long, wild hair, too, and a grief-stricken look upon her face. Megan tried to speak with her now and then, but to little effect. Sometimes the pale girl wandered in the fields, singing to herself in a lilting voice. Her tunes were invariably melancholy, but they seemed familiar.

At night Megan would see the great eels emerging from the dykes. Some of them were so vast she could not think how they had ever fitted into the ditches they occupied. Their huge bodies shimmered in the starlight as they writhed in the open fields, performing their secret rites and rituals. They were a strange sight as they coiled and twisted; vast slippery forms filling all the flat land with their sinuous, slithering secrets. She could hear the low murmuring of their many voices, but did not know their language. The black dog never came when the eels were abroad.

One evening at twilight she saw the figure of a man moving across the fields. It was unusual to see anyone, even the singing girl, at this hour. He moved in fits and starts as though he did not really know where he was going. Although his path was erratic, he seemed to be traveling roughly in the direction of the windmill. Curious but wary, Megan watched his progress. She knew he must have seen her because he paused for a second, and then turned slightly, heading purposefully in her direction. In the fading light, Megan could see the shape of his face well enough, and an ecstasy of recognition filled her being. It was as though the missing half of her spirit was returning at last, although until that instant she had not known what was gone. In a moment she was in his arms, feeling the sturdy power of his body beneath her hands and the heat of his kisses on her face and neck. He smelled of peaty earth and brackish water.

"Oh, my wench," he said, his voice low and yearning.

"I knew you would find me," she breathed, as though this confidence had underpinned her every thought since their separation. She cupped his face in her hands, and then touched his forehead before kissing the tip of his nose. It was him, all him, and every detail was gloriously familiar.

He caught her up in his arms, lifting her high and turning slowly as he looked up into her face. "My beautiful girl."

"My love," she replied. "My love… my lover."

He lowered her so she slithered down his body. Neither asked where the other had been or what had befallen them. The past was a country both of them had departed, and neither had much inclination to revisit it just yet.

Seth ran his hands over her shoulders and chest. Megan had thought she was fully attired, but it felt as though her skin was bare. Glancing down she saw that it was so, and that he also was naked, his skin gleaming in the moonlight. It had grown dark while they held each other and the moon had risen already. When she kissed him, he seemed more substantial than anything else had for a long time.

Something else was happening, something akin to the sexual passions they had shared in the old life, but more complete. She closed her eyes, but her awareness of him did not dim at all. She felt Seth filling her even though she could not say if it was his cock, his tongue or his fingers that penetrated her, or which orifices he seeped into. It was almost as though she was absorbing him through her skin while at the same time being drawn into him. She could remember what it had been like to climax with him, to lie trembling in the shared wonder of orgasm, but that seemed a small and paltry thing now,

The Shifting Heart

brief and fleeting, as they grasped after an experience of greater profundity. Now they were tasting a wonder that before they had known only as a pale reflected light. It was as though they had only ever seen the moon but now the sun blazed down upon their skin, the origin of heat and desire. The lovers were transported in this slow and ecstatic mutual penetration, this binding together of heart and soul.

Everything that had been before was but a poor shadow of the true thing, and they had not known it. They could touch, kiss and play as they had done in the past. She still had pert nipples to offer to his warm mouth, and she reveled in the sensation of his tongue upon her. When she reached down to fondle him, his cock rose just as it had always done, swelling between her fingers. She guided him to meet the yearning hole between her thighs. In he thrust, deeper and deeper driving his full length further inside her than ever before. Passion wore the forms it had always favored but now they could travel beyond them, taking the connection deeper, discovering levels of pleasure that transcended anything they had ever achieved before. He lifted her and she wrapped her legs around his middle, drawing him close. She felt as though she could take the entirety of him inside, that there was room enough for every last inch of his glorious body. His penetration of her seemed absolute, reaching up into her heart and mind as never before.

Megan saw the rise and fall of the moon, the endless slow dance of stars through the sky, and the fast spinning of the earth beneath her feet. She could feel the grass growing and the eels chanting their melancholy songs of a distant sea. The words of their whispering laments were audible, suddenly, and she realized they were singing the same haunting songs the pale girl offered to the open skies. They were singing the songs of the lonely stars locked in their eternal quadrilles to a melody wrought from the hum of fleeting lives. The lovers danced with them, their bodies glowing in starlight, twined into a single form lithe as any eel. They made their own music to rhythms of love and desire, notes of whispered passion and pleasure.

Seth was with her, around her and inside her, their minds touching as closely as their bodies. In a blinding flash of insight they both glimpsed a hint of something beyond the visions already shared. They had only just begun the journey, and there were greater wonders yet to be sought and understood. They had only sipped from the chalice of the numinous. Something bigger and yet more intense waited for them if they could but find the means to drain the glass. This coming together was not the end of the quest, Megan realized, just the beginning of another adventure. The light of ancient, dancing suns exploded within her and gushed forth around her, and she knew Seth was with her in this orgasm of the soul. For a perfect instant each knew they felt as the other did; shared the same thoughts and understanding.

Afterwards, she would sometimes wonder how they climbed down from amongst the stars and closed their ears to the eels' midnight song. She did not know. The wonder of it all faded slowly; releasing them from the spell they had woven. Gradually, her spirit crept back into the form it knew, seeking for the companion of her heart. When at last it was over, they found themselves to be just a young man and his woman clinging together, bare-skinned and tremulous before the shuddering remains of a windmill. Megan returned her feet to the ground and they stood for a while, gazing into each other's eyes and listening to the windmill creak in the dawn. The air still tingled with the aftertaste of magic.

Seth pressed her close and she rested her head on his shoulder, not wanting to ever let him go. "Don't leave me," she said. "I feel like I've been losing you and finding you forever. I don't want to lose you ever again."

"You won't," he promised. He stroked her hair, pulling twigs and leaves from amongst the tangles, and then easing out the knots with his fingers. "We can do anything, you and I."

She tilted her head back so he could kiss her. The warmth of his mouth was still a surprise and a wonder. She did not think it possible she could ever press her lips to his enough times to dull the fascination of this most simple connection. Each time they touched it was new as a sunrise. She reached for his hand, looking at each finger in turn, marveling at the perfection of his uncanny existence and wondering if there could ever be sufficient time to truly appreciate him to the full.

"I loves you," he said.

Megan had the feeling he had never said that to her before."I loves you, too, and all, my beautiful boy" she replied, echoing how he usually spoke.

He chuckled at this. "There's so much I wants to show you," he told her.

She nodded, trusting him, and willing to go wherever he led. "What has happened to us?" she asked.

He closed his eyes. "Don't you remember?"

She shook her head. "I don't remember anything much. I remember you, my love, clear as day, but I don't know what happened to us, and I don't know where we are now."

"What do it matter, though? You be happy and forget, and I'll forget it all and it'll never matter to us again. The past's dead, we don't want to go back."

"No," she agreed. "What do we do now?"

"Whatever you desire."

"Can you teach me how to change my skin?" She had wanted that, in some silent part of her soul since the first time she had seen him cast off his fur. A flickering vision of his otter form rose in her thoughts, hazy but compelling nonetheless. Her yearning for this was clear suddenly, even though she had not known it before.

"I can. You'll be anything you likes now. You'll have fur or feather, anything, everything."

"How?" she asked, believing him but not understanding his words.

"There's no law can bind us now. If you dare to, you can have anything."

Megan tilted her head to one side, thinking about this. "Are we real?" she asked. Something pressed on her thoughts, suggestive of other truths and explanations. She pushed the impression away. Better not to know or remember anything that might spoil her happiness.

"We're as real as them eels singing, and the changing moon." He smiled.

It was a good enough answer, she thought. "Show me," she said. "Show me how it's done."

He changed, and although she had seen it many times, she had never grasped the sense of it before. The skin he wore was just illusion. Any skin was illusion if you knew the right way to look at it. It was so easy to understand now that she could see properly, and Megan wondered why she had not known these things before. Such a question led back to the veiled past, and she rejected it hurriedly, not willing to journey there while the present seemed so fledgling. She knew there were things behind her she was not ready to turn and face. The knowledge of their shared condition was something she was carefully protecting herself from.

Throwing her arms wide she leaned back, raising her eyes to the great, open skies, to the vast airy realm of freedom and possibility. Seth had told her she could do anything, and she believed him. How would it feel to have that thick pelt instead of soft skin the cold wind could buffet? How would those long, sharp teeth feel, and that tail? She reached and imagined, and the answers to her questions came rapidly… it was snug in the thick furs, the wind barely touched her at all. Her jaw was longer, and she licked at her teeth, feeling them, knowing them. It was natural to raise her tail in a high question mark over her back, and she knew if she were a true otter she would leave some little ball of droppings at this moment, a message to all other otters that one of their own was abroad in the area. Where the knowledge came from she did not know, it was as if she summoned it out of the air just as she had this impression of a different body.

Looking into Seth's dark otter eyes, standing nose to nose with him, she could feel the laughter bubbling up in her, joyous and carefree. They sniffed each other carefully, becoming familiar with these new forms. Then they were away, bounding across the grass. The loping pace came readily enough, as though she had always run on four paws, and there was nothing more natural than sniffing the air and feeling the breeze in whiskers sensitive enough to find a fish in a dark pond. Seth was a little in front of her and she pounced on his tail, nipping it lightly. He turned, tumbling with her, biting playfully as he tried to fend off her feigned assault.

Chapter Thirty Three

There were flowers on the blackthorn, softening the otherwise lifeless hedgerows with patches of delicate white blossoms. Spring was truly coming as the shiny dark buds on trees fattened to bursting, promising new leaves. It was that time of year when suddenly the evenings became lighter as the darkness of winter receded. In a matter of weeks it would be May, with the hawthorn in full flower and the fair in Bury. Both Ivy and Ben had been working in the fields, he setting long rows of celery on the squire's land while she had gone to her parents, planting the flowers that would subsidize the family's otherwise meager earnings. Two of her sisters and one of her younger brothers had been kept out of school to help with the work. They eyed her warily. Hetty, the eldest, had only been four or so when Ivy first went into service. None of them really knew her. The rest of Ivy's numerous siblings were either employed elsewhere already or not considered useful enough workers.

Those were long days crouching or bending double, working plant after plant into the soil. The smell of damp peat was ever present. They seldom talked, having little to say and much to do. It was unrelenting labor, but there was nothing else to be had and money was always tight.

Several days into the work, Ben met her from the field. He carried a parcel under one arm. Ivy was surprised to see him, but there was a brightness to his face that had been long absent. He exchanged polite nods with her parents and siblings, but few words. They were all too tired, and hours of planting gave you little worth talking about. Ivy stood quietly until the rest of her family departed, and then waited to see what had brought her husband to her.

"Going well?" he asked.

Ivy contemplated the long strips of leafy plants that they had set in the ground, and nodded wearily. "Well enough. What you got there?"

"Bit of bread and cheese. I was thinking, being as it's such a nice evening, maybe we could go for a walk?"

"I don't know as I could go far, I'm about done for."

"If you be too tired…"

"I reckon I could manage a little way." It was indeed a pleasant evening and she hankered after an escape from her work. If she went home, she would only use the twilight for rug making. Although her boots had been rubbing and her feet ached, she gave him a good attempt at a smile and tried to make the best of it.

"Maybe we'll see a hare," he said. "It's the time for they."

"More like we'll startle some courting couple, it's the time of year for that, too." She chuckled.

He laughed a little with her. "You and me never did much courting," he remarked.

It was true enough. Most couples walked out for a few months – sometimes a year or more – before they made their vows. Ben and Ivy had never wandered the lanes hand-in-hand as lovers, or dawdled in the twilight exchanging tender words and passionate promises. They had married hastily and with little romance.

The young couple sat on the ridge above a dyke to share their evening meal and watch a troupe of ducks paddling in the water. The young ones were fluffy and playful, having not yet gained the more serious adult plumage.

"There's something I'd like to show you, if you aren't too tired yet?" he asked when they had finished eating.

"I'm right enough, let's see." She had half wondered if the suggestion was meant bawdily, although there had been nothing like that between them for some time. From the tone of his voice, she thought not.

He rose, and offered her his hand. "It's a little way yet."

Amongst the dykes and ditches there were a few natural streams, and they followed one of these as it meandered along the edge of a pasture where cows were grazing. At a crook in the stream the reeds grew tall and thick, clustered together in a large bed. Flashes of yellow showed where flags and kingcups were in flower. Ben pointed towards this spot. For a while, Ivy could not see what had drawn his eyes. There seemed to be nothing unusual. Gradually she discerned the well-disguised presence of a small construction. It was a ball made from old reeds and other plant debris, and she could not guess what it was for.

"What do you think that be?" he asked.

"I couldn't say."

He motioned her to sit. The grass was soft and luscious and the cows paid them no attention as the pair watched the reed ball. Ben slid one hand over hers, his touch sweetly affectionate. She ventured a shy smile in his direction, but he indicated she should keep her attention on the reeds. It was not long before their patience was rewarded. There were four of them in all, three little ones following in the wake of their significantly larger mother. They crept from the reed nest to dabble in the stream and play along its banks while the mother began her work foraging for food. Ivy had never seen young otters before, and these seemed very small.

"How old would them be?" she asked, her voice hushed.

"A month maybe, not much more."

The otters whistled to each other as they scampered up and down the bank.

"She'll move them soon, in a day or two, at most. She'll take them off down the river where there's more fish to be had."

"Do you know them?" Ivy asked, realizing these little creatures might be more than they seemed.

"The mother, her's only two and a bit, them's her first cubs."

"Are you related? Is them little ones family?"

Ben chuckled. "Could be. My dad, him liked otter company. I told you Seth were otter-born himself, and a right wild pup he were. Never did know much about his old mother, I were too little then. Could be related a bit, not too close."

"I wondered if them were yours," she admitted.

"I've not got any otter-born."

"Would you want to?"

He looked at her for quite a while before answering. "My grandmother were otter-born, but me and dad, we both came from the human side. I were so late getting my second skin him thought I might not do it at all. Him thought I weren't enough otter. I'd like an otter-born pup, keep the line going."

"Did Seth have any?"

"Him did, several, but them was wandering types, went off in a few years. You can be too much otter, and all."

"I wouldn't mind, if you wanted an otter child," Ivy said slowly. She felt she could hardly press him for fidelity when she had broken that pledge herself.

"And what about the other sort?" he asked.

"That too."

He smiled and lowered his head into the curve between her neck and shoulder. "I'd love to get a child on you," he confessed.

"Even if it don't have a second skin?"

"Even so."

Ivy considered the possibility, imagining her stomach swelling with new life and a little being of her own emerging, needing her care and attention. She knew it would be hard work to feed and clothe a small one. She knew many children died young. A child with a second skin would be challenging, indeed. She would not know how to mother the otter in it, or how to teach it those things it would most need to know. There was much to fear in child-birth and the struggles of parenthood, but she realized this was what she wanted after all. The thought of a baby filled her with warmth and optimism.

"I reckon we could have a little one," she decided.

"You don't want three or four like she?" he asked, gesturing towards the otter bitch.

"That wouldn't happen, would it?"

"Didn't I tell you I were one of twenty-seven? My old mother, she'd have two or three most years, four sometimes. Course, half of them were otters, and didn't her have a right old time of it, teaching they to catch fish. She'd be diving in them dykes at all hours getting eels, and that were right hard, her not being an otter at all, and not liking fish even."

He got some way through the monologue, straight-faced and deadly serious, before it occurred to Ivy he was teasing her.

"Oh! You…" she poked him hard, but she could not find it in her heart to be cross with him. It was the first time he had attempted such humor since the death of his brother. "Is that why her ran off to be a gypsy?"

"I'm guessing so. Her were tired of catching them eels. Twenty-seven children when you're not even thirty, I think she were worn out."

"If them were all as bad as you, she must have been mad."

"It were just that my old dad were irresistible. Runs in the family."

Ivy remembered Old Moocher, a portly man with a heavy beard, eternally grubby and disreputable. The thought of anyone considering him sexually irresistible reduced her to helpless giggles.

Ben pulled her backwards so her head was resting on his shoulder, silencing her with kisses to her neck and cheek. His mouth covered hers as his hand strayed over her stomach. His fingers drifted down suggestively, and Ivy realized just how much she wanted to feel him between her thighs, arousing her as he had done when they were newly wedded. To her disappointment, he did not make contact with her pussy, nor press down into the fabric of her clothing to give her stimulation. She reached behind her, touching his thighs with her fingers. From his talk of babies and his jesting, she thought he might be open to some advance and she inched her fingers back, seeking the telltale swell in his trousers. In this he did not fail her at all.

As her questing hands found her husband's erection, he responded in kind, rubbing her through the heavy fabric of her dress so her garments moved against her skin. Parting her legs, she invited him to delve further, and was rewarded with longer strokes that made her hot all over. It was easy enough to unbutton his trousers and work her hand into the warm, cramped space within his clothes. His tip was slick, the foreskin pulled back by the sheer magnitude of his arousal. She had never felt him so thick or long before. He moved her skirt, taking advantage of its fullness to get a hand beneath it without exposing her. His eager fingers plunged into her moist cleft, rapidly inspiring fresh gushes of liquid pleasure. With two digits pressing deep inside her sex, and his thumb working gently on her clitoris, he soon had her trembling. She wanted to do more for him, but with her hand behind her back it was difficult to do more than caress him slowly.

"Does you like that?" he asked.

She sighed her response.

"Or would you rather I were a bit more rough with you?" There was a hint of menace in his voice – a suggestion of the predatory aggression that had so hypnotized her when perpetrated by Seth. She shivered at the sound of it, partly from arousal, partly from alarm. He squeezed one of her breasts with his other hand, startling her. She was used to him being safe and gentle, she was not sure if she wanted him to become more like his feral brother had been. It occurred to her then that perhaps this had been in him all along, that he too was wild and dominant, but that he had played at being tame for her sake. He had, after all, kept the truth of his shifting nature from her. What else might he have hidden? She did not think she could ask him so direct and difficult a question. He moved, and she was forced to relinquish his cock. "What would you do with I?" she asked him tremulously.

"Only what you wants."

"Tell me what you fancy…"

She felt his face against hers, his breath cool on her skin. "Right now? I'd roll you in the grass here, get your skirts hitched up, and fuck you to within an inch of your life, my pretty wench." His hands continued their work between her legs while the effect of his words was to sharpen the intensity of her response. "I'd have you now if you'd let me. I'd give a lot to get them clothes off you, suck your boobs, and get my teeth into you." He reinforced this point by nipping at her neck and shoulder, his teeth stinging even through her dress. "There's a part of me wants to force it on you. A part of me reckons if I were rough, if I pushed and demanded, you might well give me your all. A part of me thinks you might just like that. What do you think, my girl?"

His tone sent shivers down her spine and carried her over the brink, causing her to press one final bout of trembling shudders against his hand. The threat of dominance and force aroused her more than she would ever have admitted.

"I think you liked that," he said, carefully removing his hand.

As soon as she was able to move, Ivy turned to smile her gratitude at him and cover his face with her kisses. "Would you let me do something for you?" she asked, still a little shy.

Ben smiled with a mixture of pleasure and embarrassment. "You've done a lot for me."

She slid her fingers into his pants, only to find the mighty erection was gone and the cloth damp. She looked up at him in wonder.

"About when you did," he said, guessing her unvoiced question. "You don't know what that does to me."

"I think maybe now I does," she replied. She was touched by his reaction to her pleasure.

"Much as I doesn't want to, we'd best move, my girly. It'll be dark in a bit. But don't you worry, I knows every last hedge from here to home, we'll not go far wrong," he promised.

Chapter Thirty Four

Over a rather fine dinner of roast mutton and potatoes with the squire, Reverend Gotobed found the conversation shifting in the direction of local concerns. He was developing quite an appetite for ghostly tales and improbable stories and hoped the Squire might be led that way. The red-faced and portly old man chattered away with enthusiasm, giving Septimus considerable insight into the history of the village, particularly with reference to the importance of the Gills. Other men might have found the lengthy monologues tedious, but the young vicar did not, which made him a favorite of the Squire's.

Septimus supposed it was his fen heritage showing through at last. His father had been a gentleman farmer who traced their people back almost as far as the Norman invaders. They predated even the Dutch dyke builders, and the murky water of the fens was very much in their blood. Squire Gill had an equally compelling lineage on his father's side, but his mother's people had unfortunately been of Dutch descent. Their arrival, some two-hundred years ago or more, had been unpopular with the fen-dwelling natives. The bogs and marshes were drained, depriving many of traditional employment. Even so long after the event, to be descended from the Dutch drainage engineers was something the Squire felt ambivalent about. He was proud of his ancestors' achievements, but conscious of the trouble they had caused.

"I've heard it said…" he remarked as he sipped his wine thoughtfully. "I've heard it said that a man's horizons, his physical horizons, you mark me, very much determine how broadly he can think. You take the fenlanders. We have all that great stretch of horizon, as though you might see from here to the end of the world. We're a challenging group of people, Septimus, you must own it, a challenging group. We've never been the sort to do what outsiders tell us and we never will be, you can count on that."

"I think it very likely."

"From Hereward the Wake to Oliver Cromwell, we refuse to conform," Gill added, warming to his subject. "There's that many stories of how we fought. We fought the Vikings and the Danes, the Normans and the Dutch, and we only lost because there aren't men in all the country as stout and true as those you will find in the fens."

"And we have such a wealth of folklore as well," Septimus ventured.

"That we do!" the Squire banged his fist down on the table, making the plates and cutlery rattle. "Why, there are several ghost stories pertaining to Burnham alone."

Septimus waited eagerly.

"You might not know, but there have been many sightings of a ghostly pair who walk on summer nights. A blind old man led by a boy. You know, I saw them myself once, with my very own eyes. I was walking in the avenue to this house, and I saw these two coming the other way. The boy spoke to the old man and he greeted me most politely. I never gave it a second thought, as they seemed real enough. However, recalling the stories, I turned only seconds after they passed me, and do you know? There was no sign of them anywhere. It was twilight, not too dark, and they had entirely vanished."

"Incredible."

"I certainly thought so. It had me quite rattled."

"I can well believe it. And you say they looked perfectly normal to you when you first saw them?"

"Absolutely, they looked as substantial as you do this very moment."

"I wonder if I may have had such an experience myself," Septimus began, testing carefully to see if the subject would interest his host.

"I should be delighted to hear about it."

"I may have mentioned before that I have some small interest in historical matters?"

"I recall that you did."

"I was at the abbey one afternoon when I saw a young lady as plain as you like. She said some very curious things to me. None of it made any sense. I happened to mention her to some of the parishioners – I was concerned for her wellbeing – and it was suggested to me that I had in fact seen a ghost."

The Squire's expression rapidly darkened as though an old gloom had settled upon him. Septimus had not forgotten the full intelligence he had received on the subject, and was keen to see what he could learn.

"Some girl called Meg Tuck, I was told. It all sounded very mysterious and tragic."

"We have several ghost girls," the Squire said, all boisterous good humor gone from his voice. "When I was a boy, there was Daisy Norman, who was supposed to have drowned herself in the river, and before her there was Sarah Gall, who died of a broken heart. My grandfather could remember her. I made quite a study of it at one time. Meg Tuck went missing one winter, and then where people before had seen poor Daisy from time to time, they then started seeing little Meg."

"That is curious."

"Indeed. And now I hear that young Megan West is missing. I saw her parents myself not so very long ago. Poor Mrs. West is not long for this world, I fear. I rather expect we shall have one or two sightings of her daughter soon, and that Meg Tuck will haunt us no longer."

"Do you think there is anything in it?" Septimus asked.

"These ghost girls who haunt the marshy places? They are the ones we can never quite forgive ourselves for; the ones we let slip through the cracks.

Girls ruined by love, abandoned by families, driven to madness and who knows what else."

"I thought Meg Tuck was caught in a snowstorm?" Septimus queried.

"But why was she out at night in the first place, have you ever wondered that?"

Septimus considered it tactful not to answer. He waited for a while to see if any more observations would be forthcoming. There was a distant look in Gall's eyes, and the young vicar suspected he would learn no more for now.

"All those poor ghost girls," the Squire added, more to himself than to his guest. "Every last one of them a little touched by something, I shouldn't wonder."

Septimus nodded, having nothing intelligible to offer by way of response.

"They say its bad luck to see them, round here," the Squire continued, "but I think, if you see the girls, you've already had a taste of bad luck, you've already been touched by them."

The jovial atmosphere of the early evening had gone entirely, leaving uncomfortable gloom behind it. Septimus did not wait very long before thanking his host and departing to seek his own bed.

The village was slumbering quietly when Septimus made his way home. All the talk of ghosts had left him edgy and he jumped at shadows. Every tiny night sound made him quiver. He half expected to see some specter stalking the night – some suicidal girl with flowers in her hair and a mad smile on her beautiful face.

"What if it is mere coincidence?" he asked himself, knowing only too well how strange and complex tales could be woven out of small truths that had no bearing on one another. It seemed improbable there was anything other than a narrative connection between these ghosts, but all the same, the thing seemed more sinister than ever now. Was there some connection between

Megan West's disappearance and Meg Tuck's death? And what of the others Gill had named, Sarah Gall and Daisy Norman? From the sounds of their names, both would have families still in the village. He wondered if there were others, hidden further back in time; their names forgotten. He envisaged a line of ghostly girls linked by tragedy and reaching back into distant history, each an omen for the death of the next. But where did the tragic chain begin?

It made for a wonderful story, as mysterious, romantic and troubling as you could wish for. Septimus saw with a flash of insight that it made no odds whether he found some uncanny connection between these deaths and disappearances. If such a thing existed, it would most likely lie beyond his capacity to comprehend. These phantasms belonged to the mythic life of the fen and would never place themselves within his grasp. Continuing along with this philosophy born of speculation and fine Port, he walked steadily through the night.

As he approached the house, he noticed a pale face at one of the upstairs windows. It seemed as though whoever it was watched the vicar's slow progress along the road. From this distance, and with the poor light and the sheen of glass, it was impossible to say who was there. Most likely, he thought, it would be Sarah keeping vigil against his return. Usually the thought of her sinfully desirable body was enough to cheer him, but the blank face at the window chilled him beyond all warming. He wondered if it was just a trick of the light, but he could think of nothing in the window's vicinity that would cause it. The head turned, he saw it distinctively. There was a flash of pale blond hair, and then the specter was gone.

Sarah opened the door to him at once. She too had been watching his progress, but from the little window beside the door. "What were you looking at?" she asked.

"Oh, nothing." He tried to shrug the experience off.

The Shifting Heart

"You been stood there a good quarter hour by the clock."

He said nothing, wondering how he would ever be able to sleep easily in his own bed. He reached for Sarah's hands. He needed her warm humanity and her cool pragmatism, wanting to believe that her presence might ward off the phantoms.

Chapter Thirty Five

vy sat in a chair outside the house making use of the good light to cut her cloth into suitable pieces for rug making. That morning they had finished flower planting and her parents had no further need for her. The last two rugs had been bought quickly and at a decent price. Now she could afford to pay for pieces of cheap material rather than having to scrounge off-cuts, and her patterns were more ambitious.

From time to time, she raised her head, looking out across the fields for signs of her husband's return. Along the road a boy led a large Suffolk horse towing a wide piece of farm machinery. The majestic creature's chestnut coat glinted in the sun like burnished bronze. Other people were out in the fields – an old man carrying a large sack of something, a boy herding a pig along the hedgerow, and further away, less distinct, the shapes of laborers moving over the land. There was also a girl a few fields away walking with her head down and her shoulders drawn in. Long loose hair flew about her. For a moment Ivy thought it might be Megan, and her heart leapt. At this distance it was impossible to tell, and she discarded the foolish hope. There had been no sign of Megan for too long, although she had half expected the Spring tides to leave a body on some riverbank. It seemed likely Megan had been carried downstream to be found by people who did not know her name or sorry history. Every few years the river surrendered a corpse, often battered and ruined beyond recognition.

The unexpected weight of hands on her shoulders made her start, dropping her bundle of cloth. Tilting her head back, she looked up into Ben's familiar face. He kissed her lightly.

"You're early," she said.

"We got the wall done, and there weren't anything else, so back I come."

"There's rabbit pie if you're hungry." Having collected her fallen fabric, she glanced towards the road again. The long-haired girl was approaching along the narrow bank that served as a path to the cottage. Her hands were slightly outstretched before her, as though she was reaching for something. The sight of her lifted the hairs on Ivy's arms as a cold draft might have done. This girlish figure was much of a height and build with Megan, but her face was very different, with a little up-turned nose and a mouth like a rosebud. By the time she had reached the scrubby hawthorn a few yards from the house, she appeared ethereal. Light seemed to pass through her and her body shimmered like a heat haze. As she came closer, her form grew misty, evaporating away until nothing at all remained.

Ivy shivered. "Did you see her?" she asked nervously.

"See who?"

"The wench on the path."

Ben looked round, seeing no one anywhere in the vicinity of their cottage. "Where?"

"She were on the path and then her vanished."

Ben touched her forehead, his hand cool against her skin.

"I weren't imagining it, there were a wench on the path and her's just vanished away." She could hear the panic in her voice. She knew there were myths of ghost girls and did not like to think one might have appeared so close by.

"Maybe you saw my old aunt Meg. Her died before I were born, she were my father's sister. Her died in a snowstorm. Her fell in a dyke, like your Megan did, only there weren't no one about to rescue she."

"You ever seen her?"

"Not as I knows of. But other folk reckon to have seen her, so maybe you have and all."

"You told me about her that first night," Ivy said, suddenly remembering the conversation in vivid detail.

The wind picked up. It was a cold blow coming in off the sea, and it seemed unaware that for the rest of the world, it was late Spring.

"There's a bite in that," Ben remarked.

"There is and all."

He helped carry her cloth into the cottage.

"Did your old dad live here when him were a boy?"

"Him did, and his dad before him going way back."

"So her lived here," Ivy asked, reluctant to name the unquiet dead.

Ben understood her quickly enough. "Her did, but I never saw her round here, and nor did anyone else."

"Apart from if I saw her just now."

He wrapped one arm across her shoulders and slipped the other around her waist, pulling her close. "If that were anything, it were just ghosts, and them won't do no harm to us."

"What if I sees someone else?" she asked fearfully.

"Then you sees someone else. No point fretting about what ain't happened yet, and might never happen."

She leaned her forehead against his shoulder and closed her eyes. She felt safe, held close so that nothing might harm her.

"You be maudlin, my wench."

She pressed closer against him. His hands stroked her back, helping her to put darker thoughts aside for a while.

"I knows sometimes you want to see them as have gone and sometimes you fear it. We've both of us got things unsaid, things we'll not undo, or do different. Comes a time you've got to accept it's just too late and there's nothing to do but keep on living."

She knew he was speaking as much for himself as for her. There were actions he would never be able to forgive himself for, nor ask to have excused.

"I should've seen him while I still could. I should've been more careful in the first place," he added.

Ivy hushed him gently, lifting her head to kiss his lips. There were things it was better not to think or speak of, and she did not want to be carried back into those haunted, shadowy places. Although it made no sense to her, she found she was rebelling against this talk of the dead, her body hankering instead after proofs of life. She kissed him again, drawing his tongue into her mouth. His response was eager and rapid, as though he too was keen to escape from troubled memories. The change of mood was sudden, like a summer storm. He covered her neck with hungry kisses, his hands squeezing her breasts and tweaking her nipples mercilessly.

"Come to bed," he demanded, and she had no inclination to refuse him.

He fucked with more rage and passion that she had thought possible. All the frustration and torment in his soul seemed to be pouring from him in a torrent of kisses, bites and thrusts. She submitted to the onslaught gladly, as though she might sweat away the pain of the past as she lay beneath him. He was so very hard delving down into her, touching parts of her body that had never before known such contact. His hands were on her wrists, pinning them to the bed as the weight of his body prevented her from resisting. She wanted nothing more than to submit.

She remembered the gentle boy she had lain with in months past. She could not help but recall Seth's aggression, but it was a world apart from this. That had been a thing of fleeting lust, wonderful and fearful but never meant to last. Her heart was truly in this coupling and she surrendered to it without fear. Ben did not want to merely capture her for a little while; this was an act of pure possession, and she knew it. He was filling her body, claiming her, and marking her as his. He fucked her as though his very life depended upon it, and she responded in kind, her eyes closed shut and her teeth clenched in concentration.

When he came, the entirety of her body responded; trembling and gasping as he filled her. Even as they rolled apart she knew with absolute certainty that this time she would conceive, although what made her so unshakably confident, she could not have said.

For a while they lay together, watching each other as though neither could quite believe the other was real. Their fingers touched and twined, weaving in and out of each other.

"Enough?" he asked.

The look in his eyes was sufficient to start her yearning again. She moved closer to him, stroking his chest with her fingertips and nuzzling her lips against his neck.

"I'm thinking that's a no," he laughed.

Chapter Thirty Six

It was late in the evening and the curtains were closed, making the little parlor snug and cozy. The nights were still cool enough to warrant having a small fire, and the sight of Sarah on her knees working a poker amongst the glowing coals was almost more than Septimus could bear. The position pulled the girl's plain dress tight over her hips and bottom, offering the most tempting curves to his view. Stealthily, he knelt behind her and ran his hand over her ass. She continued her work as though she had not noticed his advances.

"You are irresistible," he told her. "I can resist you no more. I must have you, Sarah."

She moved away then, shifting on her knees until she faced him across the hearth rug. "You knows what I said, Septimus. There's things I'll do, and things I'll not, and I'll not bed with you."

"You are a cruel mistress," he responded.

She stood up, a wicked smile playing about her lips. "If I were cruel, I'd make you kiss my feet. I'd make you serve me, and I'd not give you anything."

The mere threat of such treatment kindled the young vicar's enthusiasm. "How would you command me?" he asked.

"You'd have to go round on your hands and knees and you'd be my dog. You'd have a collar and a bowl. I'd make you fetch and do tricks for me. If you were a good little dog, I might let you put your head in my lap."

"If I was a dog, I might sniff your bottom," he said. "Dogs do things like that."

His response startled her, and for a few seconds she had no idea what to say. She was not yet accustomed to playing the harsh mistress.

"If I cannot have you the usual way, let me have you with my tongue?"

"I don't know…"

"You liked it well enough before," he pressed.

She blushed.

Septimus moved in, kissing her face and neck. "I want to kiss your fair breasts," he said, "and I want to kiss you between your thighs. I want to taste you, Sarah."

She made a soft moan of surrender.

"Would you let me do that? Would you let me taste you?"

"Yes…"

"Are you wearing anything under your dress?"

She nodded mutely.

"There's something else I would like to do. I should like to pleasure you, Sarah, touch you through your knickers. Would you let me do that?"

Again she nodded her consent.

"And then let me keep those knickers wet with your juices." His hands were already under her skirt, not waiting for further permission before he carried out his plan. Sarah might play at being coy and demure, but she liked to take her pleasure and he knew her modesty was largely pretence. Still, she had steadfastly refused him the prize, and he had not yet taken her. In his ongoing attempts at seduction, Septimus employed, on different occasions, almost every form of persuasion he could think of – gifts, money, compliments, appeals and begging. He had tried arousing her, and then offering his swollen manhood to assuage her lust, but even then she always declined. Although she said nothing to suggest she might be conquered, it was increasingly apparent to Septimus there was only one method by which he might perhaps win his way into the delightful young woman's exquisite pussy.

He devoted his fingers to her pleasure, smelling the musk rising from her cleft as she dripped onto her already sodden clothing. He could tell from the way she pursed her lips, and the fluttering of her eyelashes, that her orgasm was close. When he thought her at least partially sated, he whipped away his prize, crumpling her knickers into his pocket for his later enjoyment. The smell of her intoxicated him. Lowering his lips to her hot slit, he proceeded to gently fuck her with the length of his tongue. She moaned shamelessly, lifting her hips to meet his face. When he thought she might be beyond refusal, he lifted his head.

"Do you want me to finish you?" he asked.

"Please!"

He undid his fly, but she was not as transported as he had imagined. Her eyes flicked open, taking in the expanse of his revealed erection.

"It's lovely," she said encouragingly, and at the same time she closed her legs against him.

"I'm going half mad from wanting you," he professed.

She sighed, as though this could be no fault of hers. "I'd gladly give you my hands, or my mouth like we did before."

"But not the other?"

She shook her head.

"Are you truly so unrelenting? Is there nothing that might persuade you to alleviate my suffering?"

She looked at him darkly. "There might be."

"Is there anything short of marriage that might convince you?"

"Nothing."

The vicar found he had lost his ardor somewhat. Seeing his manhood droop its head, she opened her thighs again, showing him the full magnificence of her vulva. He ached to have her, but she would not relent.

"Then marriage it will have to be," he conceded. "Now can I have you?"

"Not before it all be properly done," she reprimanded.

The Shifting Heart

Septimus wrestled with his conscience. Prone and little as she was, it would be easy enough to plunge in. Her slick and eager cleft would not reject him. He rather imagined she would enjoy the unexpected penetration. Then he thought that perhaps she might not like it at all, but there would be precious little she could do to stop him having his will of her. His cock was straining anew, inspired by the images his lust had conjured. He hesitated a few seconds and finally decided he was not the man to do such a thing. Instead, he settled for lowering his head once more into the softness of her curls, applying his tongue to her flesh.

Chapter Thirty Seven

There were house martins nesting on some of the ledges. Their voices filled the air as they hunted for small insects, darting to and fro in the fading light. Voles scuttled in their grassy tunnels, hidden from the view of would-be predators as they undertook their quests for food. In the damp places, under fallen stones or where the moss was luscious, frogs lurked resplendent in their greens and browns. Ferns wavered in the breezes as grasses shook their stamens, giving their pollen to the air. The abbey ruins were quiet and still, as though paused on the brink of breathing but not yet ready to exhale.

"What are we?" Megan dreamed to herself. "Are we sky-dancing birds today? Are we long-legged spiders hiding in the forest of ferns? Perhaps we are buttercups shining in the sun together, quietly beautiful. There are always buttercups. We could be buttercups for all of eternity."

The sky was a perfect blue, unbroken by clouds but darkening gently as the sun sank low. It would change slowly to the deepest, midnight shades until at last the stars emerged to twinkle and make their progress. The green sea of grass was not so undisturbed; someone had been digging. The earth had been piled up in a mound and the turf torn off to reveal the dry, dark soil beneath. It had not rained in a while. The hole was long and rectangular, going down to quite some depth. It revealed lines of foundation stones and changing tones in the soil. At the bottom there were two stone boxes, lidless and laid side by side. They looked a little like coffins, and she wondered if they might indeed be that. They would have been inside the church when it stood. She supposed monks probably buried their dead in churches. Other people did, after all.

The Shifting Heart

Megan was close to the stone now, close enough to reach out and touch it. A hand appeared. She had fingers, feeling. Some part of her at least was a girl today. Forms came and went and she gave little thought to them. The dressed rock was cold and very smooth, as though at one time someone had carefully polished it. It was deep enough to take a body. Deep enough to take her, she realized. She lay in the stark space, watching the house martins wheeling over her head. This was the closest she would ever get to being buried. She imagined there should be some lid shutting her away to molder out of sight. There would be soil, and the little tiles of the church floor that had been carried from the abbey to enhance the beauty of her father's church. There would be people walking over her resting place, gathering for masses and psalm singing at all hours of the day and night, men who had renounced the life of the flesh treading carefully upon those who had abandoned it altogether.

They had not buried her. It was a long time before she dared to remember. Eventually, when she was strong enough to endure it, the past flooded back and she knew where to find the pitiful form she had abandoned. The river had been in full flood when she came to it on the day of Seth's death. The waters were flowing heavy and swift from all the weeks of rain. Those final moments remained a blur. She had not been thinking. A dark and powerful impulse gripped her. She fell. *Had she meant to fall?* That she could not remember, only the sliding, the slithering over mud, and the cold shock of being in water. She floated, shivering and increasingly afraid. Gradually she sank. In those moments there had been a sound like voices – the tones of young women crying and laughing together. In her delirium she imagined she felt the touch of fingers reaching for her garments. They seemed to be pulling her down.

How long had passed, she could not say. She and Seth experienced no time beyond their own awareness. The hours of starlight seemed to stretch forever, but all sense of days and the shape of seasons was gone from their world. Now it was early summer in the abbey ruins, but next time she knew herself to be thinking they might be walking some unfamiliar road in a heavy snowstorm, or riding the autumn winds on the wings of migrating swans.

She had washed up a long way down the river in a place she did not know by name. A great reed bed caught her and held her firm. Fish nibbled at her, small mouths eroding away all trace of identity until she was little more than bone and tendon slowly disintegrating, to be lost in the mud of the river's bed. The tangle of hair, riddled with a mess of twigs and plants, was all that showed above the surface. The sodden heap bore no resemblance to the person she had been. She was just debris washed up by the floods to lie unnoticed in a forlorn spot.

"Is that me?" she asked fearfully.

Seth took her hand, closing his fingers round hers. "That were you," he replied.

She shook her head, disbelieving. "I feel alive," she said.

"So did I, but I knew I weren't."

"Ivy and I buried you near the house. No one will bury me, will they?"

"The water'll have you, my wench. It's not such a bad place to lie."

Reclining in the stone bier, Megan considered her bones and wondered if anyone had found her. She thought it might have been good to lie with Seth, their flesh mingling completely in decay and the feasting of worms. To dissolve into soil at his side had a certain allure, but her corpse and his lay far apart.

"And what be you doing?" Seth sounded amused.

"Just thinking," she said dreamily, "and lying here."

"What you thinking about?"

"Bones." She emerged. Seth knew nothing about history, about monks and their ways, abbeys, ruins or burials. He knew far more about the myriad possibilities of existing, and that appealed to her far more. "Do all the dead walk, do you think?" she asked him.

"How many have you seen of they?" he replied carelessly.

"There was a girl in the meadow, but I don't know what she was. I don't know."

"Not enough to account for all the folks as ever lived, I'd reckon."

"I wonder what happens to them," she mused.

"What do it matter? It's what we do as matters."

Pressed close against him, with her hands in his hair and his fingers snaking around her narrow waist, Megan kissed her lover. Even the grave could not part them. His mouth seemed as warm as it had in life, his body as responsive to her touch. Sometimes she thought she could hear their two hearts beating in time even though there was no blood to pump and no life to sustain.

Chapter Thirty Eight

The vicar from Norsey came over especially to conduct the wedding. He was a cheerful man with thinning hair and crimson cheeks. Afterwards, they gave a tea on the vicarage lawn and Mrs. Norman, the church-warden's wife, said she supposed they would have to hire another girl now seeing as how he had married the first one. She eyed Sarah's slender figure critically, as though looking for signs of impropriety. Septimus knew full well that if he was a father so much as a day short of nine months hence it would be said he had been obliged to wed his servant. His failure to provide much material for local gossip was not for lack of trying on his part, he had to admit.

Sarah looked charming. He had paid for a dress to be made. The simple but beautifully cut garment was a pale blue that offset her complexion superbly and showed her curvy figure to good effect. Despite the new Mrs. Gotobed's humble origins, she was handling her guests with ease and some skill. He thought she would make a useful, helpful wife, all things considered, even though that had not been his primary motivation when pursuing her.

It seemed to take an intolerably long time for the various family members, upstanding citizens and assorted hangers-on, to have their fill of cakes and sandwiches. They seemed to loiter with intent, determined to extract as much for themselves as they could with no thought of the frustrations they might be causing. Septimus smiled and smiled, accepting small gifts and endless con-gratulations until he was heartily sick of the whole business. It seemed an age before the house and garden were finally free of invaders, allowing the bride and groom to finally be alone. Sarah cleared away the tea things carefully.

"Will that not wait until tomorrow?" Septimus asked, barely masking his irritation.

"The food'll spoil out here, and it'd be a shame to get any plates broken."

She was right. He looked around, but no one seemed to be close by. He set about helping, working as hastily as he could. It was rather beneath his dignity to be clearing away platters of half eaten food, but he decided pride was his lesser concern this evening.

They climbed the stairs hand-in-hand. He glanced across frequently, admiring his wife's sparkling eyes and fine figure. Her delight in their union was obvious and seeing it warmed his heart. He was inspired to think their nuptials might be blessed with considerable happiness.

"I won't be refusing you no more," she promised as they entered the bedroom.

She undressed without a hint of fear or self consciousness, and then came naked to his arms to help him from his own garments. The bed had never seemed softer or more inviting. The sight of her naked body – now his to possess – left the young vicar trembling with anticipation. There were so many delights he longed to taste and savor he barely knew where to begin. He set upon her breasts and neck, his hands reaching to part her legs. Tonight he would undertake the journey he had dreamed of for so long. Her thighs were creamy against his hands, already moist with her arousal.

Someone was giggling.

Septimus froze, straining his ears. "Did you hear that?" he asked nervously.

"Hear what, my love?" his newly wedded wife replied, moving her body slightly against his stiffened fingers.

The sound stopped, and Septimus wondered if he had imagined it. "Nothing, the wind I think," he said dismissively, determined to concentrate on the sensual feast before him and not be sidetracked further by his imagination.

They fell upon each other with refreshed vigor.

He was poised with his cock in his hand, about to consummate the marriage, when the giggling came again, putting him off entirely.

"What is it?" Sarah asked him gently. "Surely you don't be nervous?"

He could hear floorboards creaking in the next room, the empty room, the room he avoided venturing into. Caught somewhere between anger and fear, he reached under the bed and retrieved his poker. Seeing it, Sarah gave a muffled shriek, pressing her hand to her mouth to stifle her surprise. Without bothering to dress, he vacated the bedroom and threw open the door to the supposedly unused space.

He could see the figures quite distinctly. The girl had the most shapely hips and bottom his mind could have conjured up. Her skin gleamed pale and flawless. Dark hair tumbled down her back in loose curls, swaying as she rose and fell. The man was lithe and muscular, his hands upon her breasts, his features gripped by passionate intent. Septimus took a step forward, but the lovers paid him no heed.

"Excuse me?" he ventured. He had meant to shout and rail at these intruders, evicting them by force if needs be, instead he stood, spellbound, unable to tear his eyes away. Her breasts were small, like apples, and he thought they must taste as sweet. She rode like a woman on horseback, rising and falling at a gentle gait. Septimus felt his own cock stiffen in response to her efforts. He could imagine how that must feel, to be encased in feminine flesh and transported by such erotic movements. However eager for the act he had been before, this vision inflated his lust.

"Septimus?"

He turned and saw Sarah in the doorway. She was wrapped in a dressing gown, and she looked alarmed as she hurried to his side.

"Don't you see them?" he whispered.

"See who?" she replied, evidently perplexed.

"Them." He pointed towards the coupling figures. He could hear their gasps and moans of pleasure, now painfully distinct.

"Septimus, this room be empty. You be a bit touched, I'm thinking. Too much sun, too much wearing yourself out. You'd best sleep it off."

He turned, proffering the enormity of his erection. "Perhaps my unrequited lust has finally driven me mad," he said.

"Then you'd best come back to bed," she replied.

Tempting though the suggestion was, he looked back at the pair. The woman's head was thrown back, her face transfixed by an all-consuming surge of pleasure. He could read the signs of rapturous orgasm on her face. Her lips parted slightly and her long hair fell away from her graceful neck. For a moment she turned, her large eyes meeting his. Megan West, Meg Tuck, Daisy Norman, Sarah Gall… he did not know what name to give her or if the name truly mattered. He knew who she was, ominous ghost girl of the beautiful eyes, omen of strange times and of disaster, thief of unsuspecting hearts. He met the challenge in her gaze, and although his innards quivered with fear, he mastered it. Septimus refused to fall victim to dread and fought hard to retain control of himself. The ghostly lovers faded slowly away, leaving the room as empty and irrelevant as it should have been. She had been beautiful, whoever she was. He would not forget her face.

"Come to bed," his own Sarah said softly. "Come and lie with me."

He knew they would romp this honeymoon night away, and he would expunge his apprehension in joyful, sweaty congress. There would be time enough to explore each possibility his mind had conjured, and to penetrate utterly the girl he had married. He wanted to go deep inside her, filling her body with his seed. He reached out his hand. Warm fingers rescued his, towing him back into familiar waters. Arousal had not left him, and he welcomed her touch. When they lay down again, she was softly yielding beneath him. He dared not wait for fear of further distractions but plunged straight in, claiming his prize. It was all he had imagined, and more.

Bryn Colvin

As he pounded Sarah's slender form into the bed, Septimus thought how much like his own wife the ghost girl had seemed. He shuddered at the thought. The girl who bucked and groaned beneath him was safe – he had married her, she would be cared for and protected. His Sarah, with her mouth on his nipple and her hands urging him on, would never be one of the forgotten, ruined and abandoned ones. He remembered the look in the old Squire's eye, the worlds of melancholy and recrimination: "They are the ones we cannot save, the ones we cannot forgive ourselves for…" Septimus thrust hard into the warm flesh beneath him. He kissed her as though he meant to ward off death with the sheer force of his lust. Of course Sarah would be safe. The ghost girl was probably some phantasm brought on by the heat of a long day and the strain he had been under. Her presence meant nothing…

From the next bedroom he could hear the sounds of creaking boards. The rhythm matched his own, grinding away relentlessly. Beyond the thin barrier of his bedroom wall the ghosts were fucking endlessly. There was no blocking his ears to the sound of it. Looking down, he could see mortality in the face of the woman beneath him. He could see how her skin would draw tight across her bones, and then wither away entirely. Even closing his eyes would not block out the vision. Compelled to match the pace of his ghostly counterparts, Septimus was oblivious to his own pleasure and locked in rigid horror by his morbid vision.

Sarah kissed his face and whispered his name. Her gentle affection rescued him. The nightmare melted gradually, freeing him from its hideous grip. There were no longer sounds of other lovers to torment him. He was a young man in the throws of making love to his new wife. The rest was nothing more than vile illusion, and he cast it from his thoughts. The woman in his arms was flesh-and-blood, sweetly real and filled with life. There was no hint of the tomb about her; that was obvious now. Septimus half feared his wits were leaving him.

The Shifting Heart

"You be tired," she said, but there was no accusation in it.

They rolled, exchanging places, and she sat herself upon him. In this position Septimus had easy access to her breasts and could fondle her clitoris to his heart's content. He could feel the damp moisture of her sex surrounding his, and when he looked up into her face, her expression was radiant. She climaxed so prettily, her lips slightly parted and her head tilting back.

Chapter Thirty Nine

Winters could be dreadfully cruel. The last one had brought more than its share of horrors. There were always children who did not survive, and there were always tragedies. Some blurred quickly, familiar disasters too often seen to grieve those beyond the immediate family. Others could shake the whole community.

Standing at the graveside between two of her sisters, Ivy thought of other winter funerals. The little coffin they buried Rose in all those years ago came to mind, and then the shallow grave she had dug to take Seth's body. He had lain in the cold ground for more than two years.

When Sarah gave birth to her first baby almost six months previously, Ivy had not thought to visit her. She had so many cousins, and babies came all the time. It was hard to keep track of her sprawling family. Still, fragments of news came from her mother, or from Hetty, who stayed sometimes. Half the village was sure Septimus had been obliged to marry, but no sign of pregnancy showed in his wife's figure for a long time. When at last she did get with child, the little girl had come too soon and was so pitifully small that she did not survive the week. The familiarity of tragedies such as this did not lessen the misery they brought. Ivy could not begin to imagine what it must be like to lose a baby. Her own daughter had been born strong and well, and she was toddling when the news came of Sarah's loss. Ivy felt for her cousin.

Little Rosemary was a boisterous infant, full of energy and bright smiles. She had walked early, and found her otter skin in no time for all her father had feared she might not have the means. The less fortunate babe had been christened Mary.

There were several occasions when Ivy had seen her cousin after the loss of the child. Each time Sarah looked more haunted than ever. Her eyes were ringed black from sleeplessness, and she seemed forever to be looking at something undefined in the distance. Ivy had seen that look before – in Megan during her last days. She thought at the time it did not bode well and said as much to her mother, but there was little else to be done. Sarah would get over her disappointment; that was the general wisdom. But women deal with such things. They survive. Life goes on. No one would try to help her because there was nothing to be done.

Now those of them who had seen her suffer and not known what to do were gathered in the cemetery. The day was cold but, for once, the rain held off. They were burying Sarah next to her little daughter. Septimus had conducted the service himself, and watching him was painful indeed. Despite her early misgivings, Ivy felt tremendous pity for the young man who had been robbed of both wife and daughter within a year. His shoulders were stooped, and he looked like an old man.

Ivy and Sarah had never been close. They knew each other through the gossip of family members, and had shared a place of employment, but beside that there was very little to connect them. Still, Ivy had come to see her committed to the earth. There had never been chance to say goodbye to Megan properly and Seth still haunted her thoughts. She supposed, as she watched the coffin lowered into the ground, that she was here as much to say her goodbyes to those unfortunate two as well was to her cousin. There was something good and right about committing a person to the earth. You knew where they were, and that helped. Lost and unburied, Megan would have no proper mourners or a quiet resting place. If they had found her and thought it suicide, she would not have had a proper burial even then. Ivy found it hard to concentrate on Septimus' words. His voice was low and broken. He spoke more for himself than anyone else.

Some people liked to walk out in the fields and lanes, to forage for nuts and berries, to gather leaves to feed the family pig or just to view the ever-changing landscape. Others preferred to keep to their houses and gardens. Sarah was very much of the second sort, going abroad for bread and milk or to attend services, but not even straying much as a child. Why she had been out in the fields remained something of a mystery. She had told no one. There was precious little to be foraged in this season, and she was far from any home. A few people saw her on the road, but no one much remarked upon it at the time. Afterwards, no one could imagine where she had been going.

After they found her, the doctor said she had fallen and sprained her ankle. She had tried to drag herself along; anyone could see that from the state of her hands and clothes. She was plastered with mud. There was no sign of any foul play that he could observe, but her face was a mask of terror. Those who saw her pretty features frozen in horror or alarm said they would never forget the sight. Ivy was glad to have been spared it. Her mother had gone with her aunt to help prepare the body for burial. It had been a grim task and May refused to speak of it. This death had turned May into an old woman, putting grey in her hair and stealing the last color from her gaunt cheeks. She stood with her sister, Laura, and Lucy Norman, Sarah's grieving mother. They were three stricken women clinging together for support.

"What you think happened to she?" Hetty asked as they moved away from the graveside.

"I don't know, maybe there's something about that house, making her take strange, like Megan did," Gladys offered.

"Who's to say?" Ivy put in. She did not really want to discuss the subject, having spent far too long thinking about it already.

"Rum, though. Poor Sarah, I liked she," Hetty added.

Ivy thought about Megan walking barefoot on the road and dancing in the ruins. She thought about Sarah, found in the mud after a freezing night, dead from cold, or terror, or something else entirely. She knew the dead kept their own secrets and there would be no answers.

The Shifting Heart

***

Septimus walked home slowly and alone. Gall had offered him hospitality, but he could not face company. He knew they were already talking about her, making a myth of his poor dead girl. He could no more stop that than he could all the wild speculations. He guessed they would wonder if he had any part in it; that was just the way of things. They would watch his grieving and read significance into whatever he did. There was much speculation as to what had caused her death, but no answers. He wondered what he would do now, without her care and comfort. The house would be dreadfully empty and lonely. He would miss her bright humor. He would miss the taste of her lips. Septimus already guessed he would not find a girl to take her place. There was a feeling, and he could not help but share it, that ill fortune clung to the vicarage. What young woman would want to be his housekeeper? Who could dwell under a roof where two women had already been driven to distraction? He did not yet know if he would be able to bear it.

The image of her final moments haunted him. He could see it all too clearly in his mind's eye, the darkness and the cold, a woman shivering and weeping with pain and fear, and then the terrible, unbearable quiet. Her death was with him every waking moment.

There was a light burning in one of the upstairs windows. For a while he stood in the road, looking upwards. A shadow passed before the light, fluttering like some giant moth. There was no one in the house. There should have been no light, no flitting suggestion of a presence. Septimus did not know whether it was fear or elation that accelerated his weary heart. He opened the little gate and walked the few steps to his door. As his fingers touched the wood it moved, opening before him. Taking a deep breath, he crossed the threshold. He was home, whatever that might now mean for him.

Chapter Forty

From beneath the comfortable shade of a willow tree, Ivy watched the three forms splashing in the water. She struggled to tell them apart most of the time, even though one was considerably larger than the other two. Every so often a head would break the surface to bob for a while before submerging again. They were so graceful, these three, so lithe and energetic. The sight of them cheered her; easing the lines of worry from her face and making her feel young. If she leaned forwards she could watch their progress beneath the surface. The old mill pond was deep and clear, revealing the three otters as they played and hunted beneath the water. It was a peaceful sight. Ben was teaching his children how to fish.

She plaited grass stems idly, thinking how much safer and easier life always was in summer. Her sister Gladys was walking out with a lad from Bury. He came over twice a week on his bicycle to woo her. Summer leant itself to joy and pleasure, with the warmth of the sun and the plentiful supply of fresh food. Yet even on the brightest day there were certain shadows. The missing and the dead preyed on Ivy's mind although she seldom uttered their names. It was spending time at the vicarage that caused the trouble, and she knew it. Still, she felt very sorry for the Reverend Gotobed. The young man had become little more than a shadow. He spent a good deal of time with the old Squire, but none of his other parishioners had much to do with him outside of services. He was a man accursed, and to invite him in might be to invite the attention of malevolent forces.

Ivy felt she had come close enough to those specters already, and could no longer fear them. It was peculiar being back in the old house. She went twice a week to clean and cook, leaving pies and cold meats the vicar could eat in her absence. She was glad of the money. Often she would return to find the food moldering and uneaten. She seldom saw the man, but when she did he always looked worse than she remembered, with shadows under his eyes and a haunted look to him. Knowing how easily she might have faced a similar fate, cut off from those she loved most, Ivy did what she could for him. Sometimes he spoke a little of Sarah or of Megan, and she had the disturbing impression the two had intermingled in his mind. Sometimes he put his head in his hands and wept, begging forgiveness for unspoken or imagined crimes against the women he had loved. He resisted all moves to comfort him, and she had no choice but to leave him to his distress.

Even though the sun was warm on her back, she shivered. Only the previous week Mrs. Gall claimed to have seen a young woman on the Bury road with a child in her arms. She swore it was Sarah Gotobed. It was inevitable there would be stories. Like other girls who had died in exposed, lonely places, Sarah was fast becoming part of the myth. They would see her shade on the roads and in difficult times she would be a reflection of fear and a harbinger of doom, until some other poor lass lost her life and claimed the role.

"You look sad." Ben popped his head out of the water, his skin gleaming damply in the sun.

She shrugged dismissively. "I were thinking."

"Nothing good from the look of you."

"I were thinking about Sarah."

He climbed out of the water and settled on the bank beside her, resting his damp head against her shoulder. The two otter pups played carelessly, chasing each other around the pool.

"It seems so creepy, she dying like that, after Megan and all."

"I don't see it, my wench."

"Well, them both being at the vicarage, Megan vanishing off, Sarah dying in the fields… It's queer stuff, and I can't help but think there must be some reason for it all."

"Why must there?"

She considered the question for some time. "I suppose I just want it to make some kind of sense, and it don't."

"Life don't always make any sense, do it? What link could there be? It's just coincidence."

"I don't know." It was hard to explain. She felt acutely there was something more sinister at play, but she had no justification for this intuitive response. Some days the vicarage brooded, and she had to open the windows and doors to get some feeling of life back into the rooms. "It's always the girls, never the boys who die in them fields," she said after a while.

"There were little Jimmy Jenks only last summer, him were crushed when a horse fell on he."

"That were different. Him weren't alone, they know what killed he."

"What about my old dad? Him died a queer death out by himself."

"True." She supposed it had been a foolish, superstitious thought. It was the fen woman in her, hungry for the large and incredible story and making connections where none should rightly be found. Imagining a thing did not make it real. She smiled at her husband and tried to put all thoughts of ghosts and sinister coincidence from her mind.

"If you're not careful, that house'll get to you, my girl."

"It's not the house," she said. "Well, sometimes it's the house. It's me; I thinks too much."

"Then you should think a bit less and enjoy a bit more." He pulled her against him, stroking her arm and hip lightly. "There's so much to be glad for. It's brooding too much as makes folk queer. Life's cruel sometimes."

Ivy watched the otter pubs at play. They were careless and joyful, delighting in the sun and water. She could not help but smile at them.

"That's my wench," he said. His kisses covered her face, each press of his lips warming her soul. "We've got through a lot, you and me."

"That we have."

"There's some things can't be helped, and best not dwell on they."

"You're right my love. I just feel so sorry for he."

Ben shook his head, his smile indulgent. "I'd best not complain. If you'd not felt so sorry for me, things would have gone very different."

The confession surprised her. She had not realized the scale of her achievement in bringing Ben out of his grief.

"Time might help he to mend."

"I hope so."

"If you don't stop brooding, my girl, I'll put you over my knee and see if I can't paddle some sense into you."

"You wouldn't?"

"You'll see."

She made some attempt at escaping, but he was quick and strong. She was over his lap in no time, and he slapped her ass playfully a few times until she started to laugh. Then he set about tickling her until her attempts at escape sent them both rolling in the long grass.

"I've got you!" he said, grabbing her wrists and holding her still.

"That you have," she replied.

He rested his head on her chest, and she ran her fingers through his short hair. It was good to be close to him. She knew he was right – there were plenty of things to rejoice in and too much mithering over what could not be changed would serve her ill.

Sitting up she saw that one of the pups had clambered out on the far side. It gave a whistle. Ben lifted his head and responded as well as he could. The pup nodded once, and then vanished into the undergrowth. Ivy watched it go, realizing which of the two it must be. He seemed so vulnerable to her, so young and exposed to be faring for himself. The human skin he occasionally wore made him of a size with Rosemary, although he had only been born at the end of the previous summer. Ben assured her that this child of his must live the otter part of his nature, and they could not seek to make him fully human. He looked distressingly similar to Seth already, with the same careless insolence and quick temper. Ivy loved him as though he was her own. Sometimes when he came to the house he would curl up in her lap, his little head resting on her arm and his tail resting on her knees. He was already big enough that his birth mother wanted no more to do with him. The part of him that was human child craved the comforts of a motherly embrace, which Ivy was glad to provide. Being parent to her own child had brought to the fore her desire to nurture and protect.

Rosemary glided elegantly through the water towards them, and scrambled onto the grassy bank. Her arrival on land was a far less dignified affair than her efforts in the water had been. She shook the water from her pelt, and then rolled about on the grass for a while. Ivy reached down to scratch her daughter's hairy stomach. Only when her fur was dry and fluffy again did the little girl exchange it for her other form. She was still only a small child, but her otter form would mature slowly, matching her human growth. It was just as well. An otter bitch would have reached sexual maturity by now and might have her own young.

Ben dressed, knowing it would not do to be caught naked should anyone chance upon them. He threw Rosemary her dress. She ignored it, rolling in the grass to enjoy the feeling of plants and sun upon her young skin.

"Come on, my girl, you'd best get back in your clothes," Ivy told her.

The day was drawing in and it was time to head for home. The melancholy fit was gone and in its place came satisfaction and contentment. She had love enough, and wonder in her life. There were plenty of things worth rejoicing in.

The Shifting Heart

Rosemary pouted and refused to pick up the garment.

Ivy sighed and steeled herself for a confrontation.

"Her's no dressed," the child said.

"Who?" Ivy asked, looking around. There was no sign of anyone else nearby.

"Pretty lady," Rosemary giggled. "No dressed."

Her speech was still babyish, and Ivy frequently found it difficult to work out what her daughter was trying to say.

"What's this?" Ben asked, scooping his daughter up with one hand and pulling her dress down over her head with the other.

She resisted putting her hands into the sleeves for some time. Ivy entered the fray, and between them they managed to render the child presentable.

"Pretty hair," Rosemary added. "Strokey hair."

"Mummy?" Ben asked. "I think she wants to play with your hair."

"No. No Mummy. Pretty lady."

"Where?" Ivy asked nervously.

Rosemary pointed to a spot a little to Ivy's left. "Daddy?" she enquired, continuing to point beyond her mother.

Neither of her parents responded.

"No Daddy?" Rosemary tried again.

"We should be going," Ivy said, rising to her feet and looking around curiously. She wondered what her child could see. The little one was full of strange whims and fancies, forever talking to inanimate objects or greeting imaginary friends. She smiled at her daughter.

"Funny little bugger," Ben remarked. He hoisted Rosemary onto his shoulders, holding on to her small feet to stop her from falling. She giggled again.

Ivy gathered the rest of their things together and prepared for the long walk home. Her back ached and she thought there might be another little one on the way. She had already missed one bleed. Looking at her husband and child, she felt a great rush of pride and tenderness sweep through her. She could not protect them, or anyone else, from all ills, but she could treasure whatever time she had. Standing with their backs to the sun, the strong man's face echoed slightly in the expression of his pixie daughter, they seemed beautiful, indeed. She felt as though some vital piece was falling into place for her. Chains of the past loosed their hold, and she was free to step forth into the rest of her life.

"Bye bye bye, pretty lady!" Rosemary chirped from her father's shoulder, turning to wave.

Ivy glanced back. She could see no sign whatsoever of anyone along the banks of the pool. She supposed her daughter was just playing, dreaming up new friends to people her world. Living half human, half otter, she was always going to be strange. Yet for a moment she felt as though someone was watching them. It was neither an unpleasant nor an eerie sensation. She felt comforted by it.

"Bye bye bye, uncle Seth!" the infant added.

Guilty Pleasures by Maria Isabel Pita

Guilty Pleasures explores the passionate willingness of women throughout the ages to offer themselves up to the forces of love. Historical facts are seamlessly woven into intensely graphic sexual encounters.

Beneath the cover of *Guilty Pleasures* you will find intensely erotic love stories with a profound feel for the different centuries and cultures where they take place. An ancient Egyptian princess... a courtesan rising to fame in Athen's Golden Age...a Transylvanian Count's wicked bride... and many more are all one eternal woman in *Guilty Pleasures*.

0-9755331-5-0   **$16.95**

The Collector's Edition of The Lost Erotic Novels
Dr. Major LaCartilie, Editor

The history of erotic literature is long and distinguished. It holds valuable lessons and insights for the general reader, the sociologist, the student of sexual behavior, and the literary specialist interested in knowing how people of different cultures and different times acted and how these actions relate to the present. They are presented to the reader exactly as they first appeared in print by writers who were, in every sense, representative of their time: *The Instruments of the Passion & Misfortunes of Mary*–Anonymous; *White Stains* - Anaïs Nin & Friends; *Innocence* - Harriet Daimler

0-9755331-0-X   **$16.95**

The Ties That Bind by Vanessa Duriés

The incredible confessions of a thrillingly unconventional woman. From the first page, this chronicle of dominance and submission will keep you gasping with its vivid depictions of sensual abandon. At the hand of Masters Georges, Patrick, Pierre and others, this submissive seductress experiences pleasures she never knew existed. Re-print of the French bestseller.

0-9766510-1-7   **$14.95**

Cat's Collar - Three Erotic Romances
by Maria Isabel Pita

Dreams of Anubis – A legal secretary from Boston visiting Egypt explores much more than just tombs and temples in the stimulating arms of a powerfully erotic priest of Anubis who enters her dreams, and then her life one night in the dark heart of Cairo's timeless bazaar.

Rituals of Surrender – Maia Wilson finds herself the heart of an erotic web spun by three sexy, enigmatic men – modern Druids intent on using her for a dark and ancient rite…

Cat's Collar – Interior designer Mira Rosemond finds herself in one attractive successful man's bedroom after the other, but then one beautiful morning a stranger dressed in black leather takes a short cut through her garden and changes the course of her life forever.

0-9766510-0-9   **$16.95**

Available January 2006

Monique, Blanche & Alice

ALICE: When innocent young Alice goes to live with her uncle, she has no choice then but to suffer all the deliciously shocking consequences…
MONIQUE: A mysterious Villa by the sea is the setting for dark sexual rites that beckon to many a lovely young woman, including the ripe and willing Monique…
BLANCHE: When young Blanche loses her husband on her honeymoon, it becomes clear she will need a job. She sets her sights on the stage, and soon encounters a cast of lecherous characters intent on making her path to success as hot and hard as possible.

0-9766510-3-3   **$16.95**

The Collector's Edition of the Ironwood Series

The three Ironwood classics revised exclusively for this Magic Carpet Collector's edition.

Ironwood

James Carrington's bleak prospects were transformed overnight when he was offered a choice position at Ironwood, a unique finishing school where young women were trained to become premiere Ladies of Pleasure.

Ironwood Revisited

In *IRONWOOD REVISITED*, we follow James' rise to power in that garden of erotic delights. We come to understand how Ironwood, with its strict standards and iron discipline has acquired its enviable reputation among the world's most discriminating connoisseurs.

Images of Ironwood

IMAGES OF IRONWOOD presents selected scenes of unrelenting sensuality, of erotic longing, and of those bizarre proclivities which touch the outer fringe of human sexuality.

0-9766510-2-5   **$17.95**

Send check or money order to:

Magic Carpet Books
PO Box 473
New Milford, CT 06776

Postage free in the United States add $2.50 for packages outside the United States

MagicCarpetBooks@aol.com